BURGUNDY BETRAYAL

Visit us at www.boldstrokesbooks.com

By the Author

Crimson Vengeance

Burgundy Betrayal

BURGUNDY BETRAYAL

by
Sheri Lewis Wohl

2012

BURGUNDY BETRAYAL
© 2012 By Sheri Lewis Wohl. All Rights Reserved.

ISBN 10: 1-60282-654-4
ISBN 13: 978-1-60282-654-0

This Trade Paperback Original Is Published By
Bold Strokes Books, Inc.
P.O. Box 249
Valley Falls, NY 12185

First Edition: April 2012

Credits
Editor: Shelley Thrasher
Production Design: Susan Ramundo
Cover Design By Sheri (graphicartist2020@hotmail.com)

Dedication

In memory of my brother Steve.
A free spirit who lived life
on his own terms and in his own way.
"See you on the other side, Bro."

Prologue

Ballymagovern, Ireland
Samhain, 1370

Moira Magauran swiped away tears with the back of her hand. Emotion had no place this night. This was the time to harness the greatest of her powers, not to cry like a wee child. She would not give in, would not allow him to bring her to tears...again.

Heat from the bonfires scorched her cheeks, and bits of ash carried up into the air by the wind clung to her deep-red hair. She didn't brush it away. Alone on the high cliff she choked back the sobs that lingered so close and instead let the power of the dark half wash over and through her. Never before had she found the courage to reach into the darkness. She didn't hesitate now. Body quivering, fingertips tingling, she let the incredible power surge through every pore of her being. The fires, like her fury, raged.

Before tonight, fear kept her from this path. No longer. At this moment, she wanted to stand and drink in the power until it intoxicated her. The luxury was not to be had, for time was growing short. Soon others would come, beckoned by the light of the bonfires, ever ready to celebrate as was so proper on this festive night. She must hurry. For her, there'd be no celebration this Samhain.

Taking a deep breath, Moira slipped the carefully prepared mask over her face, securing it with ties at the back of her head. She dipped her hand into the bag draped across her shoulders. The bones inside were warm against her fingertips, the heat of the fire penetrating through the rough, woven fabric. She cradled the first bone and once more fought back tears. The hair woven around the leg bone of the wolf was silky, familiar. She dare not think about that now. All was as destiny decreed.

If only he'd been true. He'd taken what she'd offered, knowing from the first moment they'd touched that it came from her heart. He'd whispered of love and life, of promises for tomorrow. Ian Maguire had made her heart swell and hope bloom. She'd believed in him even though she could offer him nothing beyond her beauty and her love.

Six daughters had come before her, and six husbands secured. Only Moira remained unwed, growing older by the year, her hopes dimming with each passing month. She was born far too early, a tiny child with flaming red hair and a temper to match, to parents old and tired by the time she made her entrance into the world. She'd lived with their disappointment for all of her years. They'd wanted a boy and they'd gotten yet another girl. And a witch at that.

Still, Hugh and Avis Magauran were good people and raised her well. Avis taught her the Old Ways, knowing that as the seventh daughter of a seventh daughter, she would come into great power. No surprise to Moira. She'd known since she was very small how different she was. Ingrained in every fiber of her being, the pulse of energy accompanied her all her life.

Ian was the one who'd opened the door to reveal the true depth of her abilities. Love had made the difference and betrayal had unleashed the force. She'd thought he loved her and would marry her even given her age. At thirty, she was still beautiful though no longer young. He'd whispered it mattered not. He'd lied.

Tonight, Moira stroked her free hand across her still-flat midsection and, for a breath, closed her eyes. In a matter of weeks her secret would no longer be. All would see and know. She wouldn't be able to stay here. Not now, not with the child coming. Her birthright as a witch already set her apart. She couldn't ask her family to harbor a witch with child.

Within a fortnight, Ian would marry a woman of high birth. She would bring more with her into the marriage than the old-maid child of an elderly couple could ever hope to amass. He'd taken Moira's virtue and heart without a care or a backward glance, leaving her in the shadows to pledge his hand to another. Now, he'd pay.

Outside the bonfires, the circle had been drawn and fortified, ready for the confirmation of the spirit. Above her, the full moon hung large and swollen in the black sky, its light showering down upon the circle. The leg bone in her hand, Moira opened her eyes and walked between the two fires. She cast it into the center of the one on her right. She reached back into the bag, pulled out a second bone, also wrapped in Ian's hair, and cast it into the fire on the left.

Her arms raised, her face tilted toward the sky, Moira began to speak. "I invoke and conjure thee, oh spirits of Osthariman, Visantiparos, and Noctatur, and command thee to lay a curse upon one most wicked and deceitful. That the man known as Ian Maguire shall, from this sacred night of Samhain on, take the form of a creature of darkness, transforming each and every night of the full moon into a wolf, hereafter hunted and despised. I, by the power of seven, do command thee to lay this curse upon Ian Maguire until the one whom he has betrayed is made whole once more. Within this circle, I invoke thee, oh spirits of Osthariman, Visantiparos, and Noctatur, to do my will."

Flames from both fires shot high into the night, crackling and spitting, lighting the sky as though day had suddenly appeared. Moira pulled the mask from her face and threw it into the flames, watching until nothing of it remained but flakes of charred ash. In the distance, the faint sound of voices carried on the night air and she moved quickly. It took her but a moment to destroy all trace of the magic circle, all evidence that she had stood on the ground this night.

The voices grew louder—closer—and with one last look around, Moira melted into the darkness.

Destruction cometh;
and they shall seek peace,
and there shall be none.

Ezekiel 7:25
King James Bible

Chapter One

Nine Mile Falls, Washington
Present day

Definitely not in the job description. Or in the procedures manual. Nope, not once did anyone ever train Kara how to handle a mangled and bloody dead body. This particular dead body was so chewed up, she wasn't even sure if it was male or female. Sometimes it really sucked to be her.

On the flip side, the sight should have made her sick, yet it didn't. After the initial shock, she was mainly concerned how to secure the scene until people could get here who actually had a clue what they were looking at. She was a park ranger, not a detective, and this was way over her pay grade.

Kara plucked the cell phone off her belt and used it to take a picture. Hitting speed dial, she sent it to the ranger station where her boss, Jake Ford, was more than likely at his desk finishing month-end reports. Along with the picture, she sent a simple text: 911. Her phone rang shortly after.

Jake's voice was tense. "What the hell is that?"

"A big problem over on the northwest bank of the river between the dam and the Spokane House," she told him.

"Human?"

"Once upon a time."

"Jesus, Kara."

"No shit. You're gonna need to call the sheriff's people."

A long pause greeted her and, for a moment, she thought she'd lost him, then realized he'd just put her on hold. She heard a click and Jake's voice came through again. "They're on their way and so am I."

Under normal circumstances, she'd protest. She wasn't a delicate little flower who needed a man to hold her hand in a crisis. Nope, she was perfectly capable of handling problems all by her lonesome. Except today. Every time she glanced down at the remains of what was once a living, breathing person, chills ran up her arms. Frankly, she wasn't opposed to Jake coming along one bit.

Ten minutes later he was on the scene, and she breathed a little easier. Twenty-five minutes after that, more help arrived, only this time it came in the form of tall, dark, and serious.

As if he knew her, Jake waved at the woman who walked their way. With a steady, sure stride, she was the picture of confidence. Her eyes, though, were hidden behind dark glasses. For some reason she couldn't explain, Kara sensed she wasn't one of the sheriff's people despite the tan chinos and navy button-down shirt that looked an awful lot like a uniform.

"Cam, over here," Jake called.

"Cam?" Kara asked under her breath.

"A specialist," he whispered back. "And we're lucky to have her. She just happened to be in town at a conference. I caught her before she headed back to Montana." When the woman stopped in front of them, Jake did the introductions. "Dr. Camille Black Wolf, this is Ranger Kara Lynch. She discovered the body."

Camille Black Wolf, at least six feet tall, if not a touch over, had black hair in braids that reached to her waist and skin the color of rich toffee. Kara tamped down the urge to reach up and take off her glasses so she could see her eyes, reminding herself they were at the scene of a rather gruesome death. Camille extended a hand first to Jake and then to Kara.

"Please, call me Cam."

Her grip was warm and firm. Nice. "What kind of specialist are you, Cam?"

If she took offense at Kara's directness, she didn't let on. Her voice was even as she answered, "Wolf."

Why did that not surprise her? "You think a wolf did this?" Fat chance. There hadn't been a wolf in this part of the country for at least seventy years, if not longer. Sure, wolf packs were being reintroduced in Washington State, but not around here. Her educated opinion held that a wolf would show up out of the blue in Riverside State Park somewhere roughly between no way and never. The odds were even worse that one would then proceed to mangle a human.

Another explanation of the regular psychotic-murderer kind surely came into play here. Murder, of the serial-killer variety, had unfortunately visited Spokane in the not-too-distant past. But homegrown killer Robert Yates had been in prison for a long time now, and gruesome deaths few and far between since he took up residence at the state bed-and-breakfast.

Cam took off the dark glasses and tucked them into the breast pocket of her shirt. Kara was rewarded with the look she'd been wishing for. Her eyes were black as coal, her gaze intent on Kara's face. She had the distinct feeling she was looking not just at her, but inside her, and hell, nothing was too uncomfortable about that.

"I won't know until I study the remains."

Kara considered her with a raised eyebrow. "Why would you even think it could be a wolf?"

"The nature of the injuries." She spoke as though her point was so obvious anyone with half a brain would know.

Well, she had a whole brain and that still didn't make sense. Cam was at least ten yards from the body and certainly too far away to make a judgment call that precise. "I don't see it."

Jake broke in and threw a little light into the increasingly confusing conversation. "I sent the picture to Cam. I thought her area of expertise could be helpful." He turned to Cam. "This way. I told the guy from the ME's office not to move a thing until after you've inspected the body."

"Thank you." Cam pivoted away from Kara. As intense as her scrutiny had been a moment before, she dismissed Kara now as if she wasn't there at all. It appeared she tuned them all out the moment she squatted next to the body.

❖

Cam used every ounce of her concentration to remain calm. The scent of the other wolf was so heavy it all but gagged her. She took a few seconds as she squatted next to the body just to gather her strength and center herself. She didn't like being blindsided.

Not only had the wolf's scent enveloped her as she stepped out of her rig. The ranger's presence also distracted her tremendously. Before she'd slipped her sunglasses off, she'd been able to study her, and unaware of her scrutiny, Kara had been open and readable. Intriguing was the first word that came to mind. Cam's skin literally tingled when Kara stepped close. The ranger wasn't a were—she sensed nothing in that realm—yet something about her set Cam's nerve endings on fire.

Before this was all said and done, she wanted to spend a little more time getting to know Ranger Lynch, and not just because she sent alarm bells jingling throughout her nervous system. The short red hair was pretty spectacular, and she had a hunch the body beneath the olive-green uniform was something. Not since Bonnie had she met someone who gave off that zing of attraction, and frankly, this was about the last place she would expect to encounter it.

But she was letting a woman, albeit an attractive one, sidetrack her. Probably her imagination anyway. Four years was a long dry spell, and her hormones could just be reacting to a hot woman who made a park-service uniform look very sexy. Not what she needed today. She needed to focus on the body and what killed this human.

The scent told her two things: one, the attacker wasn't from around here. She knew the scent of every shifter within a three-hundred-mile radius. Two, the attacker wasn't a shifter, but a werewolf. According to the elders, there hadn't been a werewolf in this area for close to two hundred years. So why now? Why here?

"Cam?" Jake put a hand on her shoulder. "What do you think? Look like a wolf attack?"

Cam straightened, put her sunglasses back on, and turned away from the body. "It looks like a wolf attack but it's not. Someone just made it look that way."

"I think a very sick person did this." Coming from a few feet behind her, Kara's voice held a definite note of skepticism.

She nodded. "A sick human who made it look as though it was done by a wolf." Technically, not a complete lie. A stretch of the truth perhaps but, hey, sometimes just better to keep things close to the vest.

"He?" Jake asked.

"More than likely. I'm not trying to sound sexist. It's simply that the power it took to do this leans heavily toward a man. It could have been a woman, but I doubt it."

Kara's eyes slitted as her gaze dropped to the body on the ground, dark and bloody against the pale green of the wild grasses. "It would take one sick sonofabitch to do this."

If she only knew. "Yes, it would."

Her eyes, the color of the finest emerald, shifted back to Cam's face. As she studied her, Cam felt like Kara didn't quite buy in. Would she call the bluff? After a moment, Kara simply shrugged. "You're the expert."

She held her gaze. "Yeah, I am."

Kara arched an eyebrow. "Modest, too."

She shrugged. She'd been called a lot things but, honestly, modest wasn't one of them. "We are what we are."

Jake walked a few feet away and scanned the area, his hands in his pockets. "I don't know. Doesn't feel right to me. Hinky, if you know what I mean."

"I'd say fucked up," Kara added.

Cam raised an eyebrow but couldn't argue the point. True enough and definitely screwed up, even if she couldn't explain why. Instead, she made an offer. "I can stay a few days and do some studies in the park, if that would help?" She was pretty sure Jake would go for it.

He did. "That'd be great. We've got one of the park houses available for as long as you want. The more information you can give us the better. If we've got wolves coming in, we need to know, and we need to know what to do to guarantee their success…"

"And protect the safety of the public at the same time." Kara added quickly, a frown on her face.

Cam liked that she didn't get off topic. A friend for a lot of years, Jake was a great park ranger. But Cam was also well aware of how much it would mean to him to have wolves in his park. He wouldn't take the death of anyone lightly, though he'd be excited at the prospect of a new pack. The problem was, the kind of pack that came with this death wasn't the kind Jake or anyone else wanted in their public-accessible wilderness.

Cam nodded. "Done. Just show me the house and I'll get started right away."

Her father and the rest of the tribal council were right—as they always were—not that she'd come here with any doubt. The spirits had shown the elders what was coming, but not where. Now they knew. She had to find the werewolf and stop it before more innocent people lost their lives. The big question? Who could she trust? Her information was sensitive, to say the least, and those she shared it with, special. She'd know soon enough if she could confide in Jake and Kara.

"Kara, will you take Cam over to three and get her set up?"

"Sure thing, Jake. Dr. Black Wolf, if you want to follow me, it's only a minute from here."

Actually Cam would prefer to stay and check out the immediate area. It'd be hard to do with so many people around. Better to follow the pretty ranger and wait until dark, when the park was empty.

In a blue-and-white park-service pickup, Kara pulled out onto Highway 291 and headed south. Cam followed, making a right turn a short distance later to cross the Nine Mile Bridge that spanned the river and faced the dam. Just beyond the dam on the south side of Charles Road sat a cluster of old brick houses.

The cottages were interesting. She'd seen them a few times over the years though hadn't paid a great deal of attention. Now she studied them more closely. Ten of them altogether, five on one side of the short street, five on the other. All brick, all harking back to another time.

"They were built by the power company in the late 1920s," Kara said as she walked in front of Cam to what she assumed was number three. "They housed the dam workers for years. Now, they're pretty much empty except during the prime season, when the park service leases five a year."

"They're so nicely preserved."

And they were. The cluster of brick bungalows was well-maintained with tiny but very green yards. Despite the shared style of architecture, each was different. The fronts all had a porch but none quite the same. Some of the yards had fences, some didn't. The brick for all the houses was a beautiful aged red, though each had a different color trim. Almost like stepping back in time and the feeling wasn't unpleasant.

"The dam and the houses are all classified as historic."

"Ah, that makes sense."

"Kind of a bitch when you're actually living here and can't so much as put a nail in the wall for a picture."

She smiled. "I suppose so."

Kara smiled back and Cam liked the way her face softened. "I shouldn't complain. It's awesome out here. Couldn't ask for a better view, and most of the time it's just me and my lonesome."

"The solitude doesn't bother you?"

She shook her head at the same time she turned a key in the lock at the front door. "Not in the least. I like being alone. I'm not much of a city girl, hence my chosen occupation. Besides, I'm not completely alone. My dog, Winston, keeps me company most of the time. At least when he's not passed out asleep, as I suspect he is right at the moment. Here you go." She waved Cam in. "Home sweet home."

"Nice," she murmured when she stepped through the door.

"I'm going to head back. If you need me, call my cell."

Cam cocked her head and studied Kara. "I could if I knew your cell number."

A slight flush went up her cheeks. "Ah, yeah, that would help, wouldn't it?"

As she recited the number, Cam punched it into her phone, then saved it to the contacts list. "I'm all set."

"I'm next door so if you run into any problems here later, Dr. Black Wolf, just give me a knock."

"Thank you, Ranger Lynch."

She paused before going out, turning at the door to look at her. "Kara," she said softly.

"Kara," Cam repeated, liking the sound of it on her tongue. "And I'm Cam, not Dr. Black Wolf, please."

The tiny smile appeared again. "Cam it is." Then she was gone.

CHAPTER TWO

Faolán powered up the Centennial trail to Carlson Road and then dropped down the hill to where it intersected with Charles Road. He smiled when he saw the two people in front of one of the cottages. He'd known the woman would come. They always did. The names were different, the heritage different, but the hunters were always the same.

He stopped and pulled his water bottle from the cage on his road bike, a nice light model he'd picked up at a yard sale a couple of days after he'd arrived. Tilting his head back, he squeezed, sending cool water flowing down his throat. From his spot along the road, he could easily watch the women, while they paid little attention to a random cyclist stopped for a drink. A common-enough sight at the Nine Mile Dam Trailhead.

The hunter didn't concern him—much. The red-haired woman, on the other hand, sent every nerve in his body singing. Even from this distance, he caught her scent, the same one he'd been waiting centuries to find. As soon as he got back to his temporary home, he'd alert the others. He slipped the water bottle into the cage on the bike frame and was ready to ride away when he caught the light scent of a different woman. Again, he smiled.

She glided down next to him, trim and athletic in a pair of black bike shorts and a pink jersey shirt that hugged her in all the right places. She smelled of sweat, heat, and woman.

"Are you all right?"

He smiled, white teeth against a pleasantly tanned face. His accent was heavy as he told her, "Aye, just stopped for a bit of water."

Her long blond hair spilled from beneath a helmet, falling down her back like a golden cascade. Her smile matched his. "It is hot today, isn't it?"

He didn't miss the way she looked him over. The day was turning into one filled with pleasant surprises. "It is indeed. And where might your ride be taking you today?"

She sipped from her own water bottle. "I'm just about to turn around and head back on the trail. And you?"

"Why as it happens, I'm about to do the same. Perhaps you're up for a bit of company?"

"I wouldn't mind at all. I'm Diane." She held out a hand.

"Diane," he repeated, and took her outstretched hand in his. "I'm Faolán."

"Not from around here, are you?"

He laughed as he released her hand. "No, I'm a long way from my home in Ireland, but if I may say so, it gets lovelier here by the moment."

The wattage in her smile grew and a slight flush crept up her cheeks. "Shall we ride? I'm finishing the end of my Ironman training ride. You?"

He waved a hand back toward the hill he'd come down minutes before. "I'm a mere enthusiast. Nothing so ambitious as an Ironman race. After you."

Diane clicked into her pedals and took off ahead of him. The view was breathtaking. Her lean, muscled body was a vision. What man in his right mind didn't appreciate the body of a female athlete? He could almost taste the sweat that glistened on her smooth skin. The gods were definitely smiling on him today.

Kara stared at the fire pit. For the tenth time tonight she wished she could light it. Unfortunately, with a high fire risk, a ranger lighting one would be a real bad idea. She was just so restless tonight. When she'd finally gone to bed, sleep didn't come. Instead, she'd tossed and turned. After an hour of that nonsense, she'd slipped on shorts and a T-shirt and wandered out to the small patio behind her cottage, Winston at her heels.

With the back gate wide open, the dam was clearly visible. The lights rained down on the water as it spilled into the river, sparkling like a cascade of diamonds. At her feet, Winston stretched out on the warm bricks and snored. Despite his nasal bulldog snorts, the night was peaceful.

Shifting in her chair, Kara rolled her head, listening to the pops of her neck. Off in the distance, the hoot of an owl floated through the air, and she absently wondered what it meant. Was it good? Or bad? A vague recollection from some college reading on folk legends echoed in her mind. Something about owls was buried in the memory, but she just couldn't drag it out. Oh, well, she'd go with a good thing.

Before everything was said and done, the day turned very long. The crime tape strung from tree to tree all over the park insulted the beauty of the park. The army of law-enforcement professionals that swept through every inch of the area depressed her. Hours passed before the body was finally loaded into the ME's van and the park cleared out. Funny, once everyone was gone, it was as if nothing had happened. The bloodstain where the body lay untouched for hours had darkened the ground, but beyond that it looked normal. Wild grasses, evergreen and pine trees, and nearby, the sound of rushing water—all tranquil and ordinary. Not a single thing to signal evil had walked here.

She'd felt the evil in her bones long before Cam declared the damage the work of a man. Another day, she might have argued the point. Kara had a hard time believing a man could do something that heinous. He might live in the guise of a man, but whatever had done that was a monster without a shred of humanity. Cam might very well argue a case of semantics. She'd be wrong. Monsters were real.

The dreams started when Kara was very young. Hard to remember a time when they didn't haunt her sleep. Everyone had dreams. Hers were different. Not random images that were strange or funny or frightening. No, her dreams came true. Made insomnia rather appealing.

"Can't sleep?"

Kara screamed and jumped from her chair, one hand over her heart, the other reaching for the gun that wasn't there. Winston rolled up on his stubby legs and gave a deep-throated bark. As recognition settled, she whirled and stared. "Are you out of your mind? You just about gave me the big one."

"Sorry," Cam said. "I thought you heard me."

"Well, I didn't and neither did my dog." Yeah, she sounded like a petulant little kid but, darn it, Cam scared the crap out of her sneaking up like that. That she'd been dwelling on thoughts of monsters and demons had nothing to do with it.

"Do you mind?" She motioned to one of the chairs.

Kara sank back into her own chair and shrugged. "No."

"I really am sorry," she said as she sat and stretched her legs out. Like Kara, she was dressed casually in a pair of shorts and a gray T-shirt. Earlier, her hair had been braided, though now it hung loose. Kara had the strangest urge to run her fingers through it. Probably not a good idea. She folded her hands in her lap. Maybe it was better to focus on monsters and demons. Winston surprised her by going right up to Cam and, after sniffing her hand, lay down at her feet.

"Well," she said with a snort. "You've made a friend."

"Dogs like me."

"So I see. Winston is very particular about who he pals around with."

Cam ran a hand over Winston's smooth head. "My people have always had a way with dogs."

"Your people?"

"The Crow."

Well, that explained her dark and smoky good looks, though a flicker of a remembered history lesson sent Kara upright in her chair. "Hey," she said. "Don't the Crow *eat* dogs?" She resisted the urge to drag Winston back to her side.

Even in the darkened patio, she could see the roll of Cam's eyes. "*No.* Wrong tribe."

"I could swear—"

"You remembered stories about Indians eating their dogs. I know, I know. I've heard it a hundred times if I've heard it once, but trust me, the Crow did not and do not eat their dogs. We have always lived harmoniously with our canine companions."

"If you say so."

Cam rubbed Winston's head again. "Do you think for a moment this fine gentleman would stay at my side if he sensed I was sizing him up for a late-night snack?"

Kara studied Winston and then smiled. "You have a point."

"Now, tell me, what had you so deep in thought?"

It was stupid to tell her what had really going through her mind. Kara's thoughts had been creeping more along the lines of the supernatural, and Cam would undoubtedly think her a twit if she actually fessed up to that.

"Just wondering what would make a person do something so horrible." The truth even if it wasn't the whole truth.

In the muted glow of the back-door light, Cam studied her. Not with interest exactly. More like distrust. She looked away from her probing gaze and out toward the dam where the water flowed hard over the spillway. The sound of it crashing to the rocks below was like a muted symphony.

"Maybe it wasn't a person per se."

She whipped her head back around. Cam was still studying her and, if she was to hazard a guess, gauging Kara's reaction. "That's not what you said earlier."

She shrugged and rolled her head side to side. Her black hair rippled like silk in the moonlight. "True enough."

"But?" she murmured absently, still focused on that silky long hair.

"But out here in the dark with just you and me, maybe I can toss out ideas that others might not be able to grasp."

That got her attention. "And you think I can?" Where exactly was Cam going with this?

"I think you might," she said slowly. "No, that's not right. I know you can."

Kara let out a laugh. "Pretty good character assessment considering we've been around each other, oh, say an hour or so, give or take."

Again Cam shrugged. "Time isn't always the precursor to knowledge."

"You're cryptic, aren't you, Doc?"

This time she laughed. "I told you earlier, it's Cam."

"But you are a doctor, right?"

"A veterinarian, not a medical doctor."

"Hey, doctor is doctor in my book."

"It's really not important."

"And what is? A human killer? Or is it a wolf attack? Gotta make up your mind, Doc."

"Both."

"Okay, enough with the vagueness and innuendo. Spit it out. Who or what killed that person this morning?" The woman might be hot, but Kara's patience with this line of mystery was nonexistent. She had real-world problems to deal with.

Her eyes held hers for a long moment. "A werewolf."

It really wasn't a wise idea to kill another so soon. He just couldn't help himself. She was beautiful, strong, and the game so fulfilling. Dusk was beginning to settle when she returned to her car and hoisted the bicycle onto the rack on the roof of the compact SUV. The way the muscles in her arms rippled as she held the bike high over her head, sweat glistening like diamonds in the rosy twilight, made his cock stiffen. The spandex shorts molded to her shapely ass and her breasts were firm and high. Everything about her thrilled him.

No one else was in the circular parking lot situated high on the rise overlooking the Spokane River and the area known as the Bowl and Pitcher. Below, the river roared by the two rock formations that gave the place its name, and the hillsides were lush with lilacs, wild grasses, and pine trees. The air was heavy with the scent of wildflowers and woman. Hers was the lone vehicle in the lot.

She was sitting on the bumper taking off her cycling shoes as the sun dropped behind the mountains. He loved the night, but this time between darkness and light was magical. Only the most powerful could make the change at will, and he was stronger, faster, smarter than any that had come before him, his father included. He dropped his clothing, raised his arms, and breathed in the clear, clean air. A breeze ruffled the trees and underbrush, and the setting sun cast an orange glow all around him.

The change came. Bones shifted, skin stretched, his senses tingled and sharpened. Nothing could compete with the almost orgasmic feeling that a shift brought. He watched his hands lose the definition of fingers, thumb, palm, and mold into massive paws. Primal power soared through him. With a growl low in his throat, he announced his presence. The small creatures of the wilderness slid away in silence, leaving the hunting ground wide open for the king of predators. No one challenged him, neither human nor creature.

The woman stilled, her head tilted, a frown on her pretty face, and her eyes narrowed. This was one of his favorite parts, the moment when fear began to tickle at the back of the neck. An unidentified threat lurking just beyond vision. Slowly he began to pad in her direction. She stared into the trees, looking to the west as if something in that direction caught her attention. So wrong! But by the time she realized her error, it would be too late.

He slinked her way. Suddenly, her head whipped to the north and finally, triumphantly, he was rewarded with the expression he'd been waiting for: terror. She screamed and backed against the vehicle, cycling shoes clattering to the asphalt.

Run. He wanted the game, loved the chase. *Run.* She froze, then fumbled with the keys she'd frantically dug out of a pocket of the pretty jersey top. They tumbled from her hand. A sign. There was always a sign. He leapt out of the shadows and onto the pavement. With a cry, she spun away from the SUV and, as she did, their eyes met. She stilled, shock on her face. Then, she ran. *Yes!*

Excitement rippled through every nerve in his body, and his long legs stretched out, his paws barely touching the ground as he flew through the night. Still, he held back, not wanting the game to end too soon. His mouth watered and the smell of her sweat-drenched flesh thrilled him. He could hear her blood pound as it coursed through her body, the thump of her rapidly beating heart. Even so, he stayed just a few yards behind her. So much more pleasing when they ran, cried, and trembled as he chased.

When she veered off of the trail and plunged into the deep brush near the river's edge, he howled and charged, his paws barely touching the rocky path. Game on.

CHAPTER THREE

Cam was good at a lot of things, like taking a gorgeous moonlit night in the company of a beautiful woman and fucking it up. No big mystery why she was single. Kara now stared over at her through narrowed eyes. A hint of annoyance made her emerald greens spark, and damned if it didn't make her even more attractive. Too bad nothing could ever come of it. Once again, wrong time and place. Story of her life.

"Yeah, of course, a werewolf." Sarcasm dripped from Kara's words.

Cam didn't really expect her to buy in just yet. More than anything, she wanted to gauge her reaction to see how open her mind might be. Something about Kara prickled her skin and her mind, and she wanted to know why. To see how far she could take her into the reality of what was in the park. Besides, it also gave her a valid excuse to hang with her for a while.

A cool breeze rippled across her skin, bringing with it the smells of the night. Mixed in was Kara's unique scent. The urge to bury her nose in Kara's neck and breathe in her essence was as strong as it was confusing. She was here at the direction of the elders, not to diddle with a park ranger, even if she was smoking hot. Not exactly her style to think of a woman first and the mission second. Then again, it had been such a long time since any woman made her breath quicken.

With effort, she tore her thoughts from the strong, earthy desires and back to murder. The elders had been clear on the level of danger heading this way. Even if Kara couldn't totally wrap her head around the truth, somehow Cam would have to get her onto the same page.

"You said earlier it would take a sick sonofabitch to kill someone with such brutality."

Kara shrugged. "Yeah, sonofabitch as in human being, not some creature of folklore."

"You realize folklore grows out of human experience?"

"Yes, Doc, I'm fairly well educated too."

"I didn't mean to imply you weren't." Though it was obvious Kara believed she did.

Tilting her head, Kara studied her. "Then maybe you should tell me exactly what you did mean to imply."

Kara's body language screamed distrust. Her arms were crossed, her legs were crossed, and her eyes had narrowed to slits. Not quite the open-minded stance she'd need to make her see beyond the everyday world. Much existed in the shadow worlds that most refused to acknowledge. People didn't want to believe in evil, let alone creatures that straddled both human and preternatural existence. Cam was fortunate to have been raised in a culture that embraced all realms. She grew up proud of what she was, even if she instinctively understood she'd have two lives. One pretending she was wholly human. The other as a shape-shifter, with those she trusted implicitly. Before this was over, she hoped Kara would be one of the latter.

In the far distance, a vague sound shot a sliver of apprehension up her spine. A howl? Change in plan…that trust thing would have to come sooner rather than later. She pushed up from the chair. "I guess I'm simply trying to make a point. Don't forget to look beyond the normal, Kara. Keep your mind and your heart open."

"Look, I'm a pretty open person in more ways than one, but this thing today? Murder, Doc, straight-up murder."

"Cam."

Kara sighed, uncrossed her arms, and said, "Murder, Cam. Old-fashioned, brutal, without-a-conscience murder. No real mystery. Nothing supernatural."

Making no ground so far. "Perhaps."

She shook her head as she looked up at Cam, her eyes still wary. "You're a stubborn woman, aren't you? There's no 'perhaps' about it, and you're the one who said it wasn't a wolf attack."

True enough, just not quite all the truth. "I've seen too much to take anything at face value."

She raised an eyebrow. "Do tell."

"Another night." As much as she'd like to stay here with Kara and share her deep, dark secrets, it wasn't the time. Kara wasn't ready for the truth quite yet.

"Oh, hey, you're the one who opened this can of worms…or should I say pack of werewolves? So by rights, you owe me more of an explanation."

She nodded but didn't give in. "I do, you're right, but not now. I've said enough for tonight. It's time for me to get some sleep and you should do the same. It's not ideal for you to stay out here in the dark."

Her uneasiness was from more than just the howl she'd heard a minute ago. An unfamiliar scent wafted in the air, and she didn't like it. No, all good boys and girls needed to be in for the night.

Kara studied her. "I don't know you well enough to call it, but it almost sounds like you're worried about me."

Cam held out a hand to help her up from the chair. "It doesn't hurt to err on the side of caution. A person was killed not far from here last night. I'd sleep easier knowing you were locked up safe and sound in your bungalow."

She thought Kara would argue. But she took Cam's outstretched hand and let her pull her to her feet. Her hand was warm in Cam's, her long fingers wrapping around her palm. She liked the feel of Kara's smooth skin and strong grip so she didn't immediately let go. Instead, she gazed into her eyes and saw something she couldn't quite put a name to. It sent a shot of warmth to her center.

Kara met her gaze without blinking. "You're a strange chick, Cam Black Wolf."

She smiled, still holding her hand. "I can live with strange. I've been called much worse."

Kara's smile softened her features. "Yeah, I bet you have." She pulled her hand away and started toward the back door. "Come on, Winston. Sleep well, Doc."

"Cam," she reminded her softly as she watched the dog roll to his feet and follow Kara.

Pausing, Kara glanced back over her shoulder. "Cam."

She watched until both of them were inside the house and she heard the click of the dead bolt. Only then did she sprint to her own temporary home. Turning off all the lights, she stood near the front window and gazed into the darkness. Nothing appeared to move.

That wasn't good. After she stepped quietly onto the front porch, she stayed in the shadows and slipped out of her clothes. Cool air whispered across her skin, her muscles tensing in response, her nipples hardening. No time to waste. Breathing deeply and embraced by the darkest shadows, she began to shift.

❖

Faolán came out of the river shaking his head and sending cold water spraying in an arc around his bare skin. The rocks beneath his feet were worn smooth by the river's ever-moving water. Once on shore, he dropped to the soft wild grass, falling back to let the warmth of the earth spread through his body. The run had been fabulous. Acres and acres of wilderness to stretch his legs, the dip in the river refreshing. This place was wonderful. Beautiful and uncluttered. Fresh and clean. Plenty of mice and squirrels to chase. Clear waters to quench his thirst.

It certainly wasn't home, but few places in the world compared to his native Ireland. And he'd traveled enough to know. Still, he liked it here. Around him was a world alive and unspoiled. Too bad he wouldn't be able to stay. This could be a nice place to call home, at least for a decade or two or three. He usually moved on during the third decade, give or take. Folks started to get suspicious when they grew old and he didn't. Hard to make friends. Even harder to love.

Around here, the people were pleasant enough. Take Diane, for example. Beautiful, strong, and lovely, she was a terrific companion for the day. He'd hated to see it end. Not that he spent much time fretting about the parting. There'd be more Dianes. This place was full of friendly people who appreciated the majesty of their natural surroundings and didn't try to spoil Mother Nature's gifts.

Today's fun was enough to keep him satisfied for a while. Time to call it a night and catch up on much-needed rest. The days were growing shorter and he had a lot to get ready. They'd been looking for her for such a long time, and finally the gods had seen fit to smile on him and reveal her presence. Of course, it wouldn't be easy. When had any of it been easy?

He pushed up and brushed off bits of dry grass and dirt that stuck to his skin. The night air was growing cool against his nakedness. Definitely time to go in, particularly when in this form. Not only was he more susceptible to temperature variations, but people tended to get a little twitchy when they ran across a naked man out in public. Technically the park was closed and the chance of running into anyone slim. Still, better safe than sorry had kept him out of trouble for a good many years. He loved nothing more than a good run, but at the risk of going to jail? Never.

Climbing up the ridge, Faolán found his clothes right where he'd left them in a jumbled pile. He slipped into athletic pants and a T-shirt and, after lacing up his running shoes, took off at an easy pace. The small house he rented was near the trailhead at the Fort George Wright Cemetery, and he'd be back there in less than twenty minutes. Maybe fifteen.

None of the old boys buried in the cemetery would mind him jogging by. Probably should take a peek and see if he recognized any of the names. The late 1800s had been a very nomadic time for him, and though his passing through Fort George Wright had been brief, he still remembered a couple of men with fondness. No time for a trip down memory lane tonight. He was starving and the thought of a juicy, rare burger had him picking up the speed.

❖

Kara sat in the darkness, her fingers curled around the pendant always at her neck. Touching the familiar necklace should have comforted her. It didn't. And why should it? It just reminded her once more that she'd not been wanted. Still, she wore it. Still, her hand always went to it in moments of fear or confusion. Not surprising, even before Cam scared the crap out of her, the night had felt odd. Something wasn't right, although she really couldn't say what. After Cam left, the feeling grew even more intense. She'd like to say all the talk of werewolves was responsible for her unease, but that wasn't it…exactly.

Right now, Kara needed to go to bed. She didn't want to delve into why being around Cam even for a little while made her restless. Morning would come too quickly if she didn't hit the sack. Unfortunately, she wasn't tired. In fact, she was wide-awake. Murder so close to home could do that to a person, and then to top it off with dark and sexy Dr. Black Wolf? No wonder she couldn't sleep.

Hard to consider lying down when all she could think about were Cam's dark eyes and long, lean legs. She'd close her eyes and see the way she walked. Her stride so powerful, it made her want to touch her. And that hair—Lord, how she'd wanted to run her fingers through the glossy black strands. She shuddered thinking about it.

Crap. She didn't need this right now. She had her own problems to worry about. Not the least of which was the dead body left in her park. No, it wasn't really her park. She just thought about it that way. She'd been a ranger here since before college graduation, and Riverside State Park felt like home. This year, for the first time, it would be her home for a full twelve months.

She'd angled and pleaded until the powers that be agreed to let her stay in the bungalow year-round. Usually, the rangers were here only during the season. But with the way things had been going the last few years, it was prudent, at least to Kara, to have someone twenty-four seven at the park. The board finally agreed. She was thus the park's personal caretaker for the entire winter, aided by her trusty canine companion, Winston.

In a T-shirt and a pair of baggy pajama bottoms, Kara wandered through the darkened house, looking out the windows, plumping sofa pillows, and straightening pictures that were already level. When she got to the kitchen, she studied the closed freezer drawer for a long minute before she slid it open and pulled out a pack of cigarettes. From the cupboard near the back door, she snagged a book of matches, then stepped out onto the porch. The crack of the match sounded really loud—or did the guilt make it seem that way? At the screen door, Winston stared at her with big, accusing eyes.

"Go lay down," she whispered. "I'm only going to take a couple puffs." After a moment, he turned away, the click, click, click of his nails on the kitchen floor signaling his retreat.

With her eyes closed, Kara inhaled and let smoke fill her mouth. Good. If only smoking wasn't so unhealthy. She took a few more pulls before she stubbed the cigarette out in a soup can filled with sand. Tucked away from view on the corner of the porch, it usually went unnoticed, she hoped. Dirty little secrets needed to stay that way. Maybe now she'd be able to get some sleep. Or maybe her guilty conscience would push her even further away from slumber.

Just about to turn around and go inside, she caught movement to her left. *What the hell?* That sure looked like a wolf racing south toward Carlson Road. As quickly as it appeared, it disappeared up the hill. Kara rubbed a hand over her face and blinked. She was really tired and probably imagined it. After the discovery this morning, could be she was seeing things that didn't exist. No, not a wolf. Definitely not a werewolf. More likely a loose dog. Somebody's pet from down on Charles Road having a good time after escaping what was undoubtedly a big chain-link-enclosed yard. Yup, that was it, a loose pet.

Once inside, she checked to make sure the door was locked before heading to her bedroom. If she didn't think she needed sleep before, she sure did now. All it took was one bizarre suggestion about a werewolf from a woman she barely knew and she was seeing creatures in the mist. Sleep was definitely called for.

Peering down over the side of the bed, she smiled wryly. Winston didn't appear to suffer from the same bout of insomnia. On his fluffy, sheep's-wool-topped bed, he lay stretched out snoring like an old man. He didn't even twitch when she walked by. That was her handsome Winston, one hell of a watchdog.

She pulled back the blankets and crawled between the cool sheets. Her head against the pillows, her eyes closed, she breathed in the freshly laundered scent of the pillowcase. In a barely audible whisper, she repeated again and again, "It wasn't a wolf, it wasn't a wolf..."

CHAPTER FOUR

The cell phone rang at straight-up midnight. "Get your lazy arse out of bed."

"Fuck you, Conrí," Faolán said on a laugh. "Besides, brother, it'd be your lazy arse still in bed if you were here." Of course, it was eight o'clock in the morning in Ireland, where Conrí was more than likely sitting on the veranda drinking good strong tea and enjoying the morning sun. Knowing his brother, doing it in nothing more than a pair of boxers, if he'd even bothered to put on anything at all. Conrí was quite proud of all his God-given attributes and wasn't above sharing them with family, friends, and anyone else who happened by.

"Ah, you do know me well. Have you found her?"

"I think so."

The pause had nothing to do with the reality that they were continents apart. "You *think* so? Do I need to come over there?" Conrí asked.

"Oh, piss off."

"Piss off yourself, little brother. Time is growing short."

"Don't you think I know it? Don't you think I feel it just as you do?"

"Sometimes you get sidetracked."

"Christ, Conrí, I make one little detour and I hear about it for the next hundred years."

"That little detour cost us dearly."

Actually, as much as he hated to admit it, Conrí was right. He'd had the witch in his sights and was waiting for the rest to arrive when a pretty little wench with a lovely curvy backside and the breasts of a goddess took him to bed. Three days later when he'd crawled out of that same bed, the witch was gone. That was more than a century ago and Conrí had been throwing it in his face ever since.

"I won't make the same mistake twice."

"See that you don't. Once was more than plenty. Call me the minute you've locked down her location."

"Of course."

Faolán held his thumb on the cell phone's power button until the tiny phone went dead. He loved his brother but at times he wished he was an only child. After so many years, the same song and dance got old no matter how noble or significant. Conrí's own sense of self-importance grated on him, but that was his brother. What could he do? He loved the arrogant bastard.

When he told Conrí he thought he had her, he wasn't really lying. He knew where she was, but he had to tread carefully this time. Had to figure out exactly how to put everything in motion. He wanted to do it without Conrí's involvement. Things were much easier when his brother wasn't calling the shots. Once he had a game plan, all he had to do was call in the family and then wait for the day to arrive. Simple. Easy. No missteps this time. No costly mistakes. After all these years, to think the prophecy would finally come true was almost more than he could take in. Yet he knew this was it. He could feel it deep in his bones. She was the one.

Unable to sleep after his brother's call, Faolán went out to the kitchen and pulled a beer from the refrigerator. The only good thing he could say for the beer was it went down cold and malty. Beyond that, it was somewhat dissatisfying. These Americans simply didn't have the touch for a good brew. He'd give a lot to have a pint of something rich, dark, and stout. Of course, it had been centuries since he'd tasted anything as fine as the poitín of his youth. How the farmers of his day could brew such fiery magic from malt, yeast, barley, and sugar amazed him. Nothing today even came close.

Outside, he sat on the top step of the porch and sipped the beer. The air was thick and heavy, promising a storm. It wouldn't last long, they never did in this place, and then the air would once more be dry and warm. As if on cue, a burst of rain fell, darkening the street and washing everything clean. It lasted less than five minutes.

He wished his life could be as simple as a storm. Blow in. Blow out. Everything clear and fresh. Not his fate. Nothing could ever wash him clean.

Beer gone, he went back inside and tossed the bottle into the trash. The bed beckoned. Much business awaited, not the least of which was finding out the name of the fire-haired beauty down by the dam. He'd need to be rested and alert. Definitely no more getting side-tracked by beautiful cyclists out on the trail, regardless of how calming a few hours of sexual release could be. Conrí wouldn't just be pissed off at Faolán if history repeated itself with another gorgeous set of breasts. No, his brother would likely kill him this time—literally. Better to go the way of a priest for the duration than risk his brother's fury.

Besides, yesterday's dalliance with the lovely Diane didn't quite hold the zing he'd experienced in the old days. Without a doubt, good, clean fun. Was it satisfying? No, and he knew why. He could see her face as clearly as if she stood with him right now. It really hurt to love someone who would never love him back.

Cam ran easy at first, getting a feel for the landscape beneath her paws. The night was cool with a hint of change in the wind. A storm bringing wind and rain perhaps? Or maybe something more. No matter what approached tonight, soon the warm fall days would give way to winter, blanketing the land with snow. A rushing river, over ten thousand acres of parkland, and thick, trail-entwined woods made Riverside State Park a wolf's paradise any time of year.

But this was also a predator's paradise. The scent of blood whispered through the increasingly humid breeze, and Cam's acute sense of smell had her picking up speed. She raced through the wilderness, well hidden by pine trees until the scent became overpowering. The storm was close and she pushed to beat the rain.

At the top of the first hill, she paused, letting the warm light of the moon spill golden on her dark fur. The light empowered her and she charged down the hill, weaving through thick underbrush and over fallen trees. The transition between the Nine Mile section of the park and the Seven Mile area was far more open than she'd like. The homes that lined the road into the parking area had too many dogs and horses for comfort, none of which were very happy with the appearance of a wolf. The dogs barked, the horses whinnied. She ramped up her speed and crossed Seven Mile Road to disappear once more into the woods. The sounds of unhappy animals died away and pure instinct guided her.

At the Bowl and Pitcher overlook she paused once more, holding her head high and listening. Only the sounds of the forest animals that called the park home and the roar of the water as it swirled around and past the rock formations. In the darkness, the shapes were hard to make out. Moonlight glowed milky through the gathering storm clouds in the black velvet sky. She ran on, dropping below the trail to run in the underbrush that lined the river.

The hoot of an owl flying just overhead caused her to stumble. A shiver coursed through her from nose to tail. She stopped and peered into the sky, then saw the shadow of the owl, its wings spread wide, on the needle-strewn ground. The air whooshed as it dipped low over Cam's head before gaining altitude again. When it was gone, she ran again, trembling at the dire message the owl's appearance foretold. The elders would not be pleased.

She found the body below the old cemetery, just beyond the trailhead. Making a kill this close to the trail and to the city was dangerous. Not only was the trail within yards of where she lay, but so too was a service road utilized by the Park Service. That one would do such a thing, and in this place, gave her prey another, more frightening dimension.

Once more, Cam called the change, shifting from wolf to woman. As raindrops began to touch her bare skin, she knelt beside the body. She suspected in life this woman had been interesting. Though covered with blood and with a gaping hole in her neck, she had apparently been strong and well conditioned. Her long blond hair was now matted in dark, wet clumps, while blood was smeared over the various tattoos on her arms and legs.

Sightless eyes stared up at the black rain clouds and Cam gently closed them. "May your spirit go free," she whispered, then began to sing softly over the body. She hoped the song would lead the woman's soul to the afterlife.

Raindrops started to fall in earnest, making red stream down the dead woman's white cheeks. Cam didn't feel the moisture as she focused on guiding the woman's spirit away from this place of death and into the hands of the gods.

When she finished her plea to the ancient ones, Cam stood, narrowing her eyes. Breathing in deeply, she frowned. The scent she picked up from the woman's body confused her. The same as the man from last night's kill, yet it wasn't. Something she couldn't quite define was different. Was the werewolf sick? Was that why the scent contained a whisper of something odd? This was new, something she'd need to run by the elders.

Leaving didn't seem right and yet, for now, she'd done all she could for the woman. At this time of night, she wouldn't be able to easily explain her presence here. Particularly given that she was stark naked. Most people couldn't comprehend the truth of what she was, and she didn't care to try to make them understand right now. Again, she shifted before starting to run back toward the cottages at the dam. She hoped someone would come across the woman's body very soon. She hated to think of her lying there in the darkness and the rain.

Back at the cottage and dressed once more, Cam walked quietly over to Kara's. The house was still and quiet. *Good.* Kara needed her sleep. Evil had arrived and they would all need strength if they hoped to stop it. She laid a hand on her front door and said a prayer to the gods.

❖

Riah Preston stood alone at the large windows that looked out over the massive landscape below. Evergreens, pine, and birch trees were all dark and ominous in the night. A whisper on the breeze let her know the massive Spokane River ran hard and strong through the heart of Riverside State Park. If she stood here for a thousand years, she'd never tire of this view. Behind her in the large room, piles of boxes still unpacked were lined up against a wall. They'd been here less than a month and the boxes were never-ending. As many times as she'd moved in her half a millennia, this part never got any easier.

Almost a hundred years old, the house—or rather more of a castle—had been the pet project of an eccentric area millionaire. Abandoned only a few years after construction because of a lack of water, it remained a beauty in the rough for nearly a century. Things had changed in the intervening years and modern technology solved the water problem. Riah purchased the property five years earlier and four years later had it in habitable condition. Even after everything was done and the house ready, it remained empty. She didn't know why she'd hesitated to move in, but it just hadn't felt right.

Then, after the events several months earlier that cemented her relationship with scientist Adriana James, she'd decided it would be a good idea for the two of them to live in a place they created together. The solution had been simple: move into the castle with Adriana.

Except nothing in her life was ever really that simple. The estate was far too large for two people—so why not add a couple more? Riah's former student, friend, and colleague, Ivy Hernandez, had been killed in an epic battle against rogue vampires. Ivy's courage against raw evil had come at a very high price. Contrary to her better judgment Riah had caved at the pressure from vampire hunter Colin James and Adriana, and she had turned Ivy. That Ivy was now a creature of the night weighed heavy on Riah. She owed her for both the human life she took away and for her incredible friendship. So, along with Riah and Adriana, Ivy and Colin now lived at the estate as well.

After being alone for nearly two hundred years, Riah suddenly found herself at the center of a strange sort of family. It took a little getting used to, but she could no longer imagine her life any other way. Riah still worked as Spokane's medical examiner, with Ivy as her assistant. With her impressive credentials, it had been an easy sell to get Ivy hired on for the night shift alongside Riah. Together they took care of the business of death, finding answers for those whose lives were touched by accidents, murder, or the cruel hand of Mother Nature. At the same time, they kept their fingers on the pulse of the area, ever alert for those of the darkness.

At home, her sexy Adriana was more than just her lover. She possessed one of the most beautiful minds Riah had ever encountered. At seventeen, Adriana had been accepted into Yale, though a falling-out with her mother sent her across country to the University of Washington. To her knowledge, Adriana had never returned to New Haven or spoken to her mother again. She never talked about it and Riah didn't ask. She understood family estrangement better than most—just one more thing the two of them shared.

Adriana's mind, however, was what first brought them together. After years of working side by side, Adriana discovered the cure for the very thing that had held Riah captive for over five hundred years. The tragedy came in the form of Riah's first love, a woman she thought five centuries dead. Bitter and vengeful, Meriel Danson almost destroyed them all. They survived. The cure did not. It blew skyward in an explosion orchestrated by Meriel.

Now, Adriana was rebuilding her lab and trying to recreate the cure that would set both Riah and Ivy free.

The fourth member of their unlikely family was Colin Jamison. Adriana in her life made sense. Ivy in her life made sense. Nothing about Colin in her life did. A vampire hunter sent by the church to destroy Riah and all those like her, he was the last human on earth she would expect to find herself living with. Then again, after five hundred years of existence she should have learned that life could always find a way to surprise her. Like Riah, the battle against Meriel had changed him. Ivy's love had changed him.

Instead of foes, Colin and Riah became partners in a battle not between humans and preternaturals, but rather between good and evil. Both of them had to learn to trust, but the process had been quite enlightening. After Colin found love, he'd walked away from his life as a hunter and now worked as a protector instead of a killer. Riah seriously doubted he ever looked back.

For Colin the change was probably far more dramatic than for the rest of them. Even for Ivy, who left behind a human life to exist in the shadows. Of course, she hadn't exactly had a choice. Colin, Adriana, and Riah chose for her. Riah couldn't imagine their group without her. Alive or undead, Ivy was awesome.

Somewhere along the line, their little band of outcasts became a group of preternatural experts. Slowly they began to amass an amazing library of information and artifacts that rivaled even the church Colin formerly worked for. They helped those who needed help and destroyed those who embodied evil. Adriana had decided they needed a name something akin to superheroes and came up with the moniker: The Spiritus Group. Despite being technically undead, they were fighting for life. Drawing on her Latin, Adriana picked spiritus to represent their role as guardians of life. None of them argued with her suggestion.

Tonight, Riah was restless. Adriana was working downstairs in the lab she was putting together while Colin and Ivy were off searching for a text purported to hold the secrets of a coven of witches from ancient Ireland. That left her alone and fretting.

She wasn't sure what had her so nervous. Things in the area had been relatively quiet since they put down the rogue vampires. Not many vampires still existed in the world, thanks to Colin and the hunters that the church managed to always have at hand. It wasn't another of the dark she sensed. Something else was out there, and it tickled her mind like a bad case of poison ivy. At times she wished she had at least one psychic bone in her body. She might have strength and immortality, but precognitive abilities…not even a whisper.

"Hey, beautiful," Adriana said as she wrapped her arms around Riah's waist and kissed the back of her neck. "What are you thinking about so hard?"

Riah shook her head. "Nothing. Everything."

Adriana ran her hands up Riah's body until they molded around her breasts. "Well, I'm all sweaty and hot from unpacking. Think I'll go shower. Want to wash my back?"

Riah smiled. "Absolutely." Diversion, particularly the Adriana-initiated kind, was exactly what she needed.

❖

Kara was up at five and on her mountain bike by six. Everything over at Cam's appeared quiet. Probably still asleep. Despite her late night, Kara's eyes popped open bright and early, and she decided right now would be a great time to take a cruise through the park. The easiest and best way to see the park was to do it on a mountain bike rather than in her Park Service truck. The bike allowed her more of a bird's-eye view and the ability to power through the dirt trails.

Actually, she used the mountain bike frequently. The state park had its fair share of problems, including illegal cutting of timber, impromptu dope gardens, and the occasional homeless person who decided to take up residence. People were pretty ingenious, which usually meant they kept their endeavors to the interior areas of the park where visibility to the casual visitor on the paved trail was nil. In order to find the problems, she had to go onto the dirt trails and that meant her mountain bike.

She slid a full water bottle into a cage on the frame, put an energy bar into a bag on the top rail, and slipped her cell phone into a holder at her waist. Winston watched her from the yard, his head tipped and eyes sad. Of course, that didn't mean he was actually upset about her leaving him. Winston was one of those sad-eyed kind of dogs. As soon as she clipped the strap on her helmet, he got up and trotted to the porch, where he circled a couple of times and then lay down. Mister energetic would more than likely be in the same spot when she got back. She probably should have gotten a German shepherd who might actually want to run with her. Laughing quietly, Kara pedaled away. Winston might not be a powerful shepherd, but he was a pretty good guy. She figured she'd just have to keep him.

It took her about twenty minutes to cover the section from the Nine Mile Dam to the Seven Mile Bridge. It always struck her as kind of funny that the distance was actually more like four miles between the two spots instead of the two miles the names suggested. This section with its hills, bridge, and awesome views never failed to fill her with energy and delight.

Despite the sunshine, the air was cool. Summer was making a full-scale retreat. Pine needles and small tree branches littered the asphalt trail. A squirrel raced across in front of her, heading straight for a huge pinecone. The squirrels had been very, very busy the last few weeks. It made Kara worry the winter would be cold and long. The squirrels always knew when to lay in extra supplies. What would it be like in the cottage when the snow piled up and the freezing wind blew? Better double-check her supply of firewood before snow set in.

Not that it mattered all that much. She was guardian of the park this year, and Mother Nature could give it her best shot because Kara refused to let it drive her away. She'd waited too long for the chance to be the park's 24/7 caretaker, and nothing would send her packing. The shed was already half filled with firewood, and she had a pile of to-be-read books at the ready for those cold winter nights by the roaring fire.

Crossing into the Seven Mile stretch, Kara veered from the asphalt and onto one of the dirt trails that snaked throughout the park. Here, too, brown pine needles covered the path, and she had to dodge fallen pinecones and protruding rocks every few feet. It slowed her down but not much. To power through and around the natural obstacle course was fun.

So far nothing appeared out of place. She should probably turn around and head back, except the hairs at the back of her neck stood on end as if trying to tell her something was wrong. As hard as she searched, she couldn't see a thing. Once she reached the equestrian trails off Aubrey White Parkway, she stopped and decided it really was time to turn around, despite her anxiety. Maybe her senses were on overdrive because of yesterday's murder. Something like that was bound to make anyone a little jumpy and question things that under normal conditions wouldn't rate a second glance. Definitely time to go back.

Just as she pushed off, her cell phone rang. She grabbed it from the holder at her waist and flipped it open. "Lynch."

Jake's voice was tense. "Where are you, Kara?"

That jumpy feeling rippled along her spine at the sound of his voice. "I'm on my bike at the entrance to the horse trails."

"Good, you're close. Need you to get over to the military-cemetery trailhead."

"I'll be there in a couple minutes."

"Call Cam and then get here as fast as you can."

"What is it?" she asked. A sinking feeling told her she already knew.

"Another body."

Sometimes being right was so very fucked up. "Damn it."

"Get Cam." The call went dead.

Great. Just flipping great. This wasn't just bad, it was catastrophic. Kara looked at her phone and cursed. Jake told her to call Cam and that was all dandy, except she didn't have her number. Yesterday she'd made sure Cam had her cell number but, dummy that she was, she'd neglected to get hers. Short of hauling her ass back to the cottages on her bicycle, she had no way to call her.

She started to stuff the phone into her pocket when it rang again. "I'm on my way, Jake," she said, not bothering to look at the display.

"Kara, it's Cam." Unlike Jake, her voice was soft, sexy.

"Son of a bitch." How much weirder were things going to get?

"Excuse me?" A bit of snap crept into Cam's words.

Oops...hadn't meant to sound snarky. "Sorry. I just got off the phone from Jake and he'd asked me to call you. Problem is, I don't have your number. You calling me is almost as though you have ESP."

"Perhaps something like that." That smoky, sexy voice again.

Odd comment but she didn't have time to ask about it. "We'd like you to come to the trailhead at the old cemetery. Do you know where it is?"

"Yes."

"Please hurry."

"Another body?"

"I'm afraid so."

"I'm on my way. And Kara…"

"Yeah?"

"Be careful."

CHAPTER FIVE

Despite their closeness, Faolán hadn't shared one thing with his brother: Daphne. He didn't dare. She was special in so many ways it would be hard to describe his relationship with her to Conrí. He'd never understand. Faolán had never been the type to settle down. Not for centuries, not now. He had a taste for the impromptu, for the new and exciting.

Except, in the last few years, things were changing. For instance, his afternoon tryst with the sexy cyclist Diane wasn't quite as fulfilling as it might have been before Daphne. Which didn't make sense. He and Daphne didn't have a relationship outside of business. They came together for a common goal, period. Or, that's all it should be anyway, and it might be for Daphne. Not for him, and no matter how he might try to tell himself different, his heart knew the truth.

Yesterday, the afterglow of the afternoon sex with Diane wore off quickly and, once gone, his thoughts had drifted, as they tended to do these days, back to Daphne with her long legs, lush hair, and deep-green eyes. He could almost hear her voice and the gentle timbre of her laugh. It made him want to fly back to Ireland just to see her face. He could be holding another woman in his arms and still be thinking of Daphne. She was always with him.

She'd never been anything but polite and kind to him. If she knew that he dreamt of her or longed to press his lips to hers, she never let on. Hell, in all honesty, she probably felt nothing for him and he was simply in the throes of an old-fashioned schoolboy crush. Only, he was far from a schoolboy and knew the difference between a crush and all-consuming passion. This morning, just waiting for her call had him keyed up and ready to explode. No, what he felt for Daphne Magauran was nowhere close to a crush, and that's what made his chest tight and his knees weak.

When the phone rang, he jumped. "Christ," he muttered as he reached for the receiver. "Aye."

"Faolán." Daphne's voice was as clear as if she was standing in the next room.

A shiver of something he didn't dare describe raced up his spine. He took a silent, deep breath before he spoke. "Aye, Daphne, it's me."

"Everyone's ready." She didn't waste time on pleasantries.

"Are you coming?" His heart raced just asking the question.

"Yes. I'll be flying out of Dublin in the morning." Still matter-of-fact. All business.

"What about the others?" With one sister coming to Washington, that left five in Ireland. He didn't care if they came. He only wanted to see one.

"Mary and Adele will stay and watch the castle. Fiona, Tia, and Sheleigh will keep tabs on things from home. If anything starts to go even a little awry, they'll let us know."

Awry. Such an odd term for what could happen. What had happened at least three other times during the last six plus centuries. This time it would end differently. He didn't want to go on forever, and he sure as hell didn't want to die like this. Just once, he wanted to live like the man he'd never gotten the chance to be. If he could ever convince her he was worth it, he was the man for Daphne. He had no delusions. It would be an uphill battle.

"All right then," he said. "I'll see you when you get here."

She was silent for a moment, then said softly, "Soon, *cion.*" The connection went dead.

He went still. Cion…love. Putting the phone down slowly, he stared out the window. What had she meant? Like the mist that rolls in from the Irish coastline to blanket the moors, Daphne's endearment was obscure. He hoped it came of her heart.

He feared it was nothing more than simple affection offered to a friend in need.

❖

"Son of a bitch," Gene Cash muttered, his balding head tilted toward the corpse.

Squatting next to Gene, Kara leaned in closer to the medical examiner's investigator and peered at what he'd just exposed. The clothes on the body were shredded and bloody, making her wonder how he could make out much of anything. Not a pretty sight, and Kara couldn't stop the involuntary shudder that coursed through her entire body. Given the events of the last couple of days, the forestry program would need to add a homicide class to the curriculum.

"See that?" Gene pointed to a spot on the woman's arm.

Torn and bloody flesh. Destroyed clothing. What else was there to see? She was about to speak when her breath caught in her throat. "Yeah," she whispered. Despite the warmth of the sun, she was chilled.

"Well, see, here's the kicker." Gene rolled back on his heels. "This same mark was on that other guy we pulled outta your park."

"The same mark?" The chill turned to ice.

"Yes, ma'm. Couldn't see it until we got him all washed up but, sure as the world, found it right there on his arm. Or what was left of his arm anyway. Now this gal has it on her chest? Hope we don't have another sick sonofabitch like Yates on our hands. None of us needs that kind of bad again."

She was no serial-killer expert, yet she instinctively knew this wasn't the work of one. What exactly it was—she didn't know. Was pretty sure she didn't want to know. Kara's stomach lurched, and for a second, she closed her eyes against the sight of the bloody marks.

The intricate silver necklace at her neck now lay heavy against her flesh. She'd worn the necklace every day since her fifteenth birthday, when Mom had given it to her. A long time ago, it had belonged to her birth mother and was the only tangible piece of her birth family she possessed. The gift was meant to reassure her. All she remembered was how terrible it felt to hold it in her hand. It was the hard, cold evidence of a birth mother who never wanted her. Even in the face of that rejection, she'd slipped the silver around her neck and wore it to this day.

Staring at the same mark carved in this woman's flesh made Kara want to retch. The design was intricate but, more than that, unique. In the fifteen years since she'd slipped the sterling-silver chain around her neck, she'd never seen another like it. Now, not only was she staring at it on a murdered woman's body, but the ME was telling her it had been carved into yesterday's murder victim as well. Something was definitely rotten in Denmark.

A hand on her shoulder made her jump and nearly fall on her butt. The hand steadied her and she gazed up into Cam's concerned face. "Are you all right?"

The word *no* longed to tear from her lips. "Yeah, I'm okay."

"You don't look okay."

"Well, I am," she snapped.

Cam's voice softened. "Seriously, Kara, you're about three shades past white, and you're shaking all over."

She shrugged off Cam's hand and stepped back. "I'm fine." No, she really wasn't, but who was Cam to charge in like a white knight? She didn't need saving. Besides she wasn't even sure what she needed saving from.

Cam's eyes narrowed, but just about the time she thought she was going to argue, she simply nodded and then took a step toward the body. Hunched down beside Gene, Cam asked, "What have you got?"

Gene gave her a sideways glance and then, as he'd done for Kara, pointed out the carving in flesh. "This isn't some wolf and I don't care what it looks like. This is some new sicko running hell-bent through the park. We sure don't need this, Cam."

If she had to guess, she'd say Gene and Dr. Black Wolf knew each other. So why did everybody know the woman except her? Wasn't like she'd just moved to the area a week ago. She'd been born—well, she didn't exactly know where she'd been born—but she'd been raised in the Spokane area. Graduated from West Valley

High School out in the valley, went on to Spokane Falls Community College for her two-year degree, and then on to Pullman and Washington State University for her BA. Yes, indeed, she *knew* people, she just didn't know Cam, and it seemed like she was the only one.

Or maybe she was just being pissy because today was turning out even worse than yesterday. One death in the park was unusual, though not unheard of. Two in the space of twenty-four hours— that never happened. Now, it not only happened, it happened on her watch.

Shifting from foot to foot, Kara studied Gene and Cam while Jake talked to a couple of sheriff's deputies. A flicker of something she didn't quite get stilled her. Her attention was riveted on Cam when she saw it again. The movement was so subtle, in the normal course of events, she'd have missed it. This wasn't exactly a normal situation and nearly passed her by. As Cam watched Gene do his examination of the body, she sniffed the air. *Sniffed* like Winston when he got wind of a skunk or a cat or any other creature that didn't belong in his immediate vicinity. And more than just the way she sniffed the air, her eyes were alive—they followed whatever unique smell she caught in the scent...just like a dog...or a wolf.

❖

Cam could literally feel eyes on her. She'd been busted. *Good.* With the place crawling with law enforcement, staff from the medical-examiner's office, and park personnel, it wasn't the time or the place to press Kara on it. No, she'd wait until they were back at the cottages...alone. Last night under the stars, she'd opened this particular can of worms, and now, Kara was thinking outside the box. The right direction but she still had a long way to go.

"Whadda ya think, Cam? Ever seen anything like this before?" Gene peered up at her expectantly, his eyes big and blue behind black-rimmed glasses.

Cam shook her head as she brought her focus back to the body on the ground at their feet. "Not really. Somebody's playing games."

"Ya think?" Gene snorted.

"Seriously, this is some sick shit." She couldn't elaborate on how sick to Gene.

"What about the bites? They look canine to me." His head was cocked as he studied the torn flesh on her thighs and arms.

Cam shook her head again. "Like yesterday, they're made to look like a wolf, but a human hand had a part in all this." She needed to stop the werewolf asshole and quick. More bodies would bring more questions. She didn't know how much longer she could convince people this wasn't the work of the wolf. Gene was a sharp guy, and he'd catch on to her smoke and mirrors pretty quick if she didn't shut the werewolf down now.

Gene stood and waved to the two men standing up the trail. "Come on down, I'm done." He turned his attention back to Cam. "I hate this. You get one piece-of-crap killer cleaned out of the city, and the next thing you know, there's another one. It sucks, you know?"

Cam nodded. "Yeah, I know." Gene had no idea exactly how much she knew. Only this was no garden-variety serial killer; this was much worse.

When Gene and his crew had loaded the body and were on their way to the morgue, Cam walked back up to the trail with Kara in silence, though the energy that surged between them could power a small city. Yeah, Kara had definitely busted her, but it appeared she planned to let her make the first move.

"You want to talk about it?" Cam asked.

Kara gave her a sideways glance. "About what?"

Nice try. Cam put a hand on her arm and almost snatched it back as a jolt raced up her arm. She twitched but didn't pull away. "You know."

Kara paused and turned to face her. Her voice was low. "Not here, not now."

Interesting. She figured Kara would want to quiz her the first second she could. "Tonight then?"

She nodded. "Let me deal with this." She waved her hand back toward the base of the hill. "We can talk tonight about...the rest."

"Tonight it is."

"You need a ride back? I'm on my bike but Jake can pick you up in a service truck."

Cam shook her head. "Not necessary. These will do just fine." She pointed to her running shoes.

"I'll see you later then."

"Absolutely." She began to run north on the Centennial trail in the direction of the dam.

"Cam?"

Pausing at the top of the rise, she looked down at Kara. "Yeah?"

"Bring wine."

Chapter Six

Typically Faolán didn't bother with television. Today, he was so bored he picked up the remote and began to press buttons. "Hum," he muttered. "A hundred some channels and still nothing on."

After clicking through the lineup, he settled on the local news. As he made himself a sandwich, he half watched. At least until he caught a glimpse of something familiar. A newscaster was standing just outside the gates of the old cemetery down the road. The camera panned across emergency vehicles and police cars that filled the small parking lot. Two uniformed men pushed a gurney up the path behind the newsman, a black body bag clearly visible.

Sandwich forgotten, Faolán was shaking as he sank to the sofa and turned up the volume. *A second murder.* Two days, two murders, and both within minutes of his small rental home. A feeling of déjà vu swept over him.

A throb started behind his right eye and Faolán rubbed his temple. It was a coincidence...right? No way could it be happening again. No way. The pain grew until it was like a hot poker inside his head.

Hand trembling, he picked up his cell phone and hit speed dial. "It's happened again," he whispered when the connection went through. He hated how close to tears he felt. Tough guys didn't cry. Or so Conrí had told him again and again for as long as he could remember.

Daphne's voice had an immediate calming effect. "Are you certain?"

He thought back to the newscast. "Not completely, but I'd lay odds on it being the same."

"You can't be certain you did it."

Of course not. There must be dozens of werewolves roaming eastern Washington State. "The odds are in my favor."

"Faolán, listen to me. I don't want you jumping to any conclusions."

"No jump, darling." He appreciated her attempt at reassurance even if it was misplaced.

"Faolán, you didn't do anything," she snapped. "Just wait for me and together we'll get to the truth."

He gripped the small phone so tight his knuckles ached. "That's what I'm afraid of."

"The truth will set you free."

He laughed, he couldn't help it. "You know you sound like one of those crazy sci-fi shows?"

Her laughter was the sweetest sound he'd ever heard. "No sci fi about it, *darling*. I'm the real deal."

She was real and special and wise. He just didn't think any of it could save him. "God, I hope so."

"Wait for me."

"I'll do my best."

When he snapped the phone shut, despite everything, he felt better. Daphne would be here soon and she'd work her magic—literally. This wouldn't be a repeat of London a hundred years ago. He wouldn't let it be. All he had to do was be patient and wait. Together they were stronger, and if he held onto that belief maybe it would all work out somehow.

He didn't want to dwell on what he might have already done. Instead, while he waited he could work on getting everything else in place, starting with the beautiful red-haired park ranger.

After looking up the number on his computer, Faolán dialed the ranger station at Nine Mile dam. It rang ten times before someone picked up.

"I'm sorry to bother you," he said, working hard to intone his best American accent. "But I wanted to send a thank-you card to one of your rangers who helped me and my family last week. Real nice lady with red hair..."

In less than five minutes Faolán had what he needed. The helpful staffer was happy to give him the ranger's name, along with the address of the station where he could mail his fictitious thank-you card.

Kara Lynch.

❖

"Are you okay?" Jake was looking at her like she'd contracted some sort of communicable disease. Actually, she kind of felt like it too.

Kara nodded. "Yeah, considering how many people are getting knocked off in my park."

She didn't add that those two people also had the same symbol carved into their flesh that she wore around her neck every day. Way, way, way too creepy.

"Our park." He put a hand on her arm and squeezed. "And we have a lot of experienced folks out here ready to stop this son of a bitch before he hurts anyone else."

Without a doubt, a great sentiment. She just wasn't sure it would be so simple. Her arms folded over her chest, Kara tried to keep from shivering. Not that she was cold. The autumn was lovely. The kind that brought out the area's runners and cyclists to enjoy the trail before cold weather pushed them inside. She'd want to run and ride those trails right along with them. Under normal circumstances, she'd be full of energy and enthusiasm for the day.

Normal, of course, being the operative word, and this day was as far from normal as possible. Yesterday's murder had been unsettling. A second one, twenty-four hours later, even more so, and that was before she knew about the carvings. Everything about them reeked.

She looked at Jake's normally calm face. The storm she felt showed in it as well. "I know, Jake, and I know they'll get whoever did this, but it just feels so personal."

He put an arm around her. "That's what makes you so good at your job. Come on, Ranger. You want a ride back to the station?"

She shook her head. "No, thanks. I'll take my bike. The exercise will make me feel better. You know, release a few endorphins and all that." Besides, good speech aside, Jake didn't have a clue what was going on here. She wasn't sure she really did either, but she was getting there, and the ride back would give her some quiet time to mull it over.

"Okay, then, I'll see you at the station."

Jake turned and walked to his service truck. Not his usual light stride either. He walked like a man much older. She understood exactly.

Kara straddled the mountain bike and began to pedal up the short hill winding away from the cemetery. Only a few minutes later, she was in the heart of the park and far away from everything and everybody. She veered off the asphalt and followed dirt trails that led deep into the trees. As she moved farther away from the paved path, the trees grew closer together and the path rougher. The canvas of pine trees partially blocked the bright sunlight. The air stilled, disturbed only by the sound of her bike tires on the trail. Finally, after pushing as hard as she could, she stopped.

After dismounting, she leaned the bike against a tree, pulled off her helmet, and sank to the ground. In the solitude she pulled the chain from around her neck, the metal warm against her fingers. The unique silver pendant was so beautiful in the palm of her hand, and, more important, harmless. It glittered as it caught a shaft of light that managed to make it through the thick tree branches and would have fascinated her if only it didn't fill her with sorrow. She'd never seen anything like it. After Mom had given it to her, she'd tried to find its origins, hoping to learn something of her heritage. She'd come up with nothing. One more confirmation of abandonment by a mother and father who didn't have a place for her in their lives.

Until now. Personal didn't even begin to describe how it felt when Gene unknowingly brought the connection to her attention. It was as if someone was pointing a finger right at her. Totally irrational yet she couldn't shake the feeling she was involved. How she could possibly be connected to any of this was beyond her.

The metal grew even warmer, as if absorbing the heat of her body, when she closed her fingers around the pendant. As she held it, a burst of thunder roared overhead and lightning cracked across the sky. The unexpected cacophony made her jerk and lose her balance. She fell backward against the hard earth and everything went black.

"Moira, my love," he purred in her ear as he held her against his chest. "I will love you for eternity." He stroked her cheek, his touch gentle.

Hot tears flowed down her cheeks and she pulled away. His words, his touch empty. "Ye speak of love and yet ye pledge to another."

He tried to touch her again, his eyes sad. "I do not love her."

Her heart ached so deeply it was as if he'd cut her with a blade. "You will marry her on the morrow." She wrenched her words out on a sob.

"Aye, but my heart will always be yours." He stroked her cheek again, the kiss he pressed against her lips passionate.

Overwhelming emotion shook her. She broke the kiss, turned, and ran into the darkness. Tears streamed down her face. How could he do this to her? How could he kiss her and talk of love? Lies, all lies. His pleading voice grew ever fainter as she put distance between them. She couldn't be near him for even a moment more. She wanted only to get as far away as possible. When she'd run as long as she could, she crumpled to the hard, cold earth and sobbed.

The moon was high by the time her tears dried. Moira pushed up from the ground and looked skyward. Stars twinkled and the moonlight warmed the dark sky. The night seemed to mock her anguish. At least at first. Slowly calm washed over her before a tingling rippled through her head to toe. Her body began to hum and power roared through her limbs. Suddenly, as if the gods had spoken, Moira knew what she must do.

She brushed the leaves and dirt from her skirt and turned in the direction of home. Samhain would come with the new dawn and so too would her vengeance.

Under the light of the moon, her silver pendant glowed against her pale skin as she disappeared into the night.

When Kara opened her eyes, daylight had faded and twilight was settling in. Her head was pounding, her fingers aching. Only then did she notice that she still held the necklace in a death grip. It dropped away as she uncurled her fingers, the imprint of the design etched into her palm.

With her other hand, she rubbed the back of her head. Instead of soothing away the pain, the touch hurt...a lot. Her fingers came away bloody. "Well, isn't this just dandy," she muttered.

Shakily she stood. Stars sparkled in her vision and she wasn't sure consciousness would hang with her. Then the moment passed. Her vision cleared and her shaking knees steadied.

Taking stock, Kara was disheartened to realize the cottage was still a good five miles away. She'd like to think she was tough enough to make it back on the bike, but she had serious doubts. The shaking subsided, though her legs felt rubbery and she had the mother of all headaches. Bike in hand, she looked around and weighed her options. The thought of bouncing across the rocky trails made her eyes water. What other choice did she have? Wishing to be home wasn't going to get her there.

If she had any question about how out of it she was, it was answered when she looked up to see Jake practically on top of her. Even worse, he wasn't alone. She hadn't heard a single one of them and they weren't exactly trying to be quiet.

"Hey, Jake," she said without much enthusiasm, despite the fact she was actually quite glad to see him. Briefly she wondered why he started to run toward her.

"Steve," Jake yelled. "Over here."

He was reaching for her when the stars began to dance in her eyes again. Her grip on the bike fell away, her knees buckled, and blackness dropped over her once more.

❖

"I'm going home."

Cam smiled. The determination in Kara's voice was hard to miss even halfway down the hospital corridor. Her words conveyed intent and emotion loud and clear. The woman did have a mind of her own. She liked that about her.

In the exam room she found Jake standing with feet apart, arms crossed, and staring at Kara like a child who needed a time-out. Kara sat on the edge of the mobile bed, fully dressed and looking like she could spit nails—literally—if any had been handy.

"Hey, Jake," Cam said, putting a hand on his shoulder. "How is she?"

Jake raised both eyebrows. "Same old Kara. Pain in the ass, as usual."

Kara rolled her eyes.

Cam smiled. "Besides that, how is she?"

"A pretty good bump on the head, and the doc would like her to stay overnight for observation."

"Let me guess, she's not going for it."

"Not even for a second."

"I'm right here, you know," Kara said petulantly. "Like *right* here. I can hear every word."

"I see that," Cam said calmly. "I agree with Jake, though. You have to follow the doctor's orders and stay the night. Head injuries aren't something to fool around with."

"Good Lord," Kara exclaimed. "I've hit my head harder getting out of the car. This is no big deal."

"You blacked out. You need to stay." Why was she being so obstinate? Having spirit was one thing. Being foolish with a serious injury was something else.

"I said no." Kara's feet hit the ground and she started to leave. A little unsteady, she stumbled and instead ran face-first into Cam's chest.

Cam put her arms around her almost involuntarily, as if she needed to protect Kara. It didn't feel all that bad. She didn't feel all that bad.

"Sorry," Kara mumbled into her chest.

Cam held her out and gazed into her incredible green eyes. They were large and overly bright in a face that was far too pale. Beneath her palms, her body trembled. Cam wanted to draw her back into her arms and hold her until her body stilled. Instead, she slid her hands down Kara's arms to hold her hands. "Really, you should stay overnight."

Kara held her gaze. *Stubborn* all but screamed from her expression. "No."

Calmly Cam asked, "Why not?"

Kara didn't strike her as unreasonable or stupid. Beneath the stubbornness that appeared far from abating was something else. Despite all the people around them and the noise of the ER, she felt as though they were alone. All she saw was Kara's face and all she heard was her quiet voice.

For a long moment Kara didn't say anything, just held her quivering lips tight together. Finally she looked away and said, "I just can't."

Yes, a lot more to it. "All right." She continued to hold her hands as she shifted her attention to the doctor who'd followed her from the exam room. "I'll stay with her."

"I don't like it," the tall man with the graying hair said. "But as long as she's not alone for the next few hours…"

"Not a problem."

"You need to watch for a few things," the doctor continued.

Cam listened carefully, promised to bring her back if she had convulsions, was confused, started vomiting, or a few other things. She figured she could handle it. After all, she was a doctor even if her patients typically were of the four-legged variety. At least this patient could talk, and that was something she never enjoyed on the day job.

By the time Kara was buckled in the passenger seat of Cam's car, the night was pitch-black. She leaned back against the headrest and closed her eyes. Her color hadn't improved much but she did appear more relaxed.

Cam fingered the car key but didn't put it in the ignition. Shifting in her seat, she looked at Kara. Her eyes were still closed, her breathing slow and easy. Her earlier agitation gone.

"I meant what I told the doctor."

Kara slowly opened her eyes and gazed at Cam. "You got me out of there and I appreciate it, but you've done plenty. A ride home and I'm good. My own home, my own bed, it's all I need tonight, honest."

"Of course." Cam started the car. "And I'll be there just to make sure it's all you need tonight."

Kara might not realize she didn't make empty promises. Aside from her personal code of honor, though, she wanted to stay with her. Cam simply had no desire to leave her side. Some protective instinct rose inside and she wasn't about to ignore it. Maybe it was just the threat showing up and brushing Kara just a little too closely.

Or maybe it was something much more personal.

CHAPTER SEVEN

He stood in the shadows, his gaze intent on the row of brick houses. Darkness was on the horizon, the time of day most people were at home. Here things were different. He didn't see a soul around any of these modest homes. Where could they be? Could he possibly be in the wrong place? No, this was it. He could smell her.

Following her scent, he crossed the narrow street and climbed several steps leading to a covered porch. Her scent was strong and vibrant here, almost as though she'd been standing in this same spot only minutes before. He inhaled deeply and smiled. Yes, he was most definitely in the right place.

The lot itself wasn't large, and walking the perimeter took only a few minutes. A single-story dwelling, of which he easily identified all the main rooms, including the master bedroom, small as it was in the older home. Back when these houses were built, large master suites were a luxury reserved for the rich, and these weren't the homes of the wealthy by any stretch of the imagination. On the back porch, a can full of sand with a cigarette butt sticking out of it was tucked in a corner as if the she didn't want anyone to see it. He was surprised. Quite a dirty habit for one of her pedigree. Not to mention, a rather new twist for an old soul.

Then again, he wondered if she had any idea. It wouldn't be the first time he'd run into an oblivious mark. Not every generation was enlightened, or happy about it when they were. Most societies didn't exactly embrace witches, so families of hereditary witches tended to keep it really close. Too many stories of black magic and blood rituals kept the legends alive and the truth in the shadows. This witch might not know who or what she was.

Then again, she might be fully cognizant of it all—her power, her history, her importance. She could simply be hiding, pretending she was someone she wasn't. What they wouldn't do to try to fool him. Really? Did they think him that stupid? After so many years, he knew all the tricks, and stupid was something he wasn't now and never had been.

Wrinkling his nose at the disgusting smell wafting up from the makeshift ashtray, he walked away and continued his inspection. After a second loop of the house, he stopped at the back corner and unzipped his pants. If he was in wolf form, he'd lift his leg, but this would have to do. Now wasn't the time to make a shift.

He walked the perimeter, marking every few feet. When he'd covered the entire lot, he zipped up his pants and turned toward the car. A scent caught on the air and stopped him. The hair at the back of his neck stood up. Slowly he moved toward the house on the other side of the fence, his senses on alert.

He paused at the fence, his eyes closed. Inhaling deeply, he drew in the distinctive lupus scent. Not a werewolf, he knew his own kind intimately. What he also knew was the scent of a shifter, and this was most definitely a shape-shifter. A female, no less.

The shifter hadn't been here long. The scent was too light for it to have been around for any significant length of time. Interesting, and it put a very different spin on things. Then again, he liked complications. Mysteries that got his blood roaring didn't come around all that often. It had also been a very long time since he'd had the chance to take a shifter. Nothing felt quite like it, and his nerves almost sang with anticipation. The coupling. The killing. Ambrosia.

This trip was turning out interesting in ways he never imagined. As he finished his loop around this second house, trailing his fingers along the fence, the porch railing, the front door, he was smiling. He opted not to mark here. He wouldn't need anything so obvious to announce his presence. The shifter would know the minute she was within ten feet of the front door. Yes, the shifter would have her hackles up once she got a whiff of him. His smile turned to a low chuckle.

This was getting better by the minute.

❖

Kara drifted off after managing to stay awake the obligatory few hours requested by the ER doctor. When she awoke, the world outside the window was blanketed in a cloud-covered darkness as black as coal. Her head pounded and she ached all over, as if she'd been thrown from her bike even though that wasn't the case. She'd been sitting on the ground when everything went blank. After that, she didn't have a clue. Well, except for the weird-ass dream. Not actually like a dream. More like she was there. Like she *was* Moira, the woman who wore her necklace. Just remembering the dream creeped her out.

Across from where Kara stretched out on the sofa, Cam sat with her feet on the coffee table and a laptop across her thighs. Her head was bowed, her brow knitted. Her fingers flew across the keys. The only sound in the room, besides Winston's snores, was the click, click, click of the keyboard. It gave her a few minutes of unguarded time to study the very interesting Dr. Black Wolf.

Nice guns was her first thought. Great face was her second. She was more than just a hot bod, though, and that made her even more alluring. Casual relationships or a pretty face wasn't of interest to Kara. Life was too short to waste time on fluff. She liked a woman who was smart as well as sexy, and the good doctor did seem to possess the whole package.

Not to say that *she* did. Especially right at the moment. Before they left the hospital, Kara got a long look at herself. Not a pretty sight. Big black circles beneath her eyes made her look more like a raccoon than a woman, and her hair…nothing an expensive hairdresser and a couple hours in a chair couldn't fix. Now that she'd slept on it for the better part of the day, even worse. Yeah, she was a babe, all right, sure to impress someone like Cam.

As if sensing Kara's thoughts, Cam glanced up. A slow smile turned up the corners of her mouth and Kara thought her heart would stop. "How are you feeling?"

Her mouth was dry as she croaked, "Okay."

Cam set the laptop aside and moved to sit on the coffee table directly in front of Kara. She laid a hand on her forehead. The touch was like fire and Kara gasped. Cam snatched her hand away. "I'm so sorry."

Impulsively, Kara captured Cam's hand. "No, I'm sorry. You took me by surprise."

"I only wanted to see if you're running a fever."

Kara smiled slowly. "Oh, I'm running a fever, but not the kind you're checking for."

"Oh…" Cam drawled. "Is that a good thing or a bad thing?"

The hesitancy in Cam's voice surprised her. Cam was all suave and professional and so damned good looking. She didn't expect a woman with fears and insecurity might be underneath.

She squeezed Cam's hand. "It's a good thing."

Cam smiled back, her dark eyes almost twinkling. "Well, great. But, seriously, Kara, how are you really feeling?"

Kara let go of Cam's hand and pushed up to a sitting position. For a second everything sort of swam, and then it settled back down. "All weird things considered, pretty good. Still not quite sure what happened."

"Jake said you fell from your bike."

"See, now, that's the odd thing. I didn't fall from the bike. I'd gotten off and was sitting on the ground thinking. I saw lightning overhead and the next thing I know, I'm staring up into Jake's face. Right after I realized my head hurt like a son of a bitch."

"You didn't fall?"

"Nope."

"You're sure?"

"One hundred percent."

Cam got up and began to pace. "I don't like that."

"No shit. Doesn't really warm my cockles either, if you know what I mean."

Cam stopped pacing and tilted her head, studying Kara. "Cockles? What exactly is a cockle?"

Kara shrugged. "Beats the hell out of me, but that's what Mom always says." Some day she'd actually have to ask Mom about that.

A loud knock at the front door cut off anything else she wanted to say. Kara started to get up, Who on earth would be here this time of night? She didn't get many visitors here, definitely not in the middle of the night. Cam stopped her before her feet hit the floor.

"It's for me."

"For you?" How would anyone know Cam was here?

Cam nodded. "It'll make sense in a sec."

Kara raised an eyebrow. "Okay…I guess." She was talking to Cam's back.

Cam returned with two women moments later. Both were petite—a beautiful dark-haired woman with ivory-white skin and a voluptuous black woman. Their obvious closeness sent a wave of longing through Kara's heart. Maybe she'd hit her head harder than she thought.

"Kara," Cam said. "This is Dr. Riah Preston and Adriana James. Dr. Preston is the Spokane County Medical Examiner."

The last part of the introduction was unnecessary. Kara recognized the name immediately. Dr. Preston was well known in the Spokane area, though rarely seen in the flesh. Kind of crazy to find the mysterious doctor in her living room now.

"Kara Lynch." She stood, only mildly unsteady, and held out her hand.

Both women shook her hand and Dr. Preston said, "Please, call me Riah, and this is my partner, Adriana."

Formalities out of the way, she wanted to know what was going on.

"Okay," Kara said slowly as she looked from face to face. "Since I'm apparently the only one out of the loop here, tell me what this is all about."

Riah turned to Cam, who nodded and said, "She's ready."

"Ready?" For what? Like the day could get any stranger.

"You've got a werewolf loose in your park." Riah's explanation was very matter-of-fact, her face calm and serious.

The werewolf again! Kara resisted the urge to roll her eyes. "And what would bring you to throw that out? Seriously, first Cam and now you. Come on, both of you are educated professionals. Surely you have a better explanation for these murders than a werewolf."

Adriana patted Kara on the shoulder. "Trust me on this one, Kara. These two know what they're talking about."

"Because…"

With an eyebrow raised, Adriana leaned her head toward Cam. "Because she's a shape-shifter, and gorgeous over there," she motioned to Riah, "is a vampire."

CHAPTER EIGHT

Cam was pretty sure, between the three of them, they'd made Kara's headache even worse. It took at least an hour to explain their position, and by the time they were done, she thought they'd made a pretty good case. Without the evidence Riah brought along from the autopsies, she wasn't sure they'd have gotten Kara on board. Confronted with everything in Technicolor, she grudgingly conceded that maybe, just maybe, there was more here than met the eye. By the time they'd finished, Kara's eyes had deep, dark circles around them. Even deeper and darker than when they'd left the hospital. Time to lay off.

Kara, once more stretched out on the sofa, had drifted back to sleep. Good, she needed the rest. Gave her a chance to usher Riah and Adriana outside to show them what she'd discovered earlier. Didn't need to wave a red flag in Kara's face when she was already overwhelmed. The minute she'd stepped out of the car Cam had noticed but, at the time, didn't want to alarm Kara. She had plenty to deal with, like a head injury, hospital visits, and preternatural predators.

Out in the yard, the scent hit her hard again. The only one who could smell the distinct aroma, she had no doubt Riah and Adriana would take her at her word. At least with those two, explanations were easier. They were far from mere mortals. Well, that wasn't exactly correct. Adriana was all human. Except, she was a human with a whole lot of otherworld experience. She'd been working with a vampire for years and actually living with one for a good while. Human—yes. Mind wide open—definitely.

SHERI LEWIS WOHL

Cam walked to the fence, Riah and Adriana right with her. The closer they got, the stronger the smell.

"He's been here." She pointed to the corner post. "Actually, he's been all the way around the house, marking as he went."

Riah studied the fence. "Are you sure it's him? Maybe it was just Kara's dog."

Cam shook her head. "I wish it was as simple as a dog. The difference almost gags me."

Without a word, Adriana jogged to the car, returning a moment later with a bag. From inside, she pulled out a couple of swabs and glass tubes. "Show me where," she told Cam as she squatted near the fence. "I sure as hell can't smell it so you'll have to be the navigator here."

Cam pointed to a spot about a foot up from the ground. "There."

Adriana ran a swab over the fencepost, popped it into the tube, and secured the end cap. They repeated the process three more times. After she put the last tube into her case, Adriana straightened up and brushed dead grass from the knees of her jeans.

"I'll run tests on these and will be able to tell you definitely whether it's a he or a she, and we can take a look at what interesting little details the whiz will tell us."

"The whiz?" Cam's eyebrows rose.

"Yeah." Adriana smiled. "It's a technical term for urine. Sounds better."

"Okay. Must have missed that class in vet school."

"See that's what happens when you go to Wazzu instead of U of Dub." Adriana's smile grew bigger. "You just don't get quite the same training."

Cam laughed, enjoying, at least for a moment, the traditional rivalry between graduates of Washington State University, affectionately referred to as Wazzu, and the University of Washington, or U of Dub. Even in the darkest hours, when evil was taking the lead, something as simple as a smile could bolster her spirit.

"Well, my cougars will kick your husky ass any day of the week."

"Girls, girls, girls," Riah said. "As much as I hate to break this up, we've got more important things to worry about than who went to what college."

Adriana took Riah's arm. "You can tell she's not from around here."

"How about we all focus—" Riah pointed at Adriana's bag— "on the here and now."

"Point taken," Cam acknowledged. "Old habits and all that."

Adriana looked at Cam and winked. "Don't take it personally. Riah just doesn't understand the whole husky-cougar thing."

"And at the moment, doesn't have the time for either of you to explain it to me." She took hold of Adriana's hand and turned in the direction of their car.

True enough. They were getting sidetracked and Riah was right. Time wasn't a luxury they had. "Okay," Cam said. "Let me know what you find, and if you need me to take a look at the samples, call me."

Adriana nodded. "Will do."

After they left, Cam stood on the grass and listened to the night. The air was cool, the sky clear with a gorgeous blanket of stars. Under different circumstances, it would be romantic. Instead, an uncomfortable feeling settled over her.

She'd felt the presence of evil before. Nothing new to her or her people, yet something about this was different. Personal. As if she had a lot more to lose this time.

She didn't like it.

❖

Faolán couldn't deny the tug. It dragged at his soul, and the darker the night became, the harder it was to resist. He wanted to give in. To shift. To run. He just couldn't. It wasn't safe.

It would all be so much easier if his life followed the folktales. Sure, the full moon was great and, honestly, it did make the change quicker and smoother. But it didn't control the change. A full moon was more of a facilitator than anything else. At least to those born to the pack. Father had become what he was because a powerful witch had called a curse down on him and his family. By extension, he and Conrí were sons of a werewolf and born with the moon in their souls. All he had to do was walk out the door and call it. That quick. That simple.

Except nothing was simple anymore. What started out as a thrilling end to a long journey was turning into a nightmare. All he'd needed to do was find her and then call in Conrí and the sisters. No one murdered and definitely not by his hand…or rather his fangs.

Sitting on the front porch, elbows on his knees, head in his hands, Faolán massaged his temples. He had to calm down and wait. The end was in sight, and if he could hold on a little longer, it would all be over.

Actually, it would be a new beginning for him. The life he'd dreamed about and never possessed. So different and very strange. Yet, the thrill of it was fantastic. Everything would change, and it would be for the greater good. His family had existed in the shadowlands for too long now. He wanted free of the curse and this existence that condemned him to such loneliness.

The thoughts of a new level of existence chased away the vestiges of his headache and he smiled briefly. Yes, he could do this. He would stay inside this house, resist the urge to run, and wait for Daphne. Beautiful, sexy Daphne.

His dream of a future with her was nothing more than a fantasy. He understood that. Still, just the chance to spend an hour with her made all the difference. That little bit of time was enough. He could hold on.

The ring of his cell phone sent him jumping. *Jesus, I really do need to calm down.* He glanced at the display, not in the least surprised to see Conrí's number.

"Brother."

Conrí, in typical Conrí style, jetted right to the point of his call. "I'll be there within the hour."

"You don't even know where I'm staying."

"Of course I do. I know everything about you, Faolán. Always have. Always will."

As much as he hated to admit the truth of Conrí's words, he did think his brother possessed nearly psychic abilities. From the time they were small children, Conrí consistently knew everything about everyone. Pretty damn frightening. Always a bit of a bully, Conrí and his ability to keep tabs on Faolán was just messed up. He wanted to be his own man after all these centuries of running side-by-side with his brother. He didn't need or want Conrí's constant presence in his life.

Their father would be disappointed. He held great faith in the strength of families. Then again, when his father was born, sticking together wasn't just important; it was critical. Lives depended upon it. After father's death, he and Conrí continued to present a solid front. No one dared oppose them and no one did. They flourished in that time of respect and fear.

Those days were gone. This was a different world with very different rules. People weren't always frightened of those like him and his brother. Many understood what they were and why. Some even begged to join their ranks. Along the way, both of them turned a few here and there. It got lonely year after year, and Conrí wasn't exactly the best companion for eternity. A difficult man and a ferocious werewolf, he was feared in either form. Faolán, and most everyone else, typically gave him wide berth.

Even so, Conrí liked to be the one in charge. If Conrí didn't like the woman Faolán was seeing, she'd disappear without a word. If Conrí didn't like where Faolán was living, he made his life miserable until he gave in and went where Conrí wanted him to. It got tiresome after centuries of the same crap. The peace he'd enjoyed lately here in this Eastern Washington city had been fantastic.

He'd have liked a few more days without Conrí rolling in and taking over. Wasn't going to happen. Big brother was on his way, and he'd not only boss Faolán around until he wanted to scream, but he'd also have Daphne biting her nails before all was said and done. Same old…same old.

But what he wanted didn't matter. If Conrí said he'd be at his front door within an hour, that's exactly where he'd be. The games were about to begin.

❖

If she wasn't so damned tired, Kara would wonder what Cam, Riah, and Adriana were doing outside for so long. Actually, more than being tired, she was still trying to wrap her head around the news that Cam was a shape-shifter. She had less of a problem believing Riah was a vampire. After all, with pale, smooth skin that reminded Kara of fine porcelain, she had the look. Then there was the well-known fact she always worked at night. Most in the city figured she was simply a bit eccentric. Since she had skills that could have taken her anywhere, no one argued with her night-shift request. Now the night thing made sense in a whole new way.

Cam was a different story. Her being a shape-shifter certainly explained that sniffing moment at the body. Still, when Kara looked at her, she didn't see the slightest hint that she was anything other than human.

That was stupid. Like Kara had any idea at all what someone who wasn't all human might possibly look like. She grew up in a normal, run-of-the-mill, middle-class household. Both her parents were teachers. She was a park ranger with a degree in plant biology. She knew a lot more about the native grasses in Riverside State Park than she knew about vampires, werewolves, or any other creature not quite of this world. The one undergrad class she'd taken in folklore was the sum total of her education in anything even remotely resembling the paranormal.

Keeping Cam at arm's length would be the wise thing to do. She had enough on her hands with the creatures that roamed her park: human, reptile, and animal. All the talk of werewolves, vampires, and shape-shifters was making her already sore head hurt even more.

But she was incredibly attracted to Cam. Wouldn't her parents just love this one? It had taken them a while to adjust to the reality that Kara wasn't interested in men. Once they did, they were gracious to the few women she brought home. But having a lesbian daughter with a shape-shifting girlfriend might be asking them to stretch a little far.

She was jumping way ahead of herself. Here she was thinking about taking Cam home to meet the folks, and she hadn't even touched her or kissed those sexy, full lips. Must have seriously smacked her head and that's why she was lying here letting her imagination run full tilt. Time to let it go and worry about the werewolf in her park instead.

A darned good plan too. At least until Cam walked back through her front door. She paused in the doorway, with a quizzical expression, her dark eyes sharp and appraising. Staring at the snug Levis, blue shirt unbuttoned just enough to show a hint of her breasts, and her long hair pulled back in a ponytail, Kara silently commanded herself not to drool. Inwardly, she groaned. This was so hard.

"Excuse me?" Cam said, looking at Kara expectantly.

Ah, crap. The groan she thought she'd kept inside had apparently leaked out from between her lips. No wonder Cam looked at her like she was a nut case. "Nothing. Just a little rattling in my head when I move."

Cam came toward her, the expression on her face shifting to concern. "You should just rest."

"I feel like that's all I've done this afternoon. I need to get up and help."

"It's late and you can't do anything tonight." Cam took her by the shoulders and just as quickly dropped her hands, jumping back.

"Son of a bitch," Kara blurted.

Cam's eyes widened and she stared first at her hands, then at Kara. "You felt that too?"

"Damn straight." The shock that went through her body when Cam touched her was incredible. Frightening and thrilling at the same time. "Do it again."

Cam looked doubtful. "I don't know, that was weird."

"Speak for yourself. I thought it was pretty awesome."

A smile appeared on Cam's face and she winked. "Kind of a thrill."

"Yeah, it was. Do it again, Doc."

Moving closer, Cam put one finger on Kara's shoulder. The buzz was immediate. She looked up into Cam's face. "Feel it?"

"Oh, yeah."

"Try both hands."

She did and the buzz grew warm and vibrant. Kara smiled. "Pretty damned strange."

"I don't know if this is good," Cam said, but she didn't remove her hands.

Kara stared into Cam's eyes, liking the shifting emotions she saw there. "Kiss me."

Time seemed to stop and Kara was pretty sure she stopped breathing too. What would Cam do? Probably run back to Montana, scared off by the hallucinating park ranger. What the hell? After everything that happened, how bad could it be if Cam walked away? Just another instance of attraction derailed by wrong time and place. She'd be okay. Yeah, right. Who was she fooling? It would suck.

When Cam's head descended toward Kara's, her heart was beating so hard, she thought it might explode. Running away didn't appear to be on Cam's mind. Then Cam's lips touched hers. Gentle at first, she tasted sweet, and then as the fire between them ignited, her kiss deepened. Kara put her hands on that silky black hair, sighing at the feel of it against her palms.

She was breathless when Cam straightened up and stared at her as if she was trying to make sense out of what just happened. Kara would like to say she had it figured out, but it would be such a lie. She didn't know either. She just knew the kiss was incredible. The touch of Cam's lips against hers set all the nerves in her body on fire. As irrational as it was, she had the urge to rip off her clothes and wrap her naked body around Cam's.

Maybe not a really good idea…yet.

"I gotta go," Cam said as she whirled in the direction of the front door.

"I'm sorry," Kara said before she could rush out of the house. All her fault for pushing too hard. Would she ever learn to go slow?

Cam paused in the doorway and turned to look at her. Something like pain flashed across her face. "It's not you." Then she was gone.

CHAPTER NINE

R iah watched over Adriana's shoulder for at least an hour, amazed how oblivious Adriana was when she worked. Riah could walk in stark naked and get absolutely no reaction. Odd, the first time, and maybe even a little insulting, until she realized it wasn't personal. In fact, it had nothing to do with her. Adriana simply got so wrapped up in her work she shut out everything and everyone. The sign of a truly great mind.

When she wasn't zeroed in on work, Adriana's focus was a different story altogether, and just the thought made shivers of excitement race through Riah's body. So unbelievable. A year ago, Riah was a dedicated loner. Oh, she had friends like Ivy and Adriana, but her personal life wasn't just a closed book; it was closed, locked, and hidden so far on a back shelf it would never be found. Casual friendship, and most of the time barely even that, was about all she'd consider. When terror hit the city in the form of a pissed-off vampire who also just happened to have been Riah's lover from the sixteenth century, everything changed. A seriously fucked-up time that changed the landscape of her world in more ways than one.

Throw in a vampire hunter who came to take her head and ended up becoming an ally and a friend, and fucked-up didn't even begin to describe it. Funny how things worked out though. Ivy was turned to save her life and ended up falling for the vampire hunter. Riah gave in to her attraction to Adriana and found a soul mate. Crazy yet beautiful times.

Now craziness was back in her city. Well, not exactly in the city, as the bodies were piling up in the state park that bordered the city. A small distinction because it remained as big a problem as if the bodies were dumped at her morgue's front door.

The trails that flowed through Riverside State Park were heavily used. In a place like Spokane where outdoor activities were a huge part of the local culture, an incredible asset. People hiked, ran, biked, and walked through the park every single day. The paradise it created for an amoral preternatural creature was problematic. A hungry werewolf would find itself with a huge potential pool of unwary victims.

Riah couldn't remember the last time she encountered a werewolf. She knew a few Native American shape-shifters, like Cam, but werewolves…not so much. As a general rule, vampires and weres ran in much different circles. Even when Riah had taken human blood, and that had been hundreds of years ago, she steered clear of the weres. Not exactly to her taste. Not to mention they were usually combative, and that just wasn't good for anyone. Somehow she didn't think that had changed much over the years.

Adriana sat back on her stool and rolled her head. "Damn," she muttered. "Can't quite get this one."

"Give it a rest for today." Riah massaged Adriana's shoulders. She loved the way the muscles rippled and loosened beneath her fingers. Touching Adriana never got old, no matter how many times she did it.

"Not a bad idea." Adriana sighed and laid her cheek against Riah's hand.

"Did you find anything?"

Adriana nodded slowly. "Sort of—it's definitely lupus and it's definitely male."

Riah leaned back against the counter and studied her. Adriana's eyes looked tired and weariness darkened her already-dark skin. She wanted to take her in her arms and soothe away the care etched on her face. "What are you not telling me?"

"I can't even answer that question." Adriana rubbed her hands over her face. "It's just so damned weird. The markers are all there for a werewolf, yet something is off and I can't tell what it is. I just don't have much experience with these guys. This is my first live sample and it's unique in a way I can't identify. I wish I knew how but I don't."

"Step away for a while."

Adriana shook her head and started to turn back to her notes and slides. "If I just stay at it a little longer…"

Riah kissed the lobe of her ear. "Step away," she whispered.

A slow smile began to chase away the darkness in Adriana's face and her shoulders finally relaxed. "Why, Doctor, I think perhaps you're trying to seduce me."

"Maybe." She kissed her neck where the pulse throbbed and skimmed her hands over Adriana's full breasts. She loved the way her nipples responded immediately and a fine shudder rippled through her body.

"Well, if you're not sure, maybe I should keep working."

"Maybe you shouldn't." Riah kissed her, thrusting her tongue inside to taste the sweetness of her mouth.

Adriana met the passion in the kiss. "You win," she murmured against her lips.

Riah pulled back and gazed into her eyes. "Have I mentioned today how much I love you?"

Grabbing her hand, Adriana pulled her in the direction of the door. "Yeah, yeah, yeah. Too much talk, Doc, not enough action."

Sixty minutes right on the nose and Conrí sauntered up to where Faolán still sat on the front steps of the little house. The moon was high in the night sky and its pull was heavy on Faolán's heart. He wanted to let go and run. The scents of the night made his mouth water and his nose twitch. He tried to ignore the tremors that raced through his bones, making him shake like an old man. Sweat beaded on his forehead and his teeth ached. They always did when he put up this kind of fight. If only he could run for just a little while, he'd feel better.

Or would he? It didn't matter how many centuries he lived, killing never felt good. Even when he was young and the world was exciting and new, taking a life always left him feeling disconcerted. Both his father and Conrí had chided him for his lack of the prey instinct. What kind of wolf failed to enjoy a hunt? They taunted him, called him a freak…like they weren't! At least with Father gone, he only had to put up with Conrí's scorn.

Most of the time these days, not too bad. They lived different lives and, despite Conrí's need to keep constant tabs on him, their paths didn't cross all that often. Except during those times when they found *her*, like now. The proverbial double-edged sword.

"Sit up," Conrí snapped.

Faolán didn't move. "Fuck you, big brother."

Conrí smiled and slapped him on the back. "Delightful to see you too." He dropped down on the step next to Faolán. Vibrations rolled off Conrí's body. "Now, tell me about the woman."

He straightened up, moved away a couple of inches, and hated himself for doing it. Conrí always had that effect on him. He wondered, not for the first time, what his life would be like if big brother wasn't in it. "She's the one, no doubt about it."

"How can you be so certain?" Conrí studied his short, clean nails.

Rolling his eyes, Faolán counted to ten before he answered. "I know a Magauran when I see one."

Slowly, Conrí folded his hands in his lap. "Of course you do, Little Wolf."

The claws wanted to come out. He hated being called Little Wolf, and that tone of voice could easily destroy the calm he was holding onto by a thread. It had since the time they were children. Conrí could get under his skin faster than anyone on the planet. Perhaps it was nothing more than the way of siblings. God knows Faolán had seen it hundreds of times over the years. The centuries might change but the interaction between siblings always stayed the same.

Still, Conrí was his brother and the one person he could always depend on. In a way, they only had each other. Other werewolves existed in the world. They certainly weren't an endangered species.

He and Conrí were a special breed of werewolf, though, having been sentenced to the life because of their father's inability to keep his cock in his pants. Little changed in father's behavior through the years and, ultimately, it killed him. Werewolves might enjoy an endless lifespan, but only if they were careful. Pissing off the daughter of a local silversmith was far from careful. He'd survived that dangerous liaison in one piece and with her silver blade to remember her by. Years later, Conrí put that same blade through father's heart and promptly sent him to the hereafter. From three, they became two, and the two of them were left to navigate the world by themselves.

They both understood how they became what they were, and Faolán had little doubt his brother had passed the same fate along to any number of progeny. Hard to know how many because Conrí never stayed around long enough to know. Like their father, he played with women as long as it suited him, and then when things got complicated, like a pregnancy, Conrí either killed the offending woman or disappeared into the wind. More often, the former.

Actually, it would be surprising to learn that any of his early offspring survived. What woman in her right mind in the Middle Ages would raise a child who turned into a flesh-eating wolf? Just didn't happen. These days things were different, even if werewolves were still relegated to the shadows. People knew preternatural creatures existed, at least subconsciously. Not that it really made much of a difference. Knowing and acknowledging were two very different things. In this century, they were just as invisible as they were way back when.

The extinction of vampires had been a slow and dedicated endeavor that very nearly worked. When he was a child, vampires were around every corner. Now, they were few and far between, although he was very aware of the beautiful Riah Preston right here in River City. How she avoided the stake and sword, he didn't know.

Fortunately, werewolves weren't quite in the same category as the vampires and weren't on anyone's hit list for endangered status. That didn't mean he was happy with his life on the fringe of normal society. On the contrary, he hated what he was. Yes, he found it glorious to run through the wilderness and breathe in the essence of nature. All that aside, if he never did it again…it would be just dandy with him.

And that's exactly why both of them were here now sitting on the steps of the little house near Spokane Falls Community College. Just a few miles from where they sat, their salvation slept, if he was to hazard a guess, blissfully unaware.

"No doubt whatsoever, Conrí, she's the seventh daughter. They had her hidden well enough, and this was a pretty good choice for anonymity. "

Conrí wrinkled his nose and looked around. "True…who would think to look *here*?"

"Fate has a funny way of working things out. I'm having a drink at a Seattle bar and see a pretty park ranger in a news clip about a fire in a state park on the east side of the state."

"A ranger who just happens to look a great deal like six sisters we've been watching for years."

Faolán thought about Daphne and how he'd recognized the park ranger the first second he'd seen her face on that brief news story. "Once I got here, I knew right away I'd found her."

Conrí slapped him on the back. "Excellent, little brother. Excellent."

Standing, Faolán started toward the door. "Better get some sleep. Tomorrow's coming quick and we have a lot to do."

"Splendid idea." Conrí also stood.

His hand on the doorknob, Faolán paused and looked out at the night. "Less than a week," he whispered, not daring to let hope take flight. He'd been this close before, only to have his salvation die before she grasped her full power and set him free. This time would be different.

"Indeed. A few more days and she'll be the most powerful witch in the world."

"I can't believe we're finally going to be released from this curse." Despite how close they were, the thought remained surreal. Until it actually happened, hard to wrap his head around it.

"Free," Conrí echoed, and smiled.

❖

As Cam ran up the steps of the cottage, the muscles in her body rippled. The night air ruffled the fur on her back and, as she returned to human form, wafted cold against her bare skin. In the darkness she stood naked and alert, scanning the still night. Outside, quiet lay heavy with no cars, no people, no wildlife. It felt as if everyone and everything found their own place of comfort and hunkered down. Not a bad idea.

As she stood and listened, all she could hear was the sound of the water as it cascaded over the dam. Something more than the cold breeze across her skin or the eerie silence made the flesh on her arms tingle. The air carried the scent of danger and it resonated to her soul. Violence rippled just beneath the calm and appeared to gather energy with each passing moment. Not good.

She wasn't the only one picking up the disturbance. Just this afternoon her father had called after a meeting of the council. He relayed the message from Bruce Plainfeather, a Crow elder, and a man Cam admired greatly. The message was simple: be wary. He sensed a great evil stalking her wolf. She didn't doubt him. Bruce had the ability to part the veil separating the worlds to see what tried to hide. If Bruce said danger was present, it was, and she'd do well to keep all her senses on alert.

Frankly, she wasn't as worried for her wolf as she was for Kara and the innocent people in the park who were simply in the wrong place at the wrong time. Cam could protect herself; she'd been doing it for years. She was less confident about Kara. Not that Kara wasn't a capable woman. Obvious from the very first that she was strong and smart…and beautiful. Just thinking about her gave Cam a rush, something she didn't need right at the moment.

The desire turned her thoughts to Bonnie. The last time Cam allowed herself to get close to another woman, it hadn't ended well. That was an understatement. How she'd loved Bonnie, with her infectious smile and zeal for life. Cam always felt so much lighter and happier when she was around. Bonnie had loved her completely and there'd been magic in that. The magic died when breast cancer took her away.

Instead of forever, Cam found herself standing at the edge of a grave, staring at a steel, gray casket. That day, she made a promise to never be in a position to feel that searing heartbreak again. The easiest way to do that was not to feel at all, just keep her eye on the job.

Right now, the job was all about stopping a werewolf. If she didn't figure this out quickly, people would be hurt. She'd seen werewolves before and the carnage they left in their wake, never pretty. They thrived on the taste of flesh and blood. Unlike vampires, which used blood to sustain them, the werewolves were more about sport. It made them unpredictable. It made them dangerous.

Cam lifted her head and breathed in deeply. Nothing of consequence. For the moment, things were quiet and hopefully safe. Perhaps tonight all would be well. Except, maybe for Kara. Whatever occurred today under the canopy of blue skies and pine trees, simple or normal for that matter, had a definite paranormal feel. She'd been around enough seers and psychics to know when another dimension was touched. That happened to Kara earlier, even if she didn't want to accept it. Cam did.

And speaking of Kara, time to go back. Cam had run when things got a little too close for her comfort level. Stupid and childish on her part. She just didn't like people getting too close. She wasn't like everyone else anyway. She was a shape-shifter, and that alone had a tendency to scare the shit out of most people. She was a healer, and while that didn't scare most people, they didn't exactly understand either.

Probably the thing people struggled with most was that she was two-spirited, like her ancestor Pine Leaf. In short, Cam was a woman with a masculine side. She was, like her distant relation, a woman attracted to women. Pine Leaf was a chief with numerous wives, though Cam didn't aspire to the status of chief. The responsibility of multiple wives and of the child Pine Leaf herself bore was something she also didn't think she was up to. On the contrary, she dreamed of a simple life without the burden of love or deep emotional attachment.

She settled her gaze on the cottage next door, where a single light burned in the window. She sighed, leaned down, and picked up her clothes. When she was dressed, she squared her shoulders and headed to Kara's cottage. Not wanting to fall in love didn't mean she didn't care about or want the touch of another woman. She liked Kara and, more than that, found her sexy as hell. Touching…yeah, that would be okay.

She immediately noticed Kara's unlocked front door. Seriously, two dead bodies in under forty-eight hours and she didn't lock the door after Cam left? She was going to have to sit Kara down and have a little chat. Then she noticed her stretched out on the sofa in a T-shirt and a pair of shorts. She almost stopped breathing.

For a moment, Cam stood there and forced herself to breathe slow and even. Easier said than done. God, it was like being eighteen again and falling in love for the first time. A shock back then—not much less of a shock now.

First love burned hot and quick. When the fire of that love fizzled, she'd been heartbroken but wiser. Now, her heart took off and every nerve ending buzzed. Since Bonnie's death she'd had enough hook-ups to keep her satisfied without emotional investment. But this was different and the reality of that didn't sit well. Didn't make a bit of difference to her heart.

She jumped when Kara groaned and then rolled to her side on the sofa. Her T-shirt hiked up, giving Cam a look at smooth, creamy skin with just a hint of ink peeking above the band of her shorts. What she wouldn't give to expose that expanse of skin and uncover the image just waiting for her beneath the cloth. Fantasies didn't have to mean love. Nope, she was just horny and Kara happened to be the only hot female in the immediate vicinity.

Even so, daydreaming made no sense. She was here on business and nothing more. The elders would be less than pleased if they thought she was hitting on a woman instead of tracking down the werewolf. Actually, she'd be less than pleased if she got sidetracked. Business…all business.

As if her thoughts were audible, Kara's eyelids fluttered open. At the sight of Cam, she started to jump up from the sofa and then caught herself. A little laugh escaped her throat. "Well," she said to Cam. "You scared about five years out of me."

"Sorry."

Kara waved a hand. "No biggie. Just caught me off guard. I guess I dozed after you left. Did I make you mad earlier? If I did, I'm sorry."

Cam sank to the easy chair across from the sofa. "You don't owe me an apology. I have a lot on my mind and just reacted. Poorly, I might add. Sorry."

Moving slowly, Kara kneeled in front of Cam and covered one hand with hers. "These murders have all of us on edge. Throw in that werewolf twist and let's just say there's some sick shit going on. No apologies necessary, for either of us."

The feel of Kara's hand on hers made her heart race all over again. She hoped Kara wouldn't notice. *Please don't let her notice.*

CHAPTER TEN

S oon the sun would be up and he'd be forced back inside. He liked it here. Were circumstances different, he could see himself living in a place like this. Unfortunately, it couldn't be. He wouldn't have the luxury of lingering, and he didn't dwell on the right or wrong of that. Moving on was ingrained in his being as deeply as the need to hunt, even if he did like it here where the river was wide and the waters crystal clear. Where evergreens grew in abundance all the way from the middle of the city to the vast expanse of the state park and beyond to the Canadian border.

Now, he raced through the park, breathing in the fresh air and feeling the warm earth beneath his paws. He could run for hours, for days, and it never got old. Neither did the hunt.

When he was younger, he'd been satisfied with chasing mice and rabbits. Stalking them from the forest floor and moving like lightning. It didn't take long before his taste for the hunt grew beyond mice and rabbits. He was drawn to prey that grew progressively larger and more challenging, until only one remained that could satisfy his all-consuming hunger: humans.

The first kill gave him a buzz that was hard to explain. His wolf had been so high he wasn't sure he'd ever come down. Intoxicated, he hadn't wanted to. He'd come back from that hunt stronger and more virile in both human and wolf form. It became as addictive as a powerful narcotic.

Just thinking about hunting humans had him drooling, saliva dripping from between his long teeth, his eyes searching the night. He wanted a little sport right now. Stopping on the bluff overlooking the river, he raised his head and howled. When he quieted, he listened. Nothing. He was the king of this forest and all the beasts respected him. Wherever he went the respect was the same. Nothing dared challenge him, and if they attempted to…they died.

At the edge of the river, the bank thick with growth and the water-soaked ground soft, he lifted his nose and breathed in deeply. Shaking his big head, he let a growl rumble from between his teeth. The air was pure and clear, not a single human scent around. He pawed impatiently. There would be no prize for him this night.

He turned from the river and began to race through the trees. Just enough time to run the river's edge one last time before the first rays of daylight would begin to peek through. Even though he'd love to stay here and roam the woods, soon enough his presence would be required. If he wasn't there, too many questions would be asked, and right now, that was the last thing he needed.

Despite his overwhelming need for blood, it would have to wait. He was a smart man, an even smarter wolf, and the wolf knew a secret. Sometimes, waiting made the pleasure of killing even sweeter.

❖

Kara would like to say she got a good night's sleep, only that would be a big fat lie. After Cam came back last night she'd been anything but tired. Particularly after touching her. Oh, it was innocent enough. She'd simply put her hand over Cam's. That's it. Sort of. The moment their skin touched, her whole body came alive. She'd heard people talk about sparks flying and always thought the very idea a bunch of crap. She was now going to officially change her opinion. Some serious-ass sparks flew last night, and that didn't even include the kiss. She liked it…a lot.

Cam, on the other hand, looked like a bazooka had hit her. Not terribly encouraging. Oh, hell, that was an understatement. Her expression was downright discouraging. Kinda screamed "Back off, bitch" in a big way.

Maybe Kara was wrong about her. While she found the touch and feel of her incredibly sweet, maybe Cam didn't. For her, touching Cam was like downing a full bottle of excellent champagne, and she definitely wanted more. After seeing Cam's face, she wasn't sure the feeling was in any way mutual.

So she decided it would be a whole lot wiser not to push a thing and instead headed off to bed. Despite the awkward interlude, Cam insisted on staying. Kara didn't know why. She frankly expected a full retreat and was surprised when it didn't happen.

After everything yesterday, Kara hadn't felt too bad by the time she hit the bed. She should be dog-tired and sleep a given. But no matter how she turned or plumped the pillow or kicked off the blankets, she couldn't get comfortable. Her mind refused to quiet. Her body refused to calm, and all she could think about was tall, lean, and very attractive out on her sofa. It really wasn't fair.

About one in the morning, Kara gave up, rolled out of bed, and peeked into the living room. Cam had shed her jeans and shirt, and they were tossed across the arm of the chair. The woman herself was stretched out on the sofa in a tank and underwear. She was stunning. Kara's fingers literally buzzed again. She brought one hand up to her mouth and began to chew on a fingernail.

Lurking in the shadows like some kind of peeper was stupid. She quit chewing her nail and returned to bed. She tossed and turned, plumped the pillows, then threw them on the floor. When they hit with a soft thump, Winston raised his head, two sleepy eyes studying her curiously.

"Go back to sleep," she whispered.

He looked at her for a few seconds longer before laying his head back down on his paws.

Rolling over onto her back, Kara studied the shadows on the ceiling and listened to Winston's short, even snores. The rhythmic sound was soothing and, finally, sleep lulled her away from consciousness and she slept, albeit restlessly, for a few hours.

Now, the sun was up and she didn't intend to stay in bed one more minute. Might as well make some coffee and hope like hell the phone didn't ring again. One night without another body showing up in the park would be fabulous. A nice calm day to try to get back to normal would be fabulous.

By the time the coffee was ready, Cam stood in the kitchen doorway, fully dressed. "Good morning," she said. Her long hair hung on either side of her face and she was busy braiding the right side.

"Hey," Kara answered. "You like coffee?" She was happy she at least sounded calm and normal, though just seeing Cam made her breath quicken.

"Black and strong."

"Just my kind of woman."

Damn it. That didn't come out right. Watch Cam bolt for the door again. What was it about the woman that had Kara putting her foot in her mouth every fifteen minutes or so?

Cam smiled slowly, letting the completed braid drop. "You don't have to be so nervous around me."

"I'm sorry…" She couldn't imagine how sorry. Mortifying, actually.

"Don't be. It's not just you, you know."

Kara looked up and studied Cam's face. She didn't even try to pretend she didn't know what she meant. "I wasn't sure."

"Wasn't sure if I'm attracted to you?" Slowly she began to work on the second braid, her fingers moving deftly in the long black hair. Her eyes never left Kara's face.

"Well…yeah."

The smile moved from lazy to sexy. "I am." She let the completed braid drop to her shoulder.

"Thank God," Kara exclaimed, setting two empty mugs on the counter with a bang. "Even after that kiss, I thought you might be straight and that I'd read things all wrong and that I'd offended and you'd probably be running out of here like the devil was chasing you and—"

"Stop." Cam was laughing and holding up her hands as if to ward off Kara's barrage of frantic words.

"Ah, shit." She'd been babbling like a kid caught doing something she shouldn't. What the hell was going on with her?

When Cam finally got her laughter down to a snicker, she took one of the mugs from Kara, filled it with coffee, and sat down at the small kitchen table. "How about we put our cards on the table?"

"Okay." She wasn't quite sure what cards Cam meant. Didn't mean she wasn't game though.

"I'm one-hundred-percent lesbian."

Leaning against the kitchen counter, Kara smiled and winked. "Let's just say I'm totally down with that."

Cam winked. "Card one played."

"And card two?"

"I find you incredibly attractive."

This time Kara winked. "Once again, I'm down with that too."

Her eyes on the coffee mug she was now turning around in her hands, Cam said quietly, "I have no idea where any of this is going."

What a relief. To think the confident doctor was in the same boat was somewhat comforting. "That makes two of us."

Cam looked up at her. "And card three…"

"Three?" Kara frowned. She didn't need a card three. She pretty much liked one and two.

"Regardless of how much I'd like to kiss you again or run my hands all over your incredible body, we've got a werewolf to stop."

Kara sat down across from her and looked into her own full mug. "Yeah, you're absolutely correct. First things first. This bastard has to be stopped before anyone else dies."

"Agreed. Now, barring any more violence that might have happened in the park overnight…"

Kara stiffened and looked over at Cam. "Did you hear something?"

"No, no, no." Cam rushed to reassure her. "I think the park was quiet. I'm trying not so well to suggest that if nothing happened last night, and I don't think anything did, I'd like for you to accompany me to my home in Montana."

The request came so far out of left field, it took her a few to digest. Was it a date? Or something else? "Why?"

"I know it sounds crazy, especially with everything going on here, but I'd like you to meet a friend of mine."

She might not know Dr. Black Wolf well, but she had a distinct impression Cam didn't just want to introduce her to a friend. In the short time they'd been together, Kara was able to get a sense of her. She was deep, complicated, and more interesting than anyone she'd ever met before. She was also sharp and intuitive. If she asked Kara to meet a friend, she had a really good reason.

Cam started to explain. "Bruce Plainfeather is an elder in my tribe and one hell of a doctor and, more important, a healer. He has, for lack of a better explanation, incredible powers."

Interesting. "Like?"

Cam took Kara's hand, turning it over to study her palm. "Like being able to see something in you that no one else would ever be able to."

Kara looked at her palm and saw nothing out of the ordinary there. Then she gazed up into Cam's eyes. "Say I buy that, and at this point, I'm not ruling anything out. Why do you think there's anything to read from me that might help what's happening with the werewolf?"

Her eyes were dark, unreadable. "Call it a hunch."

"You want me to leave the park in the middle of not one, but two murder investigations because you have a hunch something inside my head might stop a werewolf?" She pulled her hand free of Cam's touch.

Cam nodded slightly "In a nutshell, yes."

Kara sat back in the chair and studied her. Not a single thing in her face or demeanor suggested she was anything beyond serious. No, she had the sense Cam was deadly serious. "It's a crazy idea, you know."

Cam nodded once more. "It won't be my first...or my last."

She didn't want to leave her house or the park. Was worried about what could happen while they were gone...while she was gone. She'd promised to take care of the park, and leaving it at such a dangerous time was just wrong. She could have said all that to Cam but instead blurted out, "I hate to leave my dog." *Lame!*

Cam took her hand again, her thumb stroking the soft skin on the back of Kara's hand. "He's more than welcome to come with us."

Kara opened her mouth to protest more, but before she could say anything, Cam stopped her. "No one will eat your dog."

"I wasn't going to say that." Not so bluntly, anyway.

Cam raised one eyebrow and studied her without saying a word.

She wrinkled her brow. "Okay, so you busted me. Maybe, and I'm just saying *maybe*, I thought it."

Squeezing her hand, Cam smiled. "You'll come then?"

She thought for a long time before she answered. It still felt a little like she'd be abandoning her responsibilities if she left even for a day. Then again, a chance to spend time with Cam didn't sound too darned bad and, technically, it was her day off.

"Yes."

CHAPTER ELEVEN

He sat in one of the hard chairs inside the Skyway Café and drank black coffee. His recon had been extremely fruitful, and now all he had to do was sit back and enjoy the moment. He loved it when a plan came together. This morning was no exception. It all came off without a hitch. He was so good at blending in, no one gave him much more than a passing glance as he walked between the small parked planes.

Hers had been easy to identify. Her scent was overpowering, the strength of it enough to make him gag. Not that he'd allow the smell of a mere shifter make him lose control. He was far too strong for that.

It took less than a minute and his work was done. Then, as easily as he'd made it out onto the tarmac, he sauntered off and into the concrete building of the café. His luck was a gift that always stood him well, his timing impeccable. He'd driven by the cottage just in time to pick up their trail. When he realized they were heading to the small regional airport, he'd immediately known what he needed to do, and he'd done it: quickly, easily, and with a deep sense of accomplishment. Sometimes he impressed himself.

Even at this time of the morning, the place was buzzing. Inside the café where model planes dangled from the ceiling, people chatted, read newspapers, and ate. Conversations were broken by the clatter of silverware and plates. The air was thick with the smell of frying hash browns, sausage, and bacon. Bright sunlight poured in through the large, unshaded windows. For the most part, no one paid any attention to a man sitting alone at a small table next to the windows. Perfect.

When the waitress brought him rare steak and eggs, he dug in. Not bad for a little place. The food was hot and hearty and he was hungry. The view was pretty nice too. Small planes would land and take off right outside the bank of windows. Even a helicopter came in while he waited. A nice way to pass a morning.

An old guy in corduroy pants and a plaid shirt with messy white hair tried to start up a conversation. With practiced ease, he managed to sidestep the entanglement. Didn't want to be rude—people remembered rude—but he wasn't into chitchat either. This was a business breakfast.

His second cup of coffee was just about gone when the plane he'd been waiting for came into view. He stood, dropped a twenty on the table, and walked outside. Pausing, he watched the little red-and-white plane gather speed as it rolled down the runway, the nose lifting right before it went airborne. As he walked to his car he was smiling. All that stood between success and disaster for the small plane was a piece of chewing gum stuck to the body. The only real question in his mind was exactly when it would fall off after the plane was in the sky. The news tonight would be interesting.

In all the time she'd been flying, Cam had never been so anxious to put the plane on the ground and get the hell out of it. She loved her little Bonanza G36 and flying it was a joy any time of the week. Today, however, the small plane was just a little too tight for comfort. No, wait, a lot too tight for comfort. This thing she was feeling toward Kara was downright prickly. From the moment they'd arrived at Felts Field in Spokane and climbed into the plane, her heart had been racing and her foot tapping.

Kara was so close, the fresh scent of her filled the tiny plane. Everything about her set Cam on an erotic edge. Not her style and, frankly, she didn't like it. One involvement of the heart was more than plenty. Yet something about Kara was drawing her in like a moth to the flame. No matter how she tried to pull back, she kept getting closer and closer to being singed.

At least Kara was more interested in what she was seeing out the windows than her pilot's obvious discomfort. Thank God for little favors.

Cleared to put down, she focused her full attention on the landing strip, bringing the plane closer and closer to the ground. Without warning, the plane lurched. Cam started, her eyes shifting to the gauge panel. *What the hell?* "Ah damn," she hissed. This can't be happening. She gripped the controls and sweat broke out across her forehead. Below, the runway loomed suddenly very large.

Kara gasped and turned wide eyes her way. "Turbulence?"

How she wished. "We're almost out of fuel." Those five words fell heavy in the small cockpit and were quickly turned into a lie. They weren't almost out of fuel. They were out. Something was terribly wrong.

"How can that be?" The terror in Kara's voice shot straight to her heart.

"I don't know." She'd checked the fuel levels before they left Spokane. They'd had plenty for this trip. More than enough.

Silence settled as a new, frightening reality dawned. The engine was dead. The plane was no longer being flown. Now it floated and that wouldn't last long. The ground seemed to roar up toward them.

Heart pounding, she began to speak into her headset. "Tower, this is Alpha 745 on approach. My engine is out. I repeat my engine is out."

Her hands shaking, she forced herself to remain calm. She tried to recall the feel of the glider her friend Chris had her fly years ago. The sensation of floating through the air and the pure power of flight came back to her. She had brought that glider to the ground without incident. She could do it now.

She hoped.

By the time the wheels touched down with a bone-rattling thump, she could barely breathe. When the plane rolled to a stop, she was up and out in the blink of an eye. Kara was right behind her.

Little Winston, oblivious to his two human companions, slept the whole way and was more than cheerful as he waited at the door for one of them to pick him up.

"Wow," Kara exclaimed, once her feet touched the tarmac. "That scared the shit out of me but you're some kind of pilot."

The fresh air helped. Cam concentrated on breathing in and out, slowly and evenly. Her heart rate was beginning to return to normal. "Scared the shit out of me too."

She looked up to see her father running across the tarmac, his face a mask of concern. Behind him airport personnel rushed toward the plane. Tall, lean, and still very handsome in his sixth decade, the senior Dr. Black Wolf enveloped her in a hug. "What happened?"

"I don't know." She was still as baffled now as when the cold truth of a dead engine entered her brain. The strength of his arms around her was comforting.

"Gas-tank puncture" came a disembodied voice from the other side of the plane.

"How…" She stepped away and ducked beneath the plane. Kara and her father peered at the hole alongside her. That mysterious little puncture nearly cost two lives.

"Well," Kara said calmly. "That sucks but, hey, the landing was a kick."

Her father burst out laughing and Cam couldn't help it. She started laughing too.

When she finally caught her breath, she said, "Kick is one way to put it. I take it you haven't flown much."

Kara shook her head. "Nope, haven't flown that much, period. My parents were more of the driving type and, honestly, we never went that far from Spokane. We're the close-to-home kind of family."

That struck her as odd. Kara came across as far more worldly than her words suggested. "Why?"

Shrugging, Kara said, "Good question. Mom and Dad were just always homebodies. They liked vacations around home, and since I grew up with that as the norm, I never really gave it much thought."

"No Disneyland then?"

Kara laughed. "Definitely no Disneyland. I've been to Silverwood over in Idaho though. Kinda the same thing."

"Silverwood?" She'd never heard of it, not that places like that were generally on her radar. She'd been to Disneyland once only because Bonnie had wanted to go. She'd had a grand time just as Bonnie'd promised she would. The memory brought a tiny smile to her lips and an ache to her heart.

Kara's words returned her to the here and now. "Yeah, it's a great seasonal amusement park with awesome rollercoasters. Stick around and I'll take you there once we take care of this whole werewolf thing. It'll be fun. That is, if you're not too squeamish. I mean, you can obviously handle a little plane emergency, but can you handle the Aftershock coaster?" She winked.

Squeamish, no, but a trip to an amusement park? She didn't think so. Too many memories she didn't want to bring to the surface. Then again, as she looked at the light in Kara's eyes, maybe it was time to move beyond painful memories.

Before Cam could think of an appropriate response, her father cleared his throat. "Any plans for an introduction here?"

"I'm sorry, Dad. This is Kara. Kara, this is my father, Lee Black Wolf. That," she pointed to the ground, "is Winston."

Extending her hand, Kara smiled. "So nice to meet you, Dr. Black Wolf."

He shook her hand and then rubbed Winston's head. "Lee, no doctor. Please."

Kara smiled, her face lighting up. "Lee it is. Are you a vet like your daughter?"

"No, not me. Cammy's the one who has a way with all animals. She's been a regular Dr. Doolittle since she was a toddler. Me, I'm a plain old boring doctor of the general-practitioner variety."

Cam nudged him with a shoulder. "Don't let him kid you, Kara. He's one hell of a GP and has done wonders for the Crow. Everybody loves Doc."

Kara's smile was broad. "Must be something in your gene pool. So far both doctors I've met in this family have been incredible. Not to mention great with a broken airplane."

"Come." Lee started to walk away from the plane. "Bruce is waiting for us, and if you think we're impressive, wait until you meet Bruce. Cammy and I had to go to college for years to learn our skills, but Bruce, besides being my partner at the clinic, was gifted by the gods. He's the real deal. We'll let these good gentlemen take care of Cammy's plane." Winston didn't need a second invitation and trotted cheerfully behind Lee.

"Well, let's go meet him then." Kara followed Lee as they walked away from the tarmac. "Enough excitement here for today. Now, I'm anxious to know if your Bruce can dredge anything out of this hard head." She tapped the side of her head.

Cam was glad things were moving quickly. Kept her mind off Kara's great body and on the problem at hand. She hoped Bruce could shed some light on Kara's apparent involvement. Something was there beneath the conscious surface, and she didn't doubt that Kara was unaware of her integral connection. They might be new acquaintances, but Cam could read people well. She could spot deception a mile away, and she saw nothing deceptive in anything Kara had said or done so far. Whatever secret Kara unknowingly held, it was buried deep. They just needed someone with the right skills to bring it out.

Despite her ability to see through a wolf's eyes, she was limited to the physical world regardless of whether she was in human or wolf form. The same with her father. Yes, they were both doctors, and, yes, they were both shape-shifters. But, that's where it ended for them. Neither possessed the abilities that would allow them to look between realms and see what was on the other side.

Not so with Bruce. She often wondered what it would be like to part the veil and glimpse another dimension. He was able to do it so effortlessly. Dad was right when he said Bruce was gifted by the gods. He could see and reach things no one else could even imagine. When she pressed him about how he got there and what he saw, he was quite reticent. Rather, he sorted and filtered what he learned and shared only what he thought was necessary. Though it was more than likely the right thing to do, it made her all the more curious.

Now, after picking Winston up and putting him in the back, the three of them crawled into her dad's Jeep. He drove them away from the small airport while she gazed out the window as the familiar landscape buzzed by. The beauty of it soothed her, her earlier discomfort fading with each passing mile. Despite the near tragedy, the trip was a good idea for both of them.

When they pulled up the gravel driveway to Bruce's house, she smiled broadly. Such a lovely home. Not large or luxurious. Nothing like the big-money homes built by the rich and famous who had descended in droves on Montana in recent years. On the contrary, it was a tidy, compact ranch house with cedar siding and a porch that ran the length of the front. Trees grew around the perimeter, providing shade and beauty, and a fair piece of privacy.

Bruce sat waiting for them on a dark-green resin chair situated near the front door, He stood as they got out of the car, a beat-up cowboy hat on his head and his hands stuck in the pockets of his well-worn Levis. Just the sight of him made her step lighter. She was on the porch in two long strides and, a moment later, wrapped in his strong arms. His comforting embrace was exactly what she needed.

After the warm hug, he held her out at arm's length. "Cammy girl, you look fit as ever."

"And you're as full of buffalo shit as ever." She laughed, pleased by his compliment despite her words.

He winked at Kara and released his grip on Cam. "She always did have a potty mouth. We all ran out of soap trying to clean this girl up. And you," he held out a hand, "must be the infamous Kara Lynch."

Kara stepped forward, shaking his outstretched hand. "Well, I'm Kara Lynch, but I'm not so sure about the infamous part."

After the handshake, Bruce tucked her hand in the crook of his arm. "Infamous or not, I'm glad you're here. Why don't we step into my parlor and let's just find out one way or the other."

When Kara turned and gave Cam a wide-eyed stare, she simply smiled and winked. Nobody resisted Bruce Plainfeather with his easy charm and welcoming personality. When he was on a fact-finding mission, forget even trying. Nope, the wise man or woman just saddled up and went along for the ride. Kara wouldn't realize it yet, but this was bound to be one hell of a journey.

❖

Riah was tired and decided to rest, if only for an hour or so. It was Samhain and the night was festive everywhere she turned. Excellent for hunting. Still, she wasn't capturing the mood. Something didn't feel right. She didn't feel right.

A big rock jutted out from the ground and she sat, smoothing the fabric of her pants. She tilted her head as she looked at her clothing and then brought her gaze up to study her surroundings. She knew this place. She and Rodolphe had hunted here. But she hadn't stepped foot here in over two hundred years. Even so, it looked different and then it struck her: the land was bare. By the time of her birth, this land had become home to a great manor house. She knew where she was...she didn't know when.

She tried to rise, but her legs refused to hold her, her feet useless. In the distance a fire lit up the night and the faint sounds of revelers floated through the air. She had to leave before she was discovered, and still she couldn't move.

A flash of movement to her left drew her attention away from herself and to the sight of a woman fleeing into the darkness. For just a moment, the woman paused and turned to Riah. Her skin was flushed, her lush red hair wild. She held Riah's gaze for a long second, then she was gone, disappearing into the night.

The gentle touch of a familiar hand drew her slowly out of the dream. Riah blinked, her eyes focusing in her dimly lit bedroom. She lay still, orienting herself. The odd sensation created by the dream clung to her uncomfortably. Not many things rattled her, but this did.

With Colin and Ivy still in Great Britain tracking down artifacts, she and Adriana were the only ones at home. She glanced at the bedside clock and frowned. Really, she should still be resting.

The early afternoon was bright, cheerful, and despite her ability to tolerate sunlight, she didn't like it. Daylight took too much out of her and she preferred to function at full strength. Particularly when something evil stalked the woods nearby.

For Adriana to pull her from a dark and dream-filled sleep meant something important was up. It wasn't like her to disturb Riah without a very compelling reason. She shook off the vestiges of her uneasy slumber.

"Wake up, wake up," Adriana murmured as she kissed along Riah's neck.

All of a sudden sleep was the last thing she was thinking about. Riah sucked in her breath at the same time her fangs lengthened. The dream was forgotten as she heard the pulse beat in Adriana's body and smelled the scent of blood just beneath her flesh. How many times had she cautioned her lover not to wake her up like this?

Adriana jumped away from Riah and picked something up from the dresser. "Relax, Dracula, I came prepared." She held out a goblet filled with crimson liquid.

"Sometimes I hate you," Riah muttered petulantly as she took the offered glass and drank. It tasted horrendous yet satisfied the craving, and that's what really mattered.

"Of course you do." Adriana kissed the top of her head, then turned away. She was out of the bedroom door before Riah had a chance to say another word.

Fifteen minutes later, sated, showered, and dressed, Riah found Adriana in the library. Hunched over at the huge antique oak desk, she had books and papers spread over the massive top. Reading glasses were perched on her nose and one hand absently rubbed her short curls. Was there anything about Adriana she didn't find alluring? She never dreamed she'd find granny glasses sexy.

"Now what was so important you disturbed me in the middle of the day?" Riah asked from the doorway.

A smile spread across Adriana's face when she looked up. "Well, hello to you too, gorgeous."

"Seriously, A, why did you wake me up? It's not like you."

Adriana took her glasses off and laid them on the desk. Her dark eyes sparkled. "Relax. You got plenty of beauty sleep, and you're gorgeous as usual."

"So you woke me up because you're hot for me?" Riah raised an eyebrow.

"Absolutely, though that's really not why I kicked your ass out of bed."

"Then why?"

"This." She pointed to the riot of books and papers. "Colin and Ivy have found some pretty interesting stuff, and I didn't want to wait until tonight for you to see it."

As if they'd heard their names, the telephone rang. The caller ID displayed a number she'd come to know well as of late: Colin's.

How the two of them became friends and colleagues was still crazy. Never in her wildest imaginings did she ever see herself as not just a friend but also a roommate of a vampire hunter. Colin had done an impressive job of eliminating almost all of the known vampires. He'd come looking for her as well, fully intending to take her head. She would have done her best to take his first.

In the strange way of the world, which she'd witnessed more than once in her lengthy lifetime, they'd ended up allies instead of enemies. Even having first-hand knowledge of the strange and unusual, their relationship ranked right up there with the strangest. Honestly, it still surprised her. But it worked, and very well in an oddly symbiotic way. Who could have ever guessed?

Adriana pushed the conference button on the desktop phone. "Speak," she said.

"Hola." Ivy's cheerful voice came over the line as clear as if they were just a few feet away. "Oh, wait," she said. "We're still in Ireland. I guess I should be saying, top of the morning, lassies."

Her laughter was light, happy. Not a small feat for a woman so recently turned to the darkness. Colin undoubtedly had a hand in Ivy's happiness and the ease with which she'd adjusted from human to undead. While not exactly taking Riah off the hook for doing something she'd vowed she never would, Ivy's contentment helped soothe her guilty conscience.

Adriana laughed too. Riah rolled her eyes. "What have you found?" She wanted to know what was happening across the pond.

"We've put our hands on some very old diaries." It was Colin this time, his voice deep and calm.

Riah ran both hands through her hair. "Irish diaries won't help us with werewolves." They needed something more concrete, like a silver bullet with somebody's name etched on it.

"Don't be so sure, Riah. I think what we have in our possession very well might."

Colin was a pretty sharp guy despite having spent all his adult life destroying vampires. Now, in particular, for together they'd discovered the path they were destined to go down. She could use her preternatural skills and Colin's hunting skills to protect the innocent—both human and not.

"How?" The diary would be pretty old, considering the wolf population in Ireland was wiped out by the late eighteenth century. She'd spent enough time in Ireland to know that wolves, the real, *Canis lupus* variety, hadn't been in those hills for a very long time.

Colin, interrupted every now and again by Ivy, explained about the diaries they'd discovered in an ancient library in Ireland. Stories of witches, curses, and a family destined to live forever as werewolves. The rumor of a witch whose lover left her pregnant and disgraced so he might marry another woman who could provide him with wealth and position was a common thread throughout the stories. They found versions of the same legends in not one but three different accounts.

Colin wound up his account by explaining, "Only a descendant of the original witch can lift the curse."

"Well, that doesn't seem too insurmountable and could have happened years ago." She wasn't following the logic that was so clear to Colin and Ivy. According to what they were saying, this whole story played out in the late fourteenth century. To bring it forward so many centuries later seemed close to impossible. As improbable as the sister of Henry VIII being undead and living in the twenty-first century, a little voice murmured in her head.

"No, you don't get it," Ivy said in a rush. Riah could almost see her animated face, her hands waving in the air as she talked.

Colin jumped in, before Ivy could finish. "It's not just any descendant. It has to be a special witch. She must be the seventh daughter of a seventh daughter, just like the witch who originally cursed the family, and she has to have reached her thirtieth birthday."

"Oh." Riah drew out the single word. "That does make it a bit more complicated."

"No kidding," Ivy said. "From what we've uncovered, there have been three instances since the original curse. Once in 1647, again in 1899, and the last one, twenty-nine years ago."

Colin chimed in again. "Twenty-nine years, eleven months, and twenty-four days, give or take."

Ivy drawled, "Given the six sisters we've seen here in grand old Ireland, she'll be tall, trim, with green eyes and beautiful red hair. Sound familiar, ladies?"

Riah and Adriana stared at each other. Riah was the first one to speak. "Oh, shit."

❖

To resist the draw to kill last night he'd had to call on every ounce of willpower he possessed. Now, as he stood in the waning daylight he wondered if he'd be able to say the same for this night. Giving in to the urge to hunt and then to kill…to feast, would be so incredibly easy. Just the thought made his mouth water and he swallowed hard. Yet, good old common sense told him to lay low and bide his time. His pot of gold was at the end of the rainbow if he had the patience. He knew where the rainbow was, and to capture the prize, all he had to do was wait a little bit longer.

Unfortunately, patience had never been his strong suit. No, he had a tendency to act now and ask questions later. Part of his charm, and no one ever said he wasn't charming. The label fit. It put people off their guard and that's just where he liked them. Such malleable creatures, those humans. And so damned predictable. He'd been watching for years to come across one who could surprise him. He was still waiting.

The current situation was little different than what he'd witnessed for eons. The advances in technology didn't account for much when it came to killers like him, and he didn't delude himself—he was a killer. Not that he made any apologies. On the contrary, he was proud of who and what he was. It delighted him to watch law enforcement scramble. They never really got it. Like now, even with all their fancy scientific tools and advances into the psychology of killers, they were racing around trying to figure out the identity of the killer in their park while refusing to see it for what it really was: a war.

He, and those like him, were superior creatures. Always had been, always would be. To simply be human was such an odd notion. He'd never been human and thus had no clue what it would be like...or if he'd even like it. Would he lose his charm? Would he lose his ability to seduce just about any woman—or man for that matter? Not something he cared to know the answer to. He and his wolf were one and he liked it that way.

The unfortunate part for everyone was the reality of this war. There was no stopping it because he, for one, didn't know how. Didn't want to know how. Ignorance in this instance truly was bliss.

The two worlds were at odds, and despite his awesome power, control wasn't always his own. The wolf wanted what the wolf wanted, and at times he didn't possess the ability to stop it. Not that he actually tried. Not that he would. He really didn't see the point.

In a matter of days, the next full moon would rise. It would be particularly powerful this year, as it was to come on All Hallows' Eve—Halloween, in this part of the world. Here they thought of it as a holiday filled with costumes, candy, and fun. Where he came from, or rather when he came from, the reality was something far more. It was a night to possess unparalleled power and knowledge. The thin veil between the worlds opened for those with special abilities. The power that would be gathered on this All Hallows' Eve came around not decades apart but centuries, and he would be there to reap the rewards of patience and vigilance.

Speaking of patience, he needed to exercise a bit of it now. Others were coming and, soon, things would be set into motion. He would be ready. Leaning against the porch railing, he raised his head and closed his eyes. Inhaling deeply he drank in the scents of the world. The cars on the nearby roads, the evergreens so abundant on the nearby hills, the faint odor of animals, large and small, from dogs to gophers. So much here for taking, and soon he would take his fill.

Chapter Twelve

To say she was nervous was putting a simple spin on it. Kara trembled from head to foot. A little embarrassing, really. She was a big girl, and Bruce Plainfeather was nothing if not gracious since the moment they met. He welcomed her into his home and made her feel comfortable. He'd given her absolutely no reason to feel nervous or embarrassed. Not to mention the way he treated Cam and her father warmed her heart. The obvious love among the three would be hard to miss even if she was blind. They were a tight-knit group and she'd been invited in. The gesture both humbled and touched her.

So why was she as nervous as if she was on a first date? Maybe because she could feel the vibrations of something unfamiliar rolling through her body? Maybe because her mind buzzed like she'd been on nothing but caffeine for days? Maybe because she was scared of what he might find? Yeah, a lot of maybes made for an overabundance of nerves.

Her thirtieth birthday was only days away, and though well aware she'd been adopted at birth, beyond the necklace she wore, she knew nothing about her birth family. That would be nothing with capital letters. Anytime she asked about her birth heritage, her barrage of questions never appeared to offend her parents. They'd simply been unhelpful. They knew nothing…or so they always claimed. She had no reason to question what they told her.

The story was always the same. Her birth mother had requested that her adoption records be sealed and that they'd have no contact. In the corner of her heart, it always made her a little unhappy to think the woman who gave birth to her didn't care to know anything about her. She tried to tell herself the woman felt she was giving Kara a better life. Sounded good, except in the back of her mind she wondered if she simply hadn't wanted Kara. As a child it haunted her. As an adult it made her incredibly sad. The only upside to the story was the loving home her adoptive parents gave her. She had a wonderful family and it didn't matter they weren't blood. They were of one heart and that's what mattered.

Now, Cam said the man in front of her had a supernatural ability that let him look into people and see what no one else could. Would he be able to see the truth inside her? If he could, did she want to know the truth? The honest answer? Yes and No.

Not knowing always allowed her to create whatever backstory she wanted. It varied from year to year, depending on her age and mood. When she was younger, she liked to think she was a princess stolen from a castle and left on the doorstep. As a teenager, her fantasies were much darker and filled with angst. As a young adult, she gravitated toward the more likely reality of a young, unmarried mother without the resources or support to raise a child alone. Nothing very unique—just the age-old story of a girl in trouble with no one to help her.

If what Cam told her was right, today she might actually learn the reality of her birth. It scared her—although not enough to turn tail and run home. For so long she'd wanted to find out who she really was, where she came from, who gave birth to her. Running away wasn't an option. Actually, it would be pretty stupid. This was her first opportunity to discover the truth. Only a fool would walk away. She took a deep breath, sat in a chair beside the massive fireplace, and held her hands out to Bruce. The fire warmed her body and his large, gentle hands held hers firmly. Not uncomfortable in any way. Rather, more like they'd known each other forever, and that gave her unbelievable reassurance.

His eyes were black and penetrating as he gazed into her face. A scar above his right eyebrow looked like a tiny crescent moon, a pale slash against smooth, brown skin. She wondered what could have made it. Was it a fight? An accident? A werewolf?

"Relax, little dove, I'm with you." He stroked her hands, his touch soft. As intense as his gaze was on her face, his words were low and soothing.

She was comfortable with him. Everything about Bruce was warm and inviting—safe. In response, her entire body relaxed as if she was melting into him. Suddenly, despite all the unknowns, this felt right. This was the place she was supposed to be at and he was the person she was supposed to be with. The universe was speaking to her.

When he began to sing, she was surprised. Not that she had any clear idea of what to expect. Still, singing never entered her mind. It was nice, though, calming. His voice was quiet, the words too soft to make out. Even if she could. Kara didn't think his song was in a language she would understand. The rhythm of his words and the melody of the song were hypnotic. The sensation of being whisked away from the warm and cozy room on a cloud was strong. If Cam and her father were still in the room, she was no longer aware of them.

Unable to hold back any longer, she screamed as pain tore though her belly. Her body felt as though it was being torn limb from limb. Out in the forest, a tiny fire casting a flickering light across her skin, she panted as she raised up on her arms, trying in vain to find a place of comfort. No matter how she moved, unrelenting pain ripped through her. Blood soaked her skirts. She gathered the sodden fabric and pulled it up. How much longer must she endure this agony? Alone.

She'd lost track of the time. Yesterday passed in a flurry of pain with periods of peace in between. Even sleep eluded her as the hours dragged by. She'd been at the bedsides of her sisters when they'd given birth. She knew what it all meant and what would ultimately come. But this...this was so much more than anything she'd ever experienced with her sisters. The pain went on and on. She prayed for there to be an end to this misery.

Now another day faded into darkness and still the child refused to come. Above her head, the full moon hung round and buttery yellow. The light cast on the forest filtered through the trees, giving the small clearing where she lay a strange sort of glow. Any other night it would be beautiful and magical. Instead, she saw everything through a veil of pain and exhaustion. She didn't know how much longer she could hold on.

Another band of pain squeezed and rocked her body, and screaming, she pushed, the effort taking the last of her strength with it. At last the crown of a dark-haired head appeared, followed only moments later by a small, still body. At first nothing happened and around her all was quiet save for her own ragged breath. Then the night was shattered by the wail of the infant girl, her twig-like arms flailing in the firelight. Tears stung her eyes, relief and gratitude swelling in her heart.

She gathered the child to her breast, wrapping her shaking little body in a soft woolen shawl. The baby quieted as she held her, green eyes blinking as if trying to see her mother's face. A tiny mouth, miniature hands, and a round head covered with what turned out to be fine red hair. She was perfect. As she rocked the little girl, deep emotion welled in her chest, flowing out first in tears and then bursting forth in waves of sobs. She didn't ever want to let her go. She knew she must.

"I will call you Kara," she whispered against the soft hair. "And you shall change the world." She had to believe that or it was all for nothing. Her beautiful little girl was special and no one could ever take that from her, even if she was the only one who would ever know.

In the distance the howl of a wolf startled them both. The baby began to whimper, her tiny voice soft in the night air. She pressed her lips against the baby's still-damp hair. "Shhh, little one. You are safe with me. I won't let anyone or anything ever harm you."

She dug deep for courage and strength, hating what must come next. The thought was almost more than she could bear, yet for her child, she would do what she had to. The baby quieted as she held her, her tiny chest rising and falling with the gentle rhythm of deep sleep. On weak and trembling legs, she rose and, cradling the baby close to her chest, walked away from the clearing and into the trees.

Time passed with little notice as she walked. Holding her daughter close, she concentrated on nothing more than simply moving forward. When she first caught sight of the house, darkness still surrounded them. The relief at finally reaching the end of her journey weakened her legs. Just a little longer. Through the small window set into the side of the house, the light of a fire flickered. This dwelling wasn't large, but it had been well built. The hand of a skilled craftsman had created this place with pride and care. The longer she gazed upon it, the more she decided the hand of God had brought them here. A child could grow up strong and healthy here. Perhaps even loved, if that wasn't wishing for too much?

This tiny girl carried the magic in her heart. Everything her mother had to give, she gave to her now. She no longer had a use for any of the gifts her heritage bestowed. Her time had come and was now waning. All that mattered was the child.

Her hands shook so hard as she neared the house, she feared the baby would wake. The child didn't so much as stir when she lay the still-sleeping infant on the ground in front of the door, her little face serene and lovely. She would love to see her emerald-green eyes once more but didn't want to wake her. Her memories would have to keep her.

It didn't please her to leave beautiful, tiny Kara on the cold ground, even though she continued to sleep. At least the earth was dry and covered with a bit of moss. Her makeshift bed was soft and warm for the short time she'd have to wait. She raised her head and studied the sky. Though stars still sparkled, the darkness was waning. Soon, the sun would rise and push away the darkness. The cool air would warm. Kara would be safe.

Inside the house the sound of movement startled her, and with one last look at her sleeping child, she turned and walked briskly away. She didn't look back.

Far from the house where her child lay, she stood on the lakeshore and stared out over the glistening water. Waves lapped gently at her feet, the water cold and clear. The sun was creeping up over the mountains and the morning was dawning glorious. For some beyond the trees the day would be one of new beginnings. For her, a day for endings. Slowly she began to walk into the lake, the blood from her skirts leaching into the water until a halo of pale pink surrounded her. The sodden fabric grew heavy, slowing her down as she moved deeper and deeper into its welcoming arms. By the time she was immersed up to her milk-laden breasts, the lake began to draw her down. She didn't struggle against the pull. With a calm born of the rightness of what she was about to do, she relaxed and allowed the water to claim her, body and soul.

Kara jerked at the sensation of water covering her face and filling her lungs. Her heart raced as she frantically reached up as if to part the water that obscured the dawn. Nothing happened. Still, she fell deeper and deeper. With her last breath, her eyes flew open and the room came into focus. No lake. No water. No death. Her heart still thudding, she looked up to see Bruce gazing intently into her face. He gently wiped tears from her face.

"Oh my God," she said barely above a whisper. The pounding of her heart was so loud in her own ears everyone had to hear it. Her breathing was ragged as she dragged herself away from the consuming panic.

Bruce's gaze was full of compassion. "So it is," he said, so softly only she could hear.

"I don't know what it means," she said, the pain beginning to subside, her heart rate slowing. Only the taste of cold water filling her mouth lingered.

"Let's take a walk," he said, rising and offering his hand.

"We'll join you," Cam said, as she and her father both began to rise.

"No," Bruce said in a firm voice, his hand held up, palm out. "This walk is for the little dove only."

Kara hesitated. How rude would it be to just walk out the front door and go home? Really, this was too much. Yeah, she got the gist of the vision. Yeah, she got that she was different. But what about her? Why was this falling on her shoulders, and why not call it a day and go home? She could put this all behind her and be a simple park ranger again.

She stood, glanced at the door. Home was on the other side. All she had to do was walk out. She sighed and took Bruce's hand.

❖

On the balcony, Riah sat on the lounger with her feet on Adriana's lap. She pored through the document copies Colin and Ivy e-mailed from Ireland. As she turned over the last page, she looked over at Adriana, eyebrows raised. This far from the city, the night sky was dark, punctuated by the light of a thousand stars. Beautiful and romantic.

"Well, that's some interesting reading," Riah commented as she laid the papers down.

Flickering light from the gas fire pit danced across Adriana's face. Not for the first time, it made Riah's breath catch. How many years did she waste pining away for Meriel when this gorgeous, brilliant woman was right in front of her? She was no dummy, yet all the time she'd thrown away on her own personal pity party was pretty stupid. The only smart thing she'd done was to finally wake up and smell the roses before it was too late. She'd be eternally grateful to Adriana for giving her the kick in the ass that finally set her free to love again.

"I wonder if she knows," Adriana mused, her words shattering Riah's reflective thoughts.

Actually, Riah'd been wondering the same thing as the story began to unfold, century after century. "I don't think so." She was pretty good at reading people, and if Kara was trying to hide something, Riah figured she'd be able to tell. If Kara did know, she was a far better actress than Riah would give her credit for.

Adriana wrinkled her brow in a look Riah now recognized as concentration. "How could she not know?"

Riah shrugged. "How could she? Think about it A, little Kara's dead, or so the vital statistics claim. She supposedly died at birth. There's even a lovely grave in Ireland to attest to her untimely passing."

Adriana absently rubbed Riah's feet. "Yeah, yeah. All that's true except I wonder how she wouldn't feel it, if you know what I mean. People feel it when they have that something extra, don't you think?"

Riah got that. "In most instances, I'd agree. I don't think this qualifies as most instances."

What Ivy and Colin uncovered was a family history of witches stretching back for centuries. Every now and again, a generation would celebrate the birth of a very special witch, a seventh daughter of a seventh daughter. That woman would have powers like no other and, according to legend, she, and she alone, would possess the ability to lift the curse laid upon the Maguire family in the year 1370. Until she did, the Maguires bore the mark of the werewolf—plain and simple—at least as far as curses went.

The problem, according to all accounts, was each time this very special witch was born, she was murdered before she reached the zenith of her powers at age thirty. For nearly seven hundred years, the Maguire family had been slave to the lunar cycles. Only one woman could free them from their lives as werewolves. Riah had a pretty good idea who that one woman was. She wasn't convinced Kara knew.

Adriana was on the same page with Riah. "How do you think she ended up here?"

If she was a mother in that same position, what might she do? Despite having the opportunity at motherhood snatched away from her, Riah thought she could understand how a mother would feel and what lengths she would go to in order to protect her offspring. "Kara was carefully placed here to protect her life and hide her true identity."

Adriana nodded. "Yeah, I get that. Just seems like such an odd place to choose."

"That's what makes it perfect. Spokane isn't exactly a hot spot of activity. It's big enough to afford a great deal of anonymity while small enough not to be a hub. They could place her with a family here and nobody would ask questions. I landed here for precisely those reasons. It's a great place to hide."

Riah got up and went to her computer. She put the pile of papers with the Irish research down next to the monitor. With just a few keystrokes, she was logged onto her computer at the ME's office. A few more keystrokes and she'd opened the autopsy reports on the two victims from the park. Clicking through the pages, she finally reached the collection of photographs.

"There." She pointed to the screen. "See that?"

Adriana leaned over her shoulder and blew out a breath. "Curiouser and curiouser," she murmured against Riah's ear.

Her breath sent a delicious shiver down her spine. "Well said, Alice."

"Lewis Carroll did have a way with words, didn't he?" Adriana kissed the top of Riah's head.

"Charles was a different sort," Riah murmured, her memories turning back to the tall man with the beautiful blue eyes and awkward walk.

"Charles?" Adriana pulled back and studied Riah's face, her eyes alight.

Riah nodded. "Lewis Carroll was his pen name. His real name was Charles Dodgson. Though I loved *Alice's Adventures in Wonderland,* I was never quite sure if I liked him that much."

"Wow." Adriana rolled back on her heels. "Another little mystery about you uncovered. My hot partner ran around with Lewis Carroll."

"Well, not exactly ran around with, more like acquainted with. But that's off-topic here. We need to find out why that," she pointed to the screen again, "is showing up on the bodies and in the journals from Ireland."

"We know why," Adriana said. "It's all connected to the park ranger."

"That's not the why. It's simply a connecting dot. Quite a few of those dots aren't, and we've got to figure out all the connections before it's too late. I don't want to see anyone else hurt or killed."

"So, what are we waiting for? Let's go visit Kara again and see what she can tell us. Maybe she knows more about the symbol than she's letting on."

Riah put her hand over Adriana's. She still didn't think Kara knew anything helpful. She really felt Kara had intentionally been kept in the dark. "She doesn't know. At least not yet. Whatever is going on here, she's not in the loop. For all she knows, this is the work of a serial killer, nothing more. I'd lay odds she has no idea about her heritage or the symbolism of the mark."

Adriana made a face and then sighed loudly. "I hate to say you're right because that just goes to your head, and Lord knows it's big enough as it is!"

Riah just grinned and winked. "But I am right."

"Yeah." Adriana laughed. "You're right. *As always.* If Kara knew anything, she'd have said something."

Riah stroked the hand she held, the familiar warmth rushing through her body. Even after living with Adriana for over a year, she still felt the excitement. For centuries she'd shut off every emotion that might open her up to love, believing it wasn't possible for her. To find Adriana, to fall in love again, was like the sunshine cutting through the darkness of her life. Her existence might be relegated to the dark side but her heart was full of light. "You're right, though, about going to see Kara. We should."

Adriana's eyes were bright and a sexy smile lit her face. "Maybe in a little bit?"

Riah pulled Adriana's face to hers. She kissed her, slow and easy, pushing her tongue past her lips. "Yes, in a little while."

❖

"Do you understand what you saw?" Bruce Plainfeather asked when they were well away from the house.

Despite the initial urge to run away, the walk with Bruce was good. No, it was great. The fresh air helped clear her head, and the simple act of moving relaxed her whole body. She was glad she didn't give in to fear and had stayed. Actually, just getting away from the confines of the house helped as much as anything. Both Cam and her father had looked at her with such barely restrained curiosity it almost hurt, and the claustrophobia brought on by the overwhelming sense of doom was painful. She had to make sense of what she'd seen and absorb the reality of what it was telling her before she even tried to explain it to anyone else.

In the distance, three bison stood on the crest of one of the rolling hills, their big bodies casting odd shadows in the gathering darkness. She smiled, the sight of the three animals comforting. Something about the power of nature to restore itself gave her a boost. Here in the quiet and calm of Montana, she was finding an inner strength she had a hunch would come in handy in the days to come.

Her hands in the pockets of her jeans, she inhaled deeply, then let her breath out slowly. Everything in the vision flashed through her mind again. What she wouldn't give for a cigarette right now. After a moment of silence, she nodded. "I think I do."

"Tell me."

She stood motionless, staring into the gathering darkness. Soon she would no longer be able to see the bison. All of a sudden, it felt a little like what she'd experienced in the vision. Cold and lonely… sad. If only one emotion came through like a sonic boom, it was the all-consuming sadness of a broken mother.

Slowly Kara told him, "She was all alone and pregnant. Her painful labor had gone on for days. Physically and mentally, she was exhausted and she lay in the clearing alone and suffering as she waited for the baby to come. She had no one to help her, no one who cared." Tears began to blur her vision and her voice shook.

When he took her hand and tucked it into the crook of his arm, she didn't protest. It felt good to touch another living, breathing person. The surreal nature of the vision still had her in its grip, and a connection with something so very real helped.

She gazed out at the present but saw the past. The sadness that washed over her was as deep as if she'd known Moira personally. "Kara was born under the stars, the child of a witch."

"Tell me what you know." His hand tightened on hers.

She studied him. "What do you want to hear? That I'm her Kara?"

He pursed his lips and nodded.

"I'm not. At least not literally, but my spirit was born that night and it is still with me in here." She patted her free hand on her chest.

"Yes." Bruce touched her cheek. "You do see and you understand. I knew you were special the moment I saw you." His smile was genuine, gentle.

For a moment, they stood together without saying a word. In the companionable silence she studied his face, deciding that she liked the honesty reflected there, the way his long black braids framed his chiseled features, and the tiny lines that gave his eyes character. She liked the way his very presence comforted her as if they'd been friends for a lifetime. She hoped they would be.

Finally she spoke. If anyone could understand what was on her mind, she felt he would. "See, that's what puzzles me. What makes me so special? A couple days ago I was just a simple park ranger, and now this." She waved her arms as if to encompass the universe.

He didn't even hesitate. "There are those whose spirits move from life to life, little dove. They can be either very special or very evil. They come when they are ready…when they are needed."

"You think I'm needed for something?" Didn't seem plausible. Special wasn't really something she ever considered herself, even in the face of the visions and her connection to the witch Moira.

His answer was quick. "Yes."

Seriously? "But what?" What on earth could she do about werewolves? Or really anything, for that matter. She was a park ranger, for heaven's sake. And magic heritage aside, not exactly a superhero.

He shrugged. "That I don't know. The universe didn't see fit to reveal that to either you or me quite yet, so all we can do is be patient."

"Wait?" Not exactly the answer she was expecting from him. In their short acquaintance, she'd already begun to think of him as the man with the answers. She was pretty sure, between the two of them, they could find what they needed to know now. They just had to try. Bruce was able to draw out so much already. Another stab at it and who knew what they could find out. She was more than ready.

His smile was wry as he patted her hand. "When it's time, it will all be revealed to you."

Now she snorted and shook her head. "Cryptic shit always drives me nuts."

His laughter was hearty. "I like you, little dove."

Kara puckered her lips and narrowed her eyes. "What's with the little-dove thing? With this," she ran a hand through her hair, "I'm more along the lines of a cardinal than a dove."

He touched her hair. "It's not the color of your hair or your skin, it's what you are. In the long-ago time, birds were all black. An injured dove brought color to the bird tribes and united them despite the differences that now set them apart. You are like that, little dove, and you will bring color and unity where it was missing."

"Okay…if you say so." She liked his story, although the thought of her as a beacon of unity? Couldn't wrap her head around that one, no matter how persuasive his argument. The loner that she tended to be didn't lend itself to bringing folks together.

With a wink, he said, "I do and you can trust me. I'm a very wise man. Now, we'd best return before Cam comes looking for you. I don't think she much liked me whisking you away."

A nice thought, though she wasn't convinced it was a very accurate one. They didn't have that kind of relationship. "I don't think she cared."

He raised one eyebrow and gave her a crooked smile. "Of course she didn't."

Chapter Thirteen

A bout goddamn time." Cam stood on the top step of the porch, hands on her hips, watching Kara and Bruce stroll toward the house. Stroll! Like she and Dad hadn't been waiting for over an hour. Her shoulders were so stiff they felt like stone, and a dull throb that had started at the back of her head threatened to explode behind her eyes. She didn't need a migraine.

While she waited the darkness grew deeper and deeper. Still Bruce and Kara didn't return. She figured the nightfall would draw them back to the house. Twice she started out after them. Twice Dad caught her before she got more than a couple feet off the porch and smoothly managed to guilt her into waiting. She wanted to scream and, hey, it worked when she was five so why not now?

Kara's eyebrows rose, her expression concerned. Her steps quickened until she was standing in front of Cam. "Did something happen?"

Okay, so maybe she came off sounding like a panicked shrew. "Well, no, but…"

Bruce brushed past her, patting her shoulder as he went by. "She's fine," he said softly. Then he and her father, followed by Winston, disappeared inside, leaving Cam alone with Kara.

The third-quarter moon was beginning its ascent, a half globe burning bright in the inky sky. In a few more days it would be round and full. She always liked full moons. Perhaps it was the wolf that shared her body. Running through the night by the warm light of the moon made her feel so alive. Or perhaps it was the romance of a dark sky, alive with moonlight and twinkling stars.

Kara was watching her intently. "What is it, Cam?"

She wished she knew. From the moment Kara and Bruce disappeared from sight, she'd been uneasy. It took a huge amount of self-control not to follow them the moment they stepped off the porch earlier. She'd wanted to be right at Kara's side, and if not right at her side, at least be close enough to keep her in sight. That she hadn't been able to do either had made her want to shift so her wolf could stand guard.

How to even answer Kara's question? Maybe just the truth? Probably the best answer. Also the scariest.

"You're under my skin." It was the best she could come up with without putting into words everything she wasn't quite ready to acknowledge.

Kara ran a finger lightly down Cam's arm. The sensation of skin against skin made her shiver and her pulse race. "Good."

"Good?" How could it be considering the chaos around them? Everything was crazy and confusing, not to mention dangerous. They couldn't afford any distraction.

Kara's smile was warm. "Makes me feel better to know you're feeling the same way I am."

"This just isn't a good time." Her protest sounded lame.

Kara shrugged. "Can't help it so it's just gonna have to be the right time."

Maybe she was right. She'd like to think so anyway. The relief that washed over her at Kara's words amazed and frightened her. Attraction was one thing but this was something quite different. Not bad, just different.

Cam captured her hand and brought it to her mouth, kissing Kara's palm. "All right then, what do we do now?"

Her head tilted, her eyes on Cam's face, Kara hesitated before she said, "I think we go in and have something to eat, and then in the morning, we'll go home to find out what this all means. First, though…" Kara drew Cam close and kissed her. "Thanks," she said against her lips. "I needed that."

So did Cam, although she didn't say so. Or do what she really wanted, which was grab Kara and hold her as if her life depended on it. The urge reeked of desperation and she hated that. Was she so starved for the touch of another woman that she was ready to cling to the first one who reached out to her? Deep down she knew that wasn't true. Kara's touch was what she longed for. Only Kara's touch. Oh, yeah, this definitely called for a time-out before she made a big fat fool of herself.

"Come on," she said, stepping away. "Let's go see what Bruce has whipped up for dinner."

By the time they ate Bruce's grilled elk steaks and fried potatoes the moon was high. Winston was by the back door, happily chomping away on a bone Bruce gave him. She'd picked at her dinner while Kara dug in with enthusiasm. Apparently visions created a healthy appetite. Not so with sexual tension. The last thing she felt like doing was eating a heavy meal. If anyone noticed her lack of interest in dinner, they politely didn't mention it.

After they said their good nights to Bruce and Cam's father drove them to her childhood home, he made some lame excuse about needing to run into town for something. He didn't realize she knew exactly where he was headed. Daddy had a girlfriend and apparently thought it would bother Cam. He was wrong. Her mother had been gone for fifteen years and, in her opinion, it was about time he went out and got a little. He was handsome and full of life, with plenty yet to share. The last thing he should worry about was whether his daughter approved. She did.

One of these days, she'd tell him the subterfuge wasn't necessary, but for now, watching him sneak around like a teenager was highly entertaining. Dad was no better at it than she'd been when, at seventeen, she'd tried to quietly slip out her window to go to a party. There he'd been, leaning against the big old pine tree in the front yard, his arms crossed and his face serious. She still remembered that busted feeling, and even though he'd frowned at her, she had a sneaking suspicion he'd been smiling inside. What poetic justice it would be to turn it around on him now. As much fun as that would surely be, for tonight she'd let him think he was getting away with his under-the-radar trip to his girlfriend's house. She'd bust him another night and enjoy every minute of it.

Once he was gone and they were finally alone, Cam lit a fire after she'd opened a bottle of wine and left it on the counter to breathe. Flames began to lick at the logs, and she went back to the wine. As she poured it into a couple of nice glasses she'd pulled from the china cabinet, her hands shook. It was silly to be this nervous. She took a calming breath, then carried both glasses out to the great room where Kara sat in front of the hearth, her legs tucked underneath her. Firelight danced off her red hair, her face turned toward the fire's glow.

Still standing, Cam handed one of the glasses to Kara. "You told me to bring wine last night and things just didn't quite work out, so thought I'd make up for it."

Kara looked up, her green eyes bright, and took the offered glass. After taking a sip, she smiled. "This definitely makes up for last night. Nice choice."

Cam lowered down beside her, not touching but close enough to feel the heat of her body. She longed to feel Kara's lips against hers once more, and it took effort to turn her thoughts elsewhere. Focusing on the werewolf and what Kara might be able to tell them was far more important than her physical needs and wants.

She asked, "What happened today?"

After taking another slow sip of her wine, Kara sighed. "What I saw today was just about as fucked up as what's happening at the park but a little closer to home, if you know what I mean."

She'd seen enough of the strange and unusual that she could relate. "Tell me."

Kara's voice was low, her words detached as if she was talking about a movie rather than a vision that took her from her comfortable world and into a realm that until now she probably didn't even know existed. She related a tale of love and betrayal, of life and death.

When her words trailed off, Cam leaned against the hearth and whistled. "How are you feeling about all that?"

She'd be totally freaked out, about like how she'd reacted when she first came face to face with her own special abilities. Definitely freaked her out. Kara, on the other hand, was handling it all much better. Pretty impressive.

Kara leaned her head back and closed her eyes. After a long breath, she opened them and gazed into Cam's face. "Well, how would you feel if you just found out you're a witch?"

She wanted to say, a bit like finding out she was a shape-shifter who took the form of a wolf. Instead she asked, "You think that's what the visions are telling you?"

Shaking her head, Kara said, "I don't think, I know. But I don't know what it has to do with your werewolves."

"Why do you keep calling them my werewolves?" To say the thing rampaging through the park was her werewolf was like saying all the squirrels were Kara's. Just wasn't so.

Kara shrugged. "I don't know. Maybe because until you showed up, a murder in the park was plain old garden-variety style and happened very rarely. Ninety percent of the time a death that crosses my path results from a fall, a heart attack, a fight between a couple of drunks. You know, normal stuff. I was more than happy to go with regular old murder now."

Cam laughed but with no trace of humor. "I hate to be the one to break it to you, but those were never garden-variety murders."

The murder of anyone never set well with her, though she'd drawn her own fine line in the sand. Simple, really. The world consisted of good people and evil people. Her purpose in the big scheme of things was to make sure the evil ones didn't prevail. If she stopped an evil soul, that wasn't murder, garden-variety or otherwise. The lives taken in Riverside State Park? Well, those were stolen away. Murder, straight-up and by the hand of evil, but never by any stretch of the imagination "regular old murder."

She didn't say any of that to Kara. The woman had enough to digest without Cam adding to what were certainly mind-numbing changes to her view of the world. Instead, they both fell silent. Cam sipped her wine and let the warmth roll through her body. In the fireplace the tamarack popped and snapped as it burned hotter and brighter, filling the air with warmth and a lovely earthy scent. Her earlier nerves were gone, replaced by a genial sense of companionship that she rather enjoyed. She was as relaxed as she could remember being for a really long time.

Kara took her hand. Still, they didn't speak. Even when Kara set down the empty glass and shifted so she was looking into Cam's eyes, still neither of them uttered a word.

Emeralds, that was what Kara's eyes made her think of. They were such a beautiful shade of green, and the way her hair framed her face, setting off the pale, smooth skin, was the prettiest thing she'd ever seen. There simply wasn't anything about Kara Lynch she didn't find incredibly attractive.

As she cupped Kara's cheek and leaned in to kiss her, Cam's pulse raced. She really didn't know where any of this was taking her, but how could it possibly be bad?

❖

Shifting from foot to foot, Faolán strained to see as passengers from the incoming Seattle flight made their way from the secure concourse to the baggage carrousels. He hated how the security here made it almost impossible to see people until they were at the end of the passageway that yawned from the forbidden ticketed-passengers-only areas. He missed the old days when a person could actually stand on the tarmac.

Finally, he saw her, a flash of red in a sea of dull and dark. Daphne Magauran saw him at the same time and smiled as she hurried in his direction, weaving in and out of older couples and around parents pushing strollers.

The light scent of her perfume reached him before she did. He wrapped her in his arms and kissed her cheek. "I'm so glad you're here." He didn't want to let her go. He really wanted to stand here drinking her in, even if everyone in the terminal stared at him like he was crazy. He felt a little crazy whenever he had a chance to touch her, and he took every one of them.

"I'm in time?" She stepped out of his embrace and studied his face. "What's happened?"

"Nothing. She's fine."

She cupped his face in her hands. "Faolán, how long have I known you?"

"Your whole life." Her finger stroked his cheek, sending a warm glow through his entire body. He wanted to feel the touch of her fingers against his skin for eternity. If only it could be so.

"Yes. So why do you think you can hide from me?" Her words were light but her green eyes were serious. She had a way of seeing through any smokescreen he put up.

"Come." He tucked her hand in the crook of his arm. "Let's get your luggage and then we can talk in the car."

Daphne was right though. He'd never been able to hide anything from her. She could read him like a book. No one else ever had that effect on him. Not once in all the years, and that was saying a lot. Truly scared him senseless. Her knowing him didn't bother him. No, what he minded was that if he failed this time, he'd lose her. He'd lost so much in his very long lifetime and, still, he'd survived it all. This was very, very different. He didn't have a shred of doubt that losing this one special woman would be the end of him.

"Now," she said as soon as they were in the car heading down the highway toward the Sunset Hill. The airport grew smaller in his rearview mirror as the trees bunched thicker along the highway. "Tell me what has you so worried about Kara's safety."

"I don't know." He gripped the steering wheel so tight his knuckles blanched. "She's fine, as far as I can tell."

She put her hand on his arm. "Tell me. I'm here now. You're safe."

The single word nearly brought tears to his eyes. She was so gracious and caring. He didn't deserve her kindness, and his safety? That was the last thing he was worried about.

"I don't know if I can." He had yet to put any of it into words, even to himself, but the cold sweat that greeted him when he awakened, well, that spoke volumes.

Her fingers stroked his arm. "Is Conrí at the house?"

Conrí? She shifted gears like she was driving a sports car. "Yes, of course. Didn't you think he would be?"

She didn't answer but said, "Stop here." She pointed to a coffee shop at the turnoff to Government Way. Tiny white lights glowed all along the line of the pitched roof. The small parking lot was empty and the only other car around sat at the drive-through window.

"You want coffee?" He put on his blinker and turned into the parking lot. He sure as hell didn't need anything to eat or drink. Would probably puke if he even tried to stomach a coffee.

If she noticed his discomfort, she didn't let on. She told him calmly, "We'll get a couple of cups and talk *before* we go to the house. Just you and me."

He still held the steering wheel in a death grip and didn't move. Seriously, coffee was not what he needed. Gently she took his hands and pulled them from the wheel. Despite not wanting to go into the little shop, he didn't resist. With her, he never did. She didn't say a word, just held his hands and waited. He thought she'd pull him from the car but she didn't.

When silence stretched on, he summoned the courage to say out loud what he'd been thinking and feeling. "I'm scared, Daphne."

She scooted as close as she could and put her arms around him. He laid his head on her shoulder as she stroked his hair. "As long as we're together, there's nothing to be afraid of."

"I think I've killed again." Ice flowed through his veins as the words left his lips, and a fine tremor ran through his body. He willed himself not to cry.

"You're not a killer," she insisted, still stroking his hair.

He was just as insistent. "Oh, but I am."

"Shhh, that was a lifetime ago. You're a different man now, Faolán."

Right…different man, same monster. "I'm a werewolf, Daphne, and nothing can change what I am and have been since the day I was born."

"You're a man, first."

Some man. He couldn't even control the wolf. "I don't know what to do."

She lifted his chin and kissed him. "We'll figure it out and we'll do it together. I don't think you killed anyone. You're not," she repeated, "a killer."

"I want to believe you." God, how he wanted to. He didn't want to hurt anyone. Never had, even though the reality was somewhat different. Now, he just couldn't be sure anyone was safe around him, especially with the full moon drawing close. That he had control over himself was a dangerous illusion for anyone and everyone close to him.

She kissed him again. "Believe it, and in a few days, my little sister is going to set you free."

He closed his eyes and said a silent prayer she was right.

❖

Kara melted into the kiss. She stroked Cam's hair, letting the loose strands flow through her fingers like ebony silk. God, how she loved that hair.

"So, Dr. Black Wolf, do I have a fever?"

Cam laid the back of her hand against Kara's forehead. A small smile turned up the corners of her mouth. "I'm sure you do."

"Oh," she fanned herself. "I think I'm feeling faint."

A stricken look crossed Cam's face. She shifted away from Kara. "Maybe the wine was a bad idea."

Kara reached over and pulled her close. "Relax, Doc. It's all good but if you're really worried, maybe you should do an exam?"

"I'm a vet, you know—"

"Très kinky! Come on." Kara stood and pulled Cam up. "Lead the way to the exam room."

Cam hesitated. "Are you sure?"

Kara put her hands on her hips. "Are you going to tell me you're not interested?"

"Oh, hell, no!" Cam grabbed her hand and pulled her up a set of stairs and into a bedroom at the far end of the hallway.

The bed wasn't big but it was big enough. Kara dropped her clothes just inside the doorway. She wasn't sure what it was about the last few days, but any reserve she might have had before Cam showed up in her life disappeared in a heartbeat. They were adults, they were alone, and they wanted each other. Sometimes letting go of everything except the moment was exactly the right thing to do.

"God, you're beautiful," Cam said as she rested her back against the door and watched her.

"You're not too bad yourself, even if you are all dressed up."

"Are you sure?" Cam's voice was still full of doubt.

Kara smiled and stretched out on the bed. "Hum, let me see. I'm naked. I'm on a bed. What do you think?"

Cam didn't say anything, just sent her jeans and shirt flying. As she walked to the bed, she slipped out of her underwear and bra. She was hot in her clothes but out of them? She was gorgeous. Slim hips, small breasts, and beautiful coffee-and-cream-colored skin. Her straight black hair fell down her back almost to her waist. It was like a sheet of black satin that made Kara's hands itch to touch it.

At the edge of the bed, Cam paused and stared down at Kara. Her eyes were so black, they were like obsidian. Under different circumstances, she didn't doubt they could be scary. Right now, they were sexy as hell. She took Cam's hand, tugging on it.

"If you don't want to, it's okay. I won't lie, I'll be disappointed, but I don't want to make you feel uncomfortable." She hoped Cam wanted to do this as much as she did.

At Kara's insistent tug, Cam lowered herself next to the bed and wrapped her arms around her. She kissed the top of Kara's head. "I totally want to do this."

Her words were tinged with something Kara couldn't quite put her finger on. "I hear a *but* in there."

Cam sighed. "I'm worried it's not the right thing to do."

"How could it be wrong?" Sure felt right to Kara.

"I like you," Cam said in a quiet voice.

All the better. "I like you too, so doesn't that make it even more right?"

"In a way, yes. It's just that I really like you, and I don't want to jump into something now and screw up things for later."

Then Kara understood and she tightened her arms around Cam's firm body. She laid her head against her breasts and breathed in the scent of her. "Won't happen."

"You sound so sure."

Hey, she was a witch, with visions, no less. So far her visions had all been about the past, but she had a really good feeling about the here and now with Cam in her arms. "I am. Now kiss me."

She did and Kara melted into the feel of Cam's lips against hers. She let her hands roam over her body, the smooth skin of her back, the firm muscles of her butt, the small, perfect breasts.

When Cam's hand slid between her legs, Kara gasped. The touch of her fingers against her clit made her hips buck. As her fingers glided inside, she groaned. Cam eased Kara down on the pillows, her hand still between her legs. Beside her, Cam lowered her head and took a nipple in her mouth as her hand moved faster between Kara's legs. The fire built so quickly, it took her by surprise. When she screamed, Cam's mouth covered hers as her hips pressed against her still-caressing fingers.

Despite feeling like her bones had turned to liquid, Kara found the energy to flip Cam over onto her back. "Turnabout," she murmured, then lowered her mouth to Cam's breast.

She let her hands roam all over Cam's body, tracing a line from her nipple to the tiny patch of hair. Slowly, she slipped a finger between her swollen labia and stroked her clit. Cam made a noise deep in her throat that made Kara smile. Oh, yeah, turnabout was so much fun.

Trailing kisses, Kara worked her way from nipples to clit. As she flicked her tongue over the nub, it hardened and Cam's hips strained toward Kara's face. Slowly, she worked her tongue in and around as Cam groaned, her hands wound in Kara's hair.

"I don't think I can hold it," Cam said in a hoarse voice. "I can't…"

Smoothing her hands over Cam's flat belly, she looked up at those black eyes that now were smoky. "Can't what?" She slipped a finger inside and slowly moved it in and out. "Hold it? Then don't. Come."

"I want it to last." She moved against Kara's hand.

"We don't have to stop at one," Kara said, and kissed the tiny patch of hair. "We have all night." She dipped lower and let her tongue work Cam's clit again. It only took a second and Cam cried out.

Kara moved up to lie next to her. Her arm thrown over Cam's waist, she could feel the tremors that still shook her body. She smiled. "Do I still get under your skin?"

Cam's laugh was shaky. "Under, in, over…yeah."

❖

Conrí was waiting at the top of the steps when he and Daphne drove into the narrow driveway. Faolán didn't have a good feel for how Conrí felt toward Daphne. Usually he could tell pretty quickly what his brother thought, but with Daphne it was almost as if he cloaked his emotions.

It bothered him only because his own feelings toward her were pretty intense. The unspoken competition between Conrí and him had been going on since day one. Conrí was always top dog, figuratively and literally. It never occurred to him that Faolán really didn't care one way or the other. More than anything he wanted to live a peaceful life, happy and normal. Small potatoes, overall. He just let Conrí play his games because it made him happy, and a happy Conrí was a very good thing for everyone involved, or even in the general vicinity for that matter.

But when Faolán became interested in a woman, a problem arose. Who or what the woman was didn't come into play. Conrí's competitiveness went into hyperdrive the second he sensed attraction. Even if Faolán was ultra-careful to keep his relationships on the down low, his brother always managed to find out and seduce the woman. Irritating as all hell, though not a problem in the big picture. It was, however, why Faolán preferred casual hookups. They were fun, they were physically satisfying, and he didn't have to worry about Conrí stirring up trouble. He also didn't have to explain the whole werewolf thing. Not exactly the typical icebreaker.

Except with Daphne, the rules changed. He could try to convince himself theirs was a straightforward business relationship between a witch and a werewolf, but it was such a lie nobody, least of all him, would be able to buy in. All his good intentions about keeping relationships simple and uncomplicated blew up when it came to Daphne.

The straight-up truth—he loved her. He needed only two things to make it right with her: to get her little sister to lift the curse so he could be human, and for Conrí to butt the hell out. Number one had a good chance of happening at long last. Number two was bound to be a challenge. Werewolf or human, Conrí was a handful and Faolán didn't see that changing anytime soon, regardless of how things eventually turned out.

Putting off the inevitable wouldn't make this better so, steeling himself, Faolán got out of the car and walked around to open Daphne's door. In true Daphne style, she was already out and headed up the stairs in Conrí's direction. Her stride was long and sure. Conrí didn't cow her at all.

"What took you so long?" he snapped.

"And lovely to see you too," Daphne said in a sweet, low voice, a smile on her face, her green eyes sparkling.

Conrí's eyes narrowed. "Where are the rest of the witches?"

"How many do you need?" She stopped on the step next to Conrí and looked him straight in the eyes. "I'm not exactly a novice, you know."

Conrí frowned, his expression dark, and turned his gaze on Faolán, dismissing Daphne without a word. "Do you intend to stand there all night or are we going to get to work on our little project?"

"What's gotten your tail in a twist?" Though Conrí usually had mercurial moods, he was particularly churlish tonight.

"I'm tired of sitting around while you two finish whatever it is you do when you're alone. Too much waiting."

"Then don't." Daphne brushed past him and went into the small house. "Get off your ass and do something constructive."

"She's a bitch," Conrí muttered, loud enough for her to hear.

He wondered what was really bugging Conrí. If not for Faolán's very real attraction to Daphne, he wouldn't have given her, or any of the sisters, a second glance. Conrí's tastes were a bit more slutty, for lack of a better description. He liked things down and dirty, and good girls never appealed to him. That hadn't changed in all the centuries they'd traveled the earth.

Conrí could throw a wet towel on a party faster than anyone he knew. What would he be like once he was fully human and didn't have his wolf for comfort? Faolán shuddered just thinking about it.

This time it would happen, and Conrí would have to deal with it. Things were different here, and they wouldn't make a single misstep. He'd see to that. The lovely park ranger would find her true calling and save them from yet another eternity of playing slave to the wolf.

He could hardly wait, but was the excitement one-sided? For years they'd talked about the day they'd be free of the curse. He'd literally dreamt about it. Hard to tell how Conrí was feeling now that the day was nearly upon them. Judging by how grumpy he was, maybe not so excited. Or maybe he was scared too. That thought made him look at his brother a little more closely.

He touched him on the arm as he went by. "Come on, brother. Let's talk about how we can keep the witch safe until the full moon."

CHAPTER FOURTEEN

Riah's fangs lengthened as she nuzzled Adriana's warm neck. Excitement rippled through her body as she slid her hands over bare flesh. Dragging her fangs along the smooth skin, she felt Adriana's immediate response. Riah didn't break the flesh, she never did. Not with her beautiful, loving partner. Part of the excitement between them involved that edge of danger so close they could almost taste it. An edge they shared and enjoyed.

To think she'd tied her own hands with self-imposed rules about love and friendship. The two could never mesh, at least in her dark, shrouded world. Friends were friends, and never lovers. Was she ever wrong. Adriana was her friend long before she became her lover, something she'd never experienced. Not even with her first love, Meriel.

She didn't want to think about Meriel now or how she had been turned into an evil, vile vampire who very nearly destroyed not just Riah, but her dear friends as well. She hated what Meriel's rage had forced her to do, but she'd have hated it even more if she'd lost Ivy. To have Ivy as a fellow vampire beat the hell out of not having her at all.

Thinking of Meriel these days no longer brought the heartache she'd endured for nearly five hundred years. Facing the evil and vindictive creature she'd become changed everything, as did the discovery that she'd stopped loving her years before. Talk about a huge surprise.

Adriana had shaken up her world, and that's what it had taken before she could actually see the truth. When she did, the chains of guilt and remorse fell away, and she was free to love again. She'd never been happier, and every day with Adriana was a gift filled with love. She didn't intend to waste a single moment.

If they were really lucky, brilliant Adriana would also recreate the cure she'd discovered right before Meriel destroyed it. It could have given Riah back her life. Adriana had rushed in to share her good news with Riah only to have Meriel orchestrate an explosion that turned everything she'd worked so hard for into ash. Now, if Adriana was successful with her recreated research, Riah would be human again. She wanted to love Adriana for the rest of her life and at the same time wanted to grow old with her. She hoped Adriana could make this dream a reality.

Adriana's hand between her legs brought Riah back to the here and now. The touch of her fingers across her clit made her stiffen and she threw her head back. Adriana lowered her head, and as she stroked, she took a nipple into her mouth. The feel of her hot lips against her skin nearly made Riah come right then. Her hips stiffened and her back arched. Adriana pulled her mouth away and whispered, "Not yet, my love."

Later, they lay together, Adriana dozing and Riah stroking her back. The peace flowing over her was amazing. The whole world could be coming apart at the seams, yet in this room, with this woman, everything was right. Not for the first time, she wondered what she'd done right to deserve Adriana.

All the years she'd spent with her sire Rodolphe were enough to damn her soul forever. What she'd become chilled her to think about. Despite centuries of trying to make amends, she never quite felt good or clean. At the end of those black years together she'd taken his head and stopped his reign of terror. Then she'd walked away from the life he'd taught her to live. She tried not to look back, but sometimes the memories still intruded.

As if sensing her melancholy thoughts, Adriana opened her dark eyes and curved her lips into a lopsided smile. "You think too much, my sexy little vamp. Turn it off and relax."

"I am relaxed," she said, even though the mere thought of Rodolphe made her shoulders tighten.

"Sure you are, and tell me you weren't thinking you don't deserve happiness or the life we're all building here together."

"I wasn't—"

Adriana put a finger to her lips. "Yeah, you were. Hate to break it to you, Riah, but you're an open book. At least to me. So quit with all the I'm-not-worthy shit and accept it. Accept me."

Riah pulled Adriana close and kissed her. "How can I do anything else?"

"That's what I've been trying to get through that thick head of yours. You can't. You're stuck with me, and Ivy and Colin. We're family now, so get used to it."

❖

Her cell phone rang way too early. The sun was barely up and Kara wasn't sure exactly how long she'd actually been asleep. The night had been fantastic and she felt great all over. Still, she needed some rest. Cam was some kind of tigress in bed…for a wolf shape-shifter.

Despite the urge to ignore the peppy little song coming out of her cell, she grabbed it. "This better be good," she muttered.

The sound of Jake's voice made her sit up. "Not even in the same universe as good. It's beyond bad."

Kara ran her hand through her hair. "Please don't tell me there's another body."

"Yeah, it's a body all right. I don't know what the fuck is going on around here, Kara, but something is very, very wrong."

His choice of words alone conveyed how messed up things were getting. She could count on one hand the number of times she'd heard Jake say *fuck*. "Tell me."

Beside her, Cam rolled over and blinked. Kara grabbed her hand. Everything was better when she touched Cam.

"This time, we found the body in the middle of the Nine Mile stretch of the trail, not far from the parking lot."

Kara closed her eyes and sighed. She could see the place in her head, and it made her heartsick to think of that lovely spot being sullied by death. People came from all over greater Spokane to run the trails, ride mountain bikes, and in general enjoy the beauty of nature. The parking lot was the starting point for most of the outdoor activities. To have it spoiled by murder just wasn't right.

"What happened this time?" She held Cam's hand against her racing heart.

"Looks the same as the last two. Where are you?"

She didn't really want to tell him. She also wasn't up to lying. "In Montana."

"Montana?"

His shocked tone didn't surprise her. He'd be even more shocked if she explained to him exactly why she'd come here. He'd think she was nuts. Given everything that had happened in the last few days, she sure wouldn't blame him. Still, no need to share everything. Sometimes less was more.

"Flew up early yesterday with Dr. Black Wolf. We'll be back in Spokane in a few hours." She glanced over at Cam, her eyebrows raised. Cam nodded in answer to her unasked question. "Just a few hours," she repeated.

"Great. I was going to call Cam next, but you can let her know. We'd like both of you at the park as soon as you can get here."

Able to hear much of the conversation, Cam held up three fingers. Kara nodded. "We'll be there in about three hours."

"Meet me at the ranger station at noon."

Cam was stroking her naked hip as Kara put the phone back on the bedside table. She wanted to roll over and run her hands down Cam's body, except she couldn't get Jake's words or the bloody visions they invoked out of her head. They made her slightly sick to her stomach.

Seeming to sense her distress, Cam took her in her arms and simply held her. It was exactly what she needed. After a few minutes, Kara pulled away. "As much as I'd like to stay here all day, we'd better make tracks."

"Unfortunately, you're right," Cam said as she jumped out of bed and headed toward the bathroom.

"Hey," Kara called out to Cam's retreating back. "How exactly are we gonna get back to Spokane? Doesn't your plane have a hole in a particularly important part?"

Cam paused. "Damn," she muttered, her face clouded. Her expression cleared just as quickly. "Not a problem. We'll just take Dad's."

"He has a plane too?" What didn't this family have?

"Sure thing, around here, everybody has a plane or two."

"Of course they do."

When they were both ready to leave Cam's comfortable childhood home, Kara went in search of Winston. She finally found him with Cam's father. She called him, but he simply looked up at her, wagged his stub of a tail, and stayed right where he was beside Lee, who sat in a lawn chair drinking a cup of coffee.

He rubbed Winston's head. "Time to go home, boy," he said a bit wistfully.

Winston didn't move, his eyes round and happy as he looked up at Lee. She'd never seen him act like this around anyone before. He was friendly enough, just not clingy, even with her. He was certainly acting clingy now.

"I'm sorry, Lee, I don't know what's gotten in to him. Come on, Winston," she patted the side of her leg, "time to go home."

Still he didn't get up and come to her. All he did was lean harder against Lee's leg.

Lee rubbed the top of Winston's head again. His eyes met hers and she saw affection in them. "If you'd like, he can stay with me until you and Cam have finished up over in Washington."

The offer, while well-intentioned she was sure, struck at her heart. Winston had been with her since he was eleven weeks old. When she brought him home he'd been a compact little bundle of energy and love. He'd become such a big part of her world it was hard to think of leaving him behind. Then again, these were far from normal times, and she didn't want to have to worry about him when she was concerned about the lives of innocent people. The werewolf obviously had little regard for human life and would have even less regard for the life of a dog. She shuddered and reconsidered Lee's offer.

"Are you sure?" she asked, her eyes on Lee's face.

He smiled and put any doubts she might have harbored to rest. "Absolutely. He's welcome here anytime, as are you. Besides, you and my girl there have to bring my plane back. Think of Winston as collateral."

She took a long last look at Winston, then nodded. As much as it tore at her heart to leave him here, he'd be safe. "Collateral he is then. Thank you."

The flight home was actually much nicer, even given that they were heading home to trouble and she'd left her buddy behind. The tension that had clouded the flight over was absent this time. Yesterday, she'd tried not to let Cam know she was aware how uncomfortable she was.

Today, they spoke little during the return flight to Spokane, and it was okay. The closeness they now shared made the silence comfortable, even soothing. Their intimacy was far from distracting. It was wonderful.

After Cam put the plane smoothly down at Felts Field and then brought it to a stop, they left it in the hands of the competent ground crews. The airport was a nice small facility and she hoped she'd have a chance to fly again with Cam, only under better circumstances. Of course the fact that they'd landed today without the crisis they experienced in Montana was a definite plus. It was everything else that weighed heavy on her heart and mind.

They tossed their bags in the backseat of Kara's parked car and headed out. The trip back to the park wasn't anywhere close to the tranquil flight from Montana. Traffic was a bitch, with Francis Avenue as packed as an LA freeway. They managed to hit every single red light from Market Street to Indian Trail. Finally, when they made it through the light at Indian Trail, they started to make some time. Rounding the curve that merged Francis Avenue into Highway 291, she kicked up the speed past the fifty-mile-per-hour limit. She risked getting a ticket on the popular stretch of highway the State Patrol loved to target. While she hesitated to use the term "speed trap," if the shoe fit…

When they pulled into the parking lot, Jake was waiting for them at the front door of the ranger station. Hands in his pockets, he paced back and forth. Even before she got out of the car she spotted the dark circles beneath his eyes and the unhealthy shade of white to his skin. She understood how he was feeling, and then some, considering the information she now had about the murders. Unfortunately, she couldn't share that with him, as much as she'd like to. Of course, even if she could tell him, she wasn't sure it would help.

"Let's take the four-wheelers," he told them as he turned abruptly and headed toward the rear of the station.

Leaving their bags in the car, they followed him. Jake jumped on a big Yamaha, and Kara opted for the smaller but still peppy Honda. Cam crawled on behind her and wrapped her arms around her waist. The feel of Cam pressed against her back empowered her; together they created a dynamic force. Twisting the throttle, she followed Jake out of the parking lot and up Carlson Road to where the Centennial Trail opened into the park. From there, it took only a few minutes to reach the spot where the body had been discovered earlier in the morning. Not hard to pick out even from a distance. The yellow tape strung around a stand of trees stood out as much as flashing neon.

Once they reached the taped-off area, Kara swung her legs off the four-wheeler and approached slowly across the rocky terrain that led away from the paved parking. Inside the yellow tape, the ground was dark, damp. Too dark. Too damp. The canopy of the trees blocked the light and cast a gray, depressing gloom. A chill slid down her spine.

Kara turned back in time to see Cam dismount from the four-wheeler. Her eyes scanned the area and, as she'd done at the other scenes, she sniffed the air. As she did, her eyes narrowed and her expression grew dark and moody. Her body stilled, although Kara had the sense she was coiled and ready to spring into action at the slightest provocation. Even in the short time they'd known each other, Kara'd come to recognize the almost supernatural calm that came over Cam at moments like this. The calm was deceptive, for beneath it lurked an energy that defied description.

"What is it?" Kara asked when Cam walked her way. Cam had something and she wanted to know what it was. The woman was so much more than a pretty face...and a hot bod.

"It's the same wolf," she said quietly so only Kara could hear. To Jake she said, "What did the victim look like?"

He stood at the edge of the yellow tape, his arms folded across his chest, his face clouded. He was breathing heavily through his mouth as if trying not to toss his breakfast.

Before he answered, he rubbed his eyes with the heels of his hands. "The same as the other two. Bloody and mangled, like some animal had made a meal of her. Do you still honestly think it's a human predator? Who would or could do something like that over and over?"

Cam walked over and put a hand on his shoulder. "Yes, I do. Look, Jake, the odds of a wolf even being in this part of the country are extremely low. To have a wolf do this kind of damage not just once, but three times, is crazy. It simply doesn't happen and it didn't happen here."

"Then why," he looked up into her face, "can't we find a single trace of a human hand?"

She shrugged. "Whoever it is, is really, really good."

Kara piped in. "Really evil, you mean." Nothing short of heinous could do what this monster has been doing. The word *evil* didn't seem an accurate description.

Cam nodded. "That too."

The phone clipped to Jake's belt rang and he walked a little away from them to answer. His voice was low and resigned. The only thing she heard clearly was, "I'll be right there."

"More good news?" Kara asked.

He turned back to face her as he put his phone away. "Gotta go meet the sheriff."

Kara had a sudden thought, but to act on it, she needed Jake gone. "We'll meet you back there in a few. Find out what the sheriff has to say. I want to take a look around first."

He gave her a nod, then went back to his four-wheeler and crawled on. Without another word, he turned it around and gunned the motor. She watched his back until he disappeared from her sight.

"What are you thinking?" Cam asked after Jake was well away. Her hand rested lightly on the back of Kara's neck. "I can tell you've got something on your mind."

It was hard to explain. As they'd stood here, Jake staring at the sodden earth and Cam searching for scents in the air, she'd sensed a vibration flowing into her body. The more she thought about it, the more she realized the same thing had happened to her at the other two crime scenes. At the time it hadn't struck her as anything other than reaction to the adrenaline brought on by the horror. Now she wasn't so sure, and that's what gave her the germ of an idea.

After everything she'd learned over the last few days, she had a strong feeling her idea had merit. With the scene left to her and Cam, she didn't see the harm in giving it a try. Nothing ventured, nothing gained.

"I'm thinking I might be able to pick up something from the earth."

Cam raised an eyebrow. "The earth?"

Kara put her hand over Cam's where it still rested against her neck. "Don't get cold feet on me now. You started all this."

Cam's hand snapped away and her face had a shocked expression. "I didn't have anything to do with any of the murders."

"No, not that! This…" She tapped her head. "The mind opening. You hooked me up with Bruce, and now all sorts of shit is running wild through my brain."

Relief washed over Cam's features. "Like?"

"Like I'm a witch."

"And?"

"And why not use it?"

The relief on Cam's face morphed into skepticism. "You know how to use it? After finding out you're a witch less than twenty-four hours ago?"

"No." She tried to explain. "But I might be able to figure out something from the bloody earth. Kind of the pentagram thing."

Cam was shaking her head. "Devil worship? That won't help anything."

"No, no. Didn't you ever study comparative religion?"

"Ah, no."

"Well, Dr. Black Wolf, then you have a big hole in your rather impressive education."

"So, enlighten me."

"The pentagram stands for the five elements. Earth, air, water, fire, and spirit. If I am a witch, I should be able to command the elements, right?"

"I suppose, but even if you are a witch, you weren't raised in the old ways, so how will you know what to do?"

Kara shrugged. Doing something, even if it was off the wall, was better than doing nothing. "I'll just have to wing it."

Cam appeared to like her answer, or her sentiment at least. "Why not?"

They lifted the tape and together stepped beneath it and onto the desecrated earth. Inside the taped-off circle the air felt heavier and its oppressive weight made her heart beat faster. She noticed Cam's eyes squint and her nose twitch as if an offensive odor assailed her senses. Kara wasn't aware of the smell as much as the sounds and feel. Slowly, the sounds became more muted, as if they were being filtered through a thick cloth. The brush of the air against her arms felt heavy and oppressive. Her skin tingled as if an electric charge passed through her. She tried to ignore it all and willed her body to relax. Easier said than done.

Taking a deep, calming breath, Kara lowered herself to the ground until she rested on her knees. Within seconds the knees of her pants were soaked through. She put her hands, palms down, on the cold, sodden earth. While she expected it to feel cold, warmth radiated from her hands up into her arms. The urge to snatch her hands away lasted only a moment. Then, sounds began to die away and all around the light began to fade until deep darkness surrounded her. When screams began to fill her ears, she still didn't pull her hands away from the earth.

❖

Faolán woke up to the sight of Daphne standing over him, coffee cup in one hand, the other hand on her hip, and a frown turning down the corners of her mouth. Despite the frown, she was a great sight to open his eyes to, even if his back ached and his legs didn't want to cooperate. The price of sleeping on the lumpy sofa was small when she was part of the equation.

"What?" He groaned as he sat up, wondering if his back would ever recover. Her expression didn't change. No sympathy or concern. She obviously had something else on her mind that had nothing to do with his aching bones. Maybe she was upset because he'd slept through to the afternoon.

"What?" he asked, unable to endure her continued silence.

"You said you weren't going out last night." Her words were clipped, though a tone of disappointment ran thick beneath them.

He pushed a hand through the tangles in his hair, wincing as his fingers caught and pulled. "I didn't."

She just tilted her head and looked pointedly at the pile of clothes on the floor. Only then did he realize he was naked. He grabbed the blanket tossed across the end of the sofa and wrapped it around his waist. In general, nakedness didn't bother him much. Wasn't so sure that was the case with Daphne, particularly right now, so he opted to cover up.

Then he studied the clothes. Though clean, they lay in a haphazard pile. Nothing strange about that. It wouldn't be the first time he stripped in his sleep. He was the kind of guy who got hot, so sleeping naked was natural for him. Given that, why the big deal with his pile of discarded clothing?

It took a few seconds more to realize Daphne wasn't focused on the pile of clothing. She was staring at the floor. Right in front of the door was a set of huge muddy paw prints that changed as they neared the kitchen, morphing from wolf to man. Now that—he didn't remember.

An icy grip took hold of his heart. "I couldn't have…"

Her eyebrows raised, she said quietly, "Apparently you did."

A cold sweat across his forehead, he choked out, "Was anyone hurt?"

She lowered herself down beside him and put the coffee mug on the low table. Picking up the television remote, she pressed a button and sound suddenly filled the room. Until this moment, he hadn't even realized the television was on. Now his stomach sank. The pretty news anchor was giving details of a breaking story, limited as they were, about the latest murder in Riverside State Park.

He took the remote from her hand and clicked the television off. He didn't want to see anymore. Didn't need to see anymore. His body began to shake and the remote tumbled from his hand, landing on the floor with a thud. Cold and sick to his stomach, he tried not to get up and run from the room. "Fuck, fuck, fuck."

Daphne wrapped her arms around him. "It's not you," she said against his hair, her voice now soft, comforting. "Even if you did run last night, you didn't hurt anyone."

He knew himself too well and what he was capable of doing. Still, ignoring his initial reaction to run away, he let his arms go around her. A much better option. "What other answer is there? You know it wouldn't be the first time." He couldn't ignore the truth even as much as he wanted to. If she was wise, she wouldn't either.

She pulled away and took his face in her hands. "I would know if you were evil. I might not be as strong as Kara, but I'm strong enough in my own right. I know evil when I touch it. You, Faolán Maguire, are not evil and never have been."

Intentionally evil? Maybe not. A killer nonetheless? Absolutely. "Then why are these people dying? I'm the one here. The one who's been here, so if not me then who?"

Her lips brushed his, and their softness made his breath catch. He pulled her close once more, his arms tight, her breasts pressed against his naked chest. How he wanted more even if he didn't deserve it.

"I don't know but together we'll find out," Daphne whispered close to his ear, her breath warm against his cold skin.

Leaning his forehead against hers, he hoped. A part of him was ready and willing. Another part of him was too afraid of what the truth might turn out to be. He tried so hard to fight what he was and failed time and time again.

"Believe me, Faolán," she said against his lips. "Trust me."

Every instinct told him to run away if he really did love her. The only way to keep her safe was to forget he ever knew her. If only it wasn't so hard. The man inside the wolf couldn't do it. He wanted to trust, needed to trust her. He needed to love her and be loved by her. "Aye."

She kissed him again, this time harder, more urgent. He let himself sink into the kiss and to breathe in the womanly scent so uniquely Daphne. He stroked her back, first through the cloth of her shift, then slipping beneath to feel her smooth, silky skin. She didn't move away.

Her kisses told him everything he'd longed to hear. He'd never put any stock in miracles, yet what was happening at this very moment was nothing short of one. "We shouldn't," he murmured. "Conrí could walk in any moment."

She stood, took his hand, and pulled him to his feet. The blanket fell away and his arousal was all too evident. No way to deny how he felt about her now. When he bent to cover himself, she shook her head.

"Leave it."

His hand hovering over the blanket, he repeated, "Conrí…"

"Conrí left half an hour ago."

He raised his hand and the blanket stayed right where it dropped. He followed her to the bedroom where he'd been sleeping before she arrived. Last night the only right thing to do was give her the privacy of the room while he took the sofa. Now, she pushed him to the very bed he'd vacated for her comfort and privacy.

He'd envisioned this a thousand times, knowing it could never be. He wondered for the briefest of moments if he was dreaming now, and she appeared to read his mind. Probably did read his mind. He sometimes forgot the power of her family and the secrets the witches held close.

"It's real. I'm real." She began to take off her clothes and all thoughts of witchcraft disappeared.

"Are you sure?" He'd never have any regrets where Daphne was concerned. He wasn't so convinced she would feel the same. She knew what he was and what he'd done. She knew all too well what he was still capable of doing. After he did something terrible, he could never undo it, and he wasn't sure she'd be able to reconcile with that.

He put on the brakes. Hands at his sides, eyes on her face, he said, "I'm a werewolf, Daphne. I can't change that. I've done horrible things I can't undo. I don't want to hurt you."

She didn't even pause. She continued to slowly undress, her eyes sparkling. "I know what you are. I've always known. Do you think that makes you any less a man?"

It made him less of everything. Less a man, less human, less moral. She deserved everything he couldn't be, and even as much as he wanted her, it hurt to think she was settling. The world could be hers, but it would take a better man than him to give it to her. He had nothing to offer.

"Yes."

Naked now, she put her hands on her hips. She was so beautiful his heart ached. Her long red hair hung in waves down her back, her hips narrow, her breasts full and firm. If he were an artist, he would paint her just like this. As it was, he'd simply have to keep this memory for as long as he lived.

"You know I love you, right?"

He snapped his head up. "What?" He shook his head, wondering how much worse things were going to get for him. First he was blacking out at night and hurting people. Now he was hearing things. There was no way Daphne had just said she loved him. No way.

Daphne gently took his hand and lowered herself next to him on the bed. "Faolán, sometimes you're simply clueless. Do you ever pay attention?"

He was afraid to hope. "I guess not."

"Why do you think I'm the sister who came all the way out here? Why do you think I'm the one who keeps in touch with you? Next to Kara, I'm the youngest of the seven sisters. This is not the way things usually work. The oldest runs the show, not one of the youngest."

Clueless described him well. She was absolutely correct. It was up to the seventh daughter of a seventh daughter to lift the curse. Through the centuries, he'd known all the sisters in each generation. The oldest sister always shouldered the duty of managing the younger sisters. Never anyone but the eldest. Until now. He'd just been so delighted to be on Daphne's radar, he'd never bothered to question why.

He might as well be honest. Didn't have much more to lose at this point. "I was afraid. I've never felt this way about anyone and I didn't want to question it." He blew out a breath. "I've never been in love before."

"Ever?" Her hand played against the hair on his chest.

"Ever."

She smiled and stroked lower. "Well, then, it just goes to show you that fate is at work. We're meant to be together. The universe wouldn't keep putting us together if it wasn't so."

Hope started to take root in his heart. He wanted to make love to her. God, how he wanted to. "Do you think?"

"I know." She kissed him hard, her tongue darting between his lips.

Pushing him back against the pillows, Daphne rolled on top of him. She was hot from head to toe and the sensation made him even harder. To hell with caution. If the gods wanted them together, who was he to argue?

CHAPTER FIFTEEN

Cam resisted the urge to grab Kara. When she knelt and put her hands on the bloody ground, a spasm had visibly rippled through Kara's body and then she'd gone completely still. So still, she could almost be dead.

Of course, that wasn't the case. The rise and fall of her chest let Cam know she was alive. Just the same, Kara wasn't with her right now, and she had no idea where she'd gone or when she'd be back. All she could do was wait, which about killed her. She wasn't used to being so powerless. It was a terrible feeling.

Cam leaned against a tree and closed her eyes. If she had to wait for Kara, she might as well make herself useful. She decided to let the sounds and smells of the park guide her. Answers were here, and hopefully between the two of them, they'd find the key before anyone else died.

The one constant in all the deaths was how the scent of the werewolf lingered around the bodies. He was old; the scent held an ancient, musty quality. Old didn't mean weak in the case of werewolves. On the contrary, it often meant powerful and dangerous. Rarely did she, or any of the other shape-shifters she knew, come in contact with werewolves of any age. They simply lived in different worlds and their paths crossed infrequently.

When they did, it usually wasn't good...like now. She was a protector. That didn't change when she was in wolf form. The same couldn't be said for the werewolves. She hated the way they took what they wanted regardless of consequences. They were predators and she'd like to see their time on earth come to an end. Cam wasn't usually in favor of the extinction of any species, but when it came to werewolves, she made an exception.

It was only a matter of time before they tracked this bastard down, and when they did, they would have one less werewolf to worry about. She'd see to that. The elders sent her here in the first place because of her skill and tenacity. She wouldn't let them down. She never did.

A noise caught her attention and she snapped back to the here and now. Kara was rising to her feet and relief flooded Cam. Before she could get to the tape, Kara had ducked under and was walking her way. She was glad to see her out of the trance-like state but didn't like the pale cast to her skin or the darkness in her beautiful green eyes. It was as though a shadow had draped over her like a heavy funeral shroud.

She caught Kara in her arms and held her tight. "What happened?" she asked against her hair.

"I saw him…it…"

"The werewolf?"

"Yes, if that's what you'd like to call him. He was like nothing I'd ever seen before. Part man, part wolf, completely evil." She shuddered.

Cam hugged her even tighter, grateful that as she held her, Kara calmed. She remembered all too well the first time she encountered a werewolf. She'd been horrified. When she shifted, her form became that of a wolf in all its glory and beauty. No one seeing her would know she was anything except a wolf.

In contrast, a werewolf didn't change into a magnificent *Canis lupus* but something that fell in between the two. Never pretty and always evil. Anyone with the misfortune to encounter one knew immediately it was something less than natural.

"I know," she whispered.

"It all played out in my head. I saw it stalk the woman and then tear into her like she was a good steak. Blood was everywhere. God, it was horrible."

Rubbing her hands up and down Kara's arms, she tried to put warmth back into Kara's cold flesh. "I know, trust me."

Kara leaned her head back and stared into Cam's face. "The worst part of all? It was like he knew I was there. At one point, he's tearing into this woman and then his head comes up. He looks right at me, his eyes black and mean, blood dripping from his jaw. A terrible smell swelled up around me and I almost threw up. I swear to God, he was looking right at me."

A shudder ran through Kara again and Cam pulled her close once more, holding her until the tremors passed. "Had to be an illusion created by your emotions."

"Could be." Kara didn't sound convinced.

Cam wasn't totally convinced either. It didn't make sense that the werewolf could look into her, especially after the fact. Then again, enough strange things had passed through her world to keep her from discounting anything, even if it sounded impossible. A good one to run by the elders and get their take. Later.

"Did you see anything else?"

Kara stepped out of Cam's embrace. She ran her hands through her hair and rubbed her temples. "Nothing except I'm absolutely positive if I run into this thing when it's in human form, I'll know it. I'll remember those eyes. I'm betting they look the same in either form he takes."

"Good." Not so good that evil was burned into her memory, but if Kara could spot it when in human form, they'd have a much easier time putting it down. If she could spot it soon, even better. Despite this one tiny edge, it wouldn't be enough. Cam was worried the werewolf would kill others before they found it.

"Come on," Kara said as she turned and began to jog toward the four-wheeler. "Let's go find this bastard."

❖

Riah didn't rest at all. There'd be a price tag on that. Now, as she sat in the dim confines of her office, weariness settled around her shoulders like a heavy cloak. She'd spent hours going through the tomes Ivy and Colin brought from Ireland. She didn't know how they'd managed to get the ancient books out of the country and at this point didn't care. That they did was enough. The information inside them was invaluable.

"Hey," Adriana said as she came through the door.

As usual, she looked great. She wore flannel pants tied at the waist and a white T-shirt. Her dark eyes were bright and clear. Her short black hair was as tidy as ever, her dark complexion flawless. The woman was hands-down hot. Was the first day Riah had seen her and she only got hotter with time. It didn't matter how many times she saw her, it never ceased to shoot a thrill right through her heart. Life could still amaze her even after five hundred years.

Adriana walked around behind Riah and gazed over her shoulder. "Weren't you poring over this when I went to bed?"

Riah nodded. "Yes, but this is a gold mine. So much of what's happening here tracks with what Colin and Ivy uncovered in Ireland and England."

"England? I thought they were in Ireland this whole time."

"They followed a hunch down to London."

Adriana went over to the small refrigerator built into the floor-to-ceiling cabinets on the far wall. She pulled a plastic pack from a shelf and placed it in a tiny microwave, included in the cleverly designed wet-bar setup. For herself, she punched a button on a fancy coffee machine and waited for the few seconds it took to brew a rich, fragrant cup of coffee. About the time it was done, the bell on the microwave sounded. She took the packet from inside, snipped one end open, and poured the crimson liquid into a crystal cup.

Handing Riah the cup, she lowered herself into a comfortable chair and propped her feet up on the desk. She sipped at the coffee and smiled. "So, you gonna tell me about the hunch or do I have to guess?"

Riah drank quickly and didn't smile. Leave it to Adriana to notice when her energy was flagging and go into restore mode. Left alone, Riah probably would have sat here reading until she was barely able to move. Her energy level skyrocketed. The bagged blood might taste like crap but it did its job admirably.

"Something a librarian mentioned to Colin. She told him about the legends of the witches, which is what got them on that particular trail."

"The seventh-daughter thing, right?"

"Makes sense when you think about it. Most people have at least heard of the more common folk legends about the seventh son being lucky and all that. So, to me it makes sense that the seventh daughter of a seventh daughter would be incredibly powerful, particularly if that seventh daughter is a witch."

Adriana held up her coffee cup and tipped it in Riah's direction. "It might also make sense then that some people wouldn't feel real warm and fuzzy about that seventh daughter."

"Exactly my thought. If she's powerful enough to lift a seven-hundred-year-old curse, what else could someone like that do? The possibilities are mind-boggling."

"I wouldn't be surprised if a society still skulked around out there to knock off people like her. You know, like descendants of the European witch hunters or the good, pious folks from Salem."

"Or like the vampire hunters." Riah thought about Colin and his former occupation. She'd run from people like him ever since that dark and rainy night when her life had been forever altered. He'd seen the light, so to speak, though he was also the exception rather than the rule. The hunters were still out there and she still looked over her shoulder.

"Yeah." Adriana took another sip from her mug. "Which means we've got some work ahead of us or unsuspecting hikers won't be the only ones in danger of getting knocked off."

"Now you know why I've been up all this time."

"True that, sister. Now," Adriana all but pushed Riah out of her chair, "you go rest and let a trained researcher do some work."

She didn't really want to go rest. Still, she couldn't argue with Adriana. If she had any hope of getting a step ahead of this werewolf, a hundred and ten percent was where she'd need to be. She just wanted to understand exactly what they were up against, and the materials Colin and Ivy had brought with them held secrets they needed to dig out. A few more hours would go a long way toward getting what they'd need.

Any argument with Adriana to stay here and keep digging would go precisely nowhere. Even though Riah was a vampire, a very powerful one at that, she was no match for that tiny spitfire. Adriana had a will of steel, and Riah learned early on that it was easier to agree. Granted, fights could have their upside—makeup sex was incredible. Today just wasn't one of those days that merited a battle. Makeup sex would just have to wait for another night.

She left the library and Adriana, who was hunched over the books, reading glasses perched on her nose. She climbed the massive staircase to the second floor. Their suite was one of the first set of rooms completed after they decided to make the place home. At about seven hundred square feet, it had all the private space they could wish for. A fire burned in the fireplace, the scent filling the room. Obviously Adriana anticipated Riah's return and tried to make the room cozy and inviting. She was incredible when it came to the little details that made Riah feel relaxed and comfortable.

Riah particularly liked the bed, modeled after the one she'd seen in the Houston Art Museum years ago. The big bed had been designed for the White House, though it never ended up being used there. Massive, it looked just right here in the big room. The wood gleamed, the bedding luxurious. Perfect for making love. Right now, she'd be satisfied with the scent of Adriana on the pillows as she lay back and closed her eyes.

When he emerged from the bedroom, Faolán spied Conrí pacing on the front porch. Though he felt fantastic after making love to Daphne not once, but twice, some of the glow faded as he studied his brother through the window. He struggled to hold onto that good feeling as he watched Conrí stomp back and forth.

Conrí must have sensed his presence for he turned, glared at Faolán, and started to head into the house. He held a smoking cigarette between two fingers, ash dropping as he walked. Meeting him at the door, Faolán put a hand on his chest and pushed him back outside. Didn't need him stinking up the place.

"No smoking in the house."

"You're a fucking twat, you know that, little brother." His lip curled in an unattractive sneer.

Big news flash. Conrí had been calling him one name or another for hundreds of years. At one time, it would have hurt him. Not anymore. Frankly, he was tired of his brother. He was a rude, obnoxious ass. One more benefit to the lifting of the curse. They would both finally grow old and die. And then...he'd finally be free of Conrí. Blood or not, it was time.

"Don't give a fig, Conrí. You're not going to stink up the house with that fag."

Conrí flicked the cigarette butt into the yard. "Well, while you've been fucking the witch, I've been doing some work. One of us has to keep an eye on what's important."

His hands curled into fists. It would be so easy to break Conrí's nose. He'd feel better, but it really wouldn't accomplish much at the moment. Better to take the high road. Usually it was with him. Conrí loved to fight, whether with him or strangers. Blood excited him. Faolán didn't want to get him started today. His moment of satisfaction wouldn't last long anyway. Conrí would kick the shit out of him. Faolán could start it but his brother would end it. That was always the way of it.

He did want to know where Conrí had been. "What exactly have you been doing?" Even though he hadn't been paying attention to what was happening outside the bedroom door, he was pretty sure Conrí had only recently returned to the house.

"I went to check out the witch." He dug out a crumpled pack of cigarettes from his pocket.

"And?" He expected to find Conrí much calmer, considering they knew where she was, except he was clearly agitated. It probably bothered him to know he and Daphne were now lovers. It always bothered him when Faolán had someone in his life. This was different. Despite the jab earlier, it wasn't the unexpected coupling that was bothering his brother. He could see it in his eyes. Something else was eating at him.

He looked at the cigarettes and seemed to change his mind. He stuffed the pack back into his pocket. "She wasn't there."

Faolán's heart began to race. "What do you mean she wasn't there?" She had to be.

"I mean not there, as in gone."

"That can't be. She was just there yesterday."

Conrí's face was dark, angry. "Do I look like I'm fucking making this up? Not a sign of her around the house. Even the stupid little dog is gone."

He tried to tamp down the rising panic. This could be a disaster. "We've got to find her." This couldn't be happening. Not again.

"No shit."

Daphne walked out of the house and joined them on the porch. She looked beautiful in blue jeans and a light-blue button-down shirt, her red hair hanging loose. He wanted to go back inside, rip the clothes off her, and make love again for hours. To forget what Conrí was telling him.

Instead, he took her hand and looked into her beautiful green eyes. "Your sister is gone."

Daphne shook her head. "You're wrong." Her gaze moved away from him to meet Conrí's straight on. Pride swelled in his chest just witnessing her strength in the face of Conrí's disapproval.

"I'm never wrong," he snapped.

"Well," she said as she squeezed Faolán's hand. "You're wrong this time."

"And you're a fucking gash."

Faolán started to lunge toward Conrí, but Daphne's soft touch held him back. Calmly she said, "And you're a tuilli so that makes us about even."

The effort it took not to laugh nearly made him choke. She couldn't have jabbed back at him any better than that. God, how he loved this woman.

Conrí's face turned red, his dark eyes black as night. Without another word, he spun and stalked to his car. Together they watched him back out of the driveway and disappear down the quiet street.

"I'm sorry," he told her when they were alone.

"About what?"

"Conrí."

Her laughter brightened his whole world. "Him? He doesn't matter. Never has, in my humble opinion."

"He's rude and hurtful."

"Yes, he is all that, but again, he doesn't matter. You," she squeezed his hand once more, "matter. Kara matters, but Conrí... not so much."

"You're incredible." He kissed her, then studied her beautiful green eyes. "What did you mean, she's still around?"

She patted her chest. "I feel her here. She might not be at her home, but she's close. I've been able to feel her since my plane neared Spokane. She was gone for a bit but she's back."

The woman amazed him at every turn. Beautiful, loving, and an intuitive witch. How did he ever get so lucky? "Well, then, let's find her."

She kissed him this time. "Yes, let's."

CHAPTER SIXTEEN

K ara got out of the car and stopped. Her house, her driveway, both very familiar. Yet something was distinctly different. She stood motionless and closed her eyes. Sounds swirled around her. Smells assailed her nostrils. The air whispered across the skin at the back of her neck. A new sense of awareness she hadn't experienced before enveloped her, and quite surprisingly, she didn't find it frightening. Pretty much the opposite, actually.

"What is it?" Cam asked from behind her.

She held up her hand, saying nothing. Something in the air almost whispered in her ear, but she couldn't quite make out the words. A good psychologist might say she was hearing things or maybe even in the early stages of schizophrenia. She knew different. Something was happening to her, all right, and it wasn't mental illness. Murders aside, it was exciting.

After a couple of minutes, she opened her eyes. "He was here."

Something passed over Cam's face that she couldn't quite define. "I know."

Still studying Cam's face she wondered what she meant. "You know?"

Cam nodded and frowned. "I could smell him that first night. He marked the whole area." She waved her hand in a gesture that encompassed both Kara's cottage as well as the one Cam had been assigned.

Hurt and anger mixed as the import of her words sunk in. "You didn't tell me." How could Cam have left her in the dark like that? How much more did Cam know about what was going on around here and wasn't telling her?

"No. I didn't want to worry you."

Worry her? It wasn't like she was twelve. "I'm a big girl."

"It's not that. Of course you're capable of taking care of yourself. It's just that werewolves are different. Far more dangerous than anything you've ever come across."

"You think?" She didn't mean to sound so sarcastic, but come on. How stupid did Cam think she was?

"Kara." She drew her name out. "If I'd told you a few days ago that a werewolf was stalking you, would you have believed me?"

Okay, so maybe she had a point. "Probably not."

"Probably?" Cam raised one eyebrow.

"Fine…No."

"You would have thought I was crazy."

Hit that one dead-on. Hot as she might be, she would have written her off as a nut job. "That might be true, but with everything that's happened since, why hold back on me now?"

"I wasn't holding back on you. Honestly, I wasn't even thinking about it."

Okay, so that was more than likely the truth. In the last twenty-four hours, her life had changed dramatically. Everything she knew, or thought she knew, had altered. Mom and Dad would have some explaining to do. Cutting Cam a little slack probably wasn't out of line.

Before she could say as much, Cam's cell phone rang. Kara watched her flip it open and hold it to her ear. "All right," she said. "See you at seven."

"What?" Kara asked when Cam stuffed the little phone into her pocket

"That was Riah. They've got some information that may help us. They'll be here after dark."

For a second, she drew a blank on the name before it hit her. "The vampire."

"Actually, two vampires."

"Great, they're multiplying."

Cam laughed. "No, there have been two all along, It's just that one of them was in Ireland and recently returned with some information I think you'll find very interesting."

Kara raised both eyebrows. "You mean more interesting than sleeping with a shape-shifter, finding out a werewolf is killing people in my park, and discovering that I'm more than likely an uber-powerful witch?"

"Oh, yeah." Cam draped an arm around her shoulders and kissed her on the side of the head. "More interesting than that."

"Wonderful," Kara said dryly.

❖

Dusk was settling when Riah rose. She showered, dressed in her black leather pants and black vest. She pulled her hair back and braided it. She didn't think she'd need her weapons but put her favorite dagger into the sheath at her hip anyway. Sometimes it paid to be safe rather than sorry. Besides, it always made her feel better when she was armed.

As much as she'd have liked to stay downstairs and finish going through the things Colin and Ivy brought back, Adriana was right to push her to rest. The difference was amazing. Before this was all said and done, she'd need all the power she could gather. The two things that always worked for her were blood and rest. Enough of both and armed to the teeth, she was unstoppable.

Not that she was terribly worried about a little werewolf. They were powerful too, no doubt about it. Just not at her level. Most of the time, vampires and werewolves got along by giving each other plenty of space. Every once in a while, though, she'd encountered a rogue. It was the kind of werewolf folk legends were made of. Nasty, bloodthirsty, and remorseless, they were evil and must be taken down. This was one of those times and she was just the girl to do it.

It was bad for all the preternaturals when one went rogue. People liked to pretend that none of them existed. The humans simply didn't like things that lived in the shadows, be they vampires, werewolves, ghosts, or witches. They knew, at least in the back of their minds, that preternaturals were here and shared their world. They just chose to pretend things were different. They created their own false reality. She didn't have that luxury.

For the most part, the false reality worked for the human population. Like Riah, others of the darkness simply existed among the humans by keeping a low profile. It worked for everyone at least until someone went off, like now. It was one reason the Spiritus Group came into being. Until the time when Adriana might finally rediscover the cure to vampirism and give Riah and Ivy back their humanity, they were sentenced to the darkness.

They could succumb to their fate and become creatures of evil, or use what they possessed to fight against those preternaturals that endangered them all. They chose the latter. Between the four of them, two vampires and two humans, they would do what they could to keep all of them safe. It was the best they could do with circumstances none of them chose.

Downstairs, Adriana was leaning over the desk, head to head with Colin. Ivy was standing with her back against the window watching them. She looked up when Riah came in and then tilted her head in the direction of the other two. "They've been like that for the last hour."

"Are they making any ground?"

"Actually I think they are. Hey, handsome, you got a plan for us?"

Colin looked up. His hair, a little long, tumbled into his eyes. "We've got two ways to come at this."

"And your suggestion?" Riah asked.

"We divide and conquer."

"I don't like splitting up."

"Hear him out." Adriana stepped over to Riah and put her arms around her waist. In her ear she whispered, "It makes me hot when you put on leather, baby."

Riah's heart raced at the quiet words. Would she always feel this way? How would she feel when Adriana grew old and died while she stayed young and vital? No matter when or how it happened, it would break her heart.

She squeezed Adriana's hand and said to Colin, "So tell me your thoughts."

By the time he was done, Riah thought he had as sound a plan as they could hope for, given everything. She still hated the idea of splitting up. Hated even more the thought that Adriana would once again be in the path of danger. Unlike Ivy and her, she wasn't a vampire. Unlike Colin, she wasn't a trained vampire hunter. The three of them had advantages that Adriana didn't possess. She was a scientist who loved a vampire. What could she do, beat the werewolf with one of her test tubes? She wanted her to stay in the safety of the estate and work in her laboratory. Colin, Ivy, and she should do any wet work that might become necessary.

"Oh, fuck off," Adriana said when Riah told her as much.

Ivy laughed out loud and Riah scowled at her. "Come on, Riah," Ivy sputtered between chuckles. "She's earned the right to do battle at our side."

"Yeah!" Adriana stood with her feet slightly apart, her hands on her hips. "I can hold my own, ladies and gentleman. A delicate chick I'm not."

Colin took a step away from Ivy. "I tend to agree with Riah. If you get hurt, we'd lose more than just your life."

Adriana seemed to consider the argument, then shook her head. "Nice try, folks, but I've backed up my research, what little I've been able to recreate, in triplicate. No more exploding houses will set me back this time. As to being a warrior, I've worked hard to be a part of this team, and if you think you're going to leave me behind on our first official outing since we formed the Spiritus Group, well, you're out of your collective fucking minds."

For a moment the room was silent. Colin burst out laughing first. Then Riah and Ivy joined in. Riah put out her hand. Colin put his hand over hers, Ivy followed. Adriana was smiling as she put a hand on top.

"Let's go kick some werewolf ass," Adriana yelled.

❖

The pull of the moon was killing him. He was born to run, to hunt, and holding back was as far from natural as possible. Too many people around now. The danger level too high. He had to be patient. The path to possessing the power of the seven was clear. Once he had it, he would be free and never again have to look over his shoulder wondering when the next witch would show up to threaten his way of life. He'd stopped them before, only he'd failed to grasp the whole picture. Stopping the seventh daughter wasn't enough. He had to take their power as his own. Now that he knew the truth, this time he'd have it all.

Forty-eight hours stood between him and victory. Now, he needed to attend to another issue. Any great plan was rife with complications, and this one was no exception. Earlier, he'd come through the park and scouted. As the trail wound north from the Aubrey White Parkway parking area, he located a secluded spot where he could leave his bag. Sufficiently hidden from view, he was confident no one would discover it until he could get back to reclaim it.

His confidence paid off. Now he left the trail and returned to the spot where he'd stashed the bag. Dusk had come and gone, leaving the park cloaked in darkness that deepened with each passing minute. The moon that was only a night away from full gave the darkness a gray shimmering glow. He could see well so all that remained was to get ready and wait.

From the bag he pulled the individual pieces of the rifle and began to assemble. From the bag's inside pocket he removed two silver bullets and loaded them into the rifle. He stretched out on the ground, the barrel resting on the fallen log in front of him.

A few moments to adjust the night scope and he was ready. All he had to do now was wait. He was very, very good at waiting.

Around him the sounds of nature provided a soothing lullaby. Several deer leapt out of the cover of trees and brush, heading for the river below him on the other side of the asphalt trail. A young doe rushed through the underbrush, either running away from something larger or trying to catch up with the two on the way to the river. The rustle of grasses to his left announced a garter snake on the move, undoubtedly looking for a warm place to curl up. An owl hooted somewhere in the distance. None of it drew his attention away from the scope. Though they were all prey, they weren't the prey he waited for.

His muscles began to twitch as the waiting dragged on. Still he didn't move. The night grew darker and the sounds louder. A skunk tottered by within three feet, taking no notice of him as he lay with the rifle held steady. Briefly he wondered if he would be cheated out of the hunt. Just as quickly as the thought popped into his mind, he dismissed it. The night was his. The victory would be his too.

Another fifteen minutes and his patience was at last rewarded. The sound was light but distinctive. Four massive paws striking the earth heralded the wolf's approach, the light wind sending the scent his way. Exactly what he waited for—at last. He smiled as he peered through the scope. It would only be a matter of seconds now. He moved his finger into position on the trigger. Closer…closer…he squeezed.

Chapter Seventeen

Cam was a little surprised when Kara suggested they take a ride. She'd thought Kara would want to rest or, at the very least, go back to the ranger station. They did neither. Kara drove her into the city and through an old neighborhood on the South Hill with plentiful brick homes and ubiquitous tall maple trees. She stopped at a small house just off High Drive and 29th Avenue. It had a decidedly English cottage feel to it and was tidy, freshly painted, and welcoming.

The surprise was the two people who walked out to greet them. He was tall and slender, with a shock of white hair. She was shorter and wider, with short blond hair. Kara's parents, and they looked absolutely nothing like her. If she had any doubts about them not being her biological parents, she didn't anymore.

For three hours, the four of them sat on the cozy back patio and talked. Actually, she and Kara mostly listened as her folks told a story of a tiny little girl smuggled out of Ireland and into the United States. Of how she was the seventh daughter born to Myra Magauran, herself a seventh daughter. And of how she finally evolved into Kara Lynch, the normal daughter of a middle-class family who grew into a tall, beautiful park ranger.

Except the story was far more complicated than simply a family who adopted a daughter through less-than-normal channels. That kind of thing happened every day all over the world. But Kara's biological parents sent her away never knowing where or who she was, in order to keep her safe. Kara wasn't just a witch with hereditary powers, but a witch with powers second to none. It was all pretty heady stuff, even for Cam, who'd seen more than her share of strange and unexplainable things.

Given the silence in the car as they headed back to the little houses by the dam, she was certain Kara was feeling equally blown away. How could she not be as astounded as Cam? She put a hand on Kara's arm.

"We'll figure this out together. I'll talk to the elders and see what light they can shed on things." This was strange enough even the elders might not be able to make sense of it. Then again they had a way of getting to the heart of anything.

Kara didn't look away from the road as she negotiated the heavy traffic and more than her share of red lights on North Division. It took forever before they reached Highway 291, leaving the obnoxious, stifling traffic. Or at least that's the way it seemed to her.

"I'm just having trouble digesting everything that's been thrown at me the last few days. How the hell can all this be true? Seriously, Cam, how can this be? How can everything I thought I knew be wrong? I don't know what's real anymore."

Good questions and she wished she had good answers. Her own special powers were harder than hell to explain. People were creeped out more than they were intrigued when they found out what she could do. Her Crow heritage fascinated them...the shapeshifting freaked them out. Being different was okay if it concerned humans. Throw in a little paranormal and suddenly okay was about the last thing it was.

So, how could she help Kara digest everything the two people she trusted most in the world had just told her? How could she help her accept the lies even if they'd been told with the best of intentions? A momentous task that she'd tried to buck up for.

"You're asking a shape-shifting lesbian Crow how you can be a witch?"

A smile twitched at the corners of Kara's mouth. "Point taken. I guess I didn't really think that one all the way through. I've been feeling sorry for myself since we left my parents, or the people I thought were my parents, like I'm the only one with issues. Poor little me."

"They are your parents in every way that matters. That hasn't changed. You have to remember they were—are—protecting you. All your parents, both biological and adopted, love you enough to try and shelter you, even knowing that you might someday hate them for the lies. That's pretty powerful love, if you ask me."

Kara pulled the car into the driveway of her cottage and turned off the ignition. She sighed, then turned to look at Cam, her green eyes sad. "Intellectually I know you're right. But here," she patted her chest, "it feels like betrayal."

"Think of it this way. You've always known you were adopted, right?"

Kara nodded.

"So you always knew you were raised by parents who really, really wanted you."

"True."

"This only adds to that. Not only did they really, really want you, but they took you knowing the danger it could put all three of you in. Still, they didn't let that stop them. That's some seriously awesome love, no matter how you cut it."

Kara dropped her head to the steering wheel, silent for a heartbeat. Cam didn't try to interrupt her thoughts or interpret her feelings. She simply waited.

When finally Kara looked up, her eyes sparkled. "You're a very wise woman, Cam Black Wolf."

Cam smiled and took Kara's hand. "No, not really. I've just had some very good teachers."

Kara stroked Cam's cheek. The touch of her fingers sent shivers through her body. She pressed her lips against Kara's. "We'll do this together," she whispered as she kissed her again.

The sound of another vehicle directly behind their car abruptly ended the kiss. She grabbed the door handle and flung the door open. Every nerve ending was on high alert, at least until she recognized the petite figure getting out of the other car.

"Jesus, Riah, you damn near gave me a heart attack."

Riah shrugged. "Not to worry, I'll give you CPR."

Cam rolled her eyes. "Five hundred years old and still a smart-ass."

"It's a gift."

Kara was standing beside her now and Cam took her hand. "What's going on?" Riah's appearance, particularly after her vague phone call earlier, hopefully had an encouraging explanation. But the hairs stood on the back of her neck. Never a good sign.

"Inside." Riah inclined her head toward the house. "We need to talk."

❖

Faolán felt a little bad about coming out tonight. Daphne tried hard to talk him into staying, but he couldn't resist the call. He wasn't alone either. Conrí beat him out the door and Faolán was close on his heels, literally. The pull of the moon won despite Daphne's considerable influence to the contrary. She was a powerful force in his life. The moon was more powerful.

Now as he stretched out his legs and ran, his doubts about the wisdom of the choice disappeared. The muscles in his body rippled and warmed as he covered the rocky, pine-needle-strewn ground. At the river's edge he paused to dip his head into the cool, clear water. He loved the way it flowed over his teeth and down his throat, the taste refreshing. He stuck his head all the way under to let the water soak his fur and cool his skin. As he came up, he shook from head to tail, water flying in every direction. Magnificent.

He'd lost sight of Conrí shortly after they left the house and didn't give much thought to where he'd gone. His brother didn't always seem to grasp the fundamental thrill of a good long run. He failed to appreciate all that surrounded them. Running together, running as a pack was the way of the wolf, except they weren't quite wolves. As much as Faolán would love to imagine himself as the regal wolf, he couldn't embrace the lie. While in this form he closely resembled a wolf, it took little more than a glance to see that he really wasn't one.

The differences between him and a wolf went beyond physical appearance. He loved to run alone without Conrí at his side. For hundreds of years they'd been together. Not every day, sometimes not even every year. Still, after centuries of existence side by side, he found that more and more he cherished the times he was blissfully alone. He often wondered if Conrí did too, although he never asked.

Now, as he ran from the water's edge and up the gently sloping hill, he breathed in the wonderful scents of the woods. Here the evergreens had a distinctive smell that he liked more each day. The grasses were thick and varied, some short and green, others tall and ornamental, waving in the breeze as he ran by. The wildlife was abundant and varied. He could almost envision himself living in this area. Living and running and loving a beautiful witch.

Not tonight though. Tonight he was just a visitor, free and content. He was the wolf, and the wolf wanted to soar through the woods and let the warmth of the moon spill onto his fur, making him feel totally alive and incredibly powerful. For now, it was enough.

As he crested the small rise, his chest heaving, his legs warm from the run, he sensed another presence. Not another wolf. He and Conrí would be the only wolves in these woods. A coyote perhaps? He knew they roamed the hills, but typically the smaller animals steered very clear of any werewolf, Faolán included. Smaller and so often sickly scrawny, coyotes were the ugly stepchildren of the lupus world. If it was a coyote he heard now, it would disappear as soon as it caught either scent or sight of him.

For a moment, he paused, listening. Nothing. Perhaps he was hearing things. His front paws stretched out as he put his whole body into the run. He heard the crack first, then felt the poker-hot pain in his back leg. Suddenly, instead of running, he was tumbling over and over, the rocks of the hill biting into his flesh, tearing out clumps of fur as he rolled. Overhead the moon beckoned, the stars sparkled, and a bird cawed.

And then, nothing but blackness.

❖

Kara sat and stared at the table. Or, rather what was laid out on the table. She'd spent the better part of an hour listening and still it all sounded impossible. If things weren't quite so crazy, she'd pat herself on the back for being such a good listener. Keeping her mouth shut and her ears open was the theme of the entire day. Not that it made any of it less surreal, from the conversation with her parents to the incredible tale Riah just finished relating.

The *Book of Shadows* quivered as it lay in the middle of the round oak table, or at least that's what it looked like. The leather cover was cracked with age, the pages yellowed and delicate, covered with beautiful script still dark and very legible. She propped her elbows on the table, her chin in her hands, and stared. Cam, Riah, and Adriana stared back. No one moved. No one said a word.

"So." She finally broke the silence. "You think that with this book, I can stop the murders?"

"In a nutshell, yes," Riah answered.

"I need to read it?"

"Yes."

Kara drummed her fingers on the table. "And of course, it's in English, right?"

"More like Gaelic."

"Aha." Exactly how was that going to work? She'd taken a foreign language in high school and college, but like most in this part of the country, she'd picked Spanish. Wouldn't do her much good translating a book written in Gaelic.

Adriana smiled, her eyes bright. "I worked on the translation all day."

"You understand Gaelic?" Would the surprises ever stop coming with these two?

Some of the sparkle went out of Adriana's eyes. "Well, no...I used some online tools."

Kara leaned back in her chair and crossed her arms over her chest. "Call me insane, but you want me to use this book, based on your online translation, to call up magic I didn't even know I possessed to stop some crazy-ass werewolf killer? That about sum things up?"

Riah nodded slowly. "Afraid so."

Cam laid a hand on Kara's shoulder, the warmth of her touch reassuring. "This doesn't feel good to me."

Didn't to her either. On the other hand, she didn't exactly see a whole lot of other options. "It's all we've got."

Cam sighed. "Crap."

She let her fingers walk the table until they were an inch away from the leather-bound book. The vibration was evident even without touching it. What would happen if she actually touched it? An academic argument, considering she didn't really have a choice. She wasn't going to ignore the possibility that she could help. She didn't know how or what she could do; she just knew she had to try.

Taking a deep breath, she wrapped her hands around the book. The second she touched it, her whole body began to buzz and shadows tinged the edges of her vision. The smell of smoke filled her nostrils while the sounds that only moments before had filled her small home faded away.

She knelt by the fire and put another log on it. A sharp stone cut through the thin fabric of her dress and into her knee. She ignored the pain and focused on the fire. Flames shot skyward and warmth brushed over her skin. A few more pieces of wood and the fire roared higher than her head. All was ready. She was ready.

Beside her, the book rested on the moss-covered ground. Picking it up, she held it to her chest. The heat from the fire had warmed the leather, the heat flowing through her bodice across her swollen breasts. Everything she knew, all that she'd learned, was written on its pages. It had been difficult to complete, writing was such a labor, but she'd been creating it since she'd discovered her gift and the true nature of her powers. Everything was there—all her knowledge, all her wisdom.

Now it was all for nothing. She couldn't undo her mistakes, ever, and the truth of that weighed heavy on her soul.

She put a hand on her distended belly and, feeling the child move inside, sighed. It wouldn't be long now and she must be ready. The baby would come very soon and everything had to be done before that day arrived. She would have no time afterward, no second chances.

Taking a deep breath, she reached into the blaze and tossed the book into the heart of the fire. Flames licked her hands and heat burned her, the flesh rising in tiny blisters. Pulling her hands away, she tilted her head skyward as the flames soared. With the fire as hot as Hades, it would consume the book in seconds, destroying the secrets as lies had consumed and destroyed her life.

The fire raged as if something otherworldly fueled it, but it didn't destroy a single page. She couldn't stop the tears as they began to slide down her cheeks. At the edge of the fire, she dropped her head into her hands and cried, salty tears stinging her burned skin.

She stayed at the edge of the fire as the flames grew smaller, until at last only glowing embers were left. Still she didn't move. Her sobs filled the night as the book lay in the center of a pile of ashes, untouched and unharmed.

CHAPTER EIGHTEEN

A cramp in her leg shot Cam up and out of her chair. "Son of a bitch," she muttered as she tried to walk it off. Talk about poker hot. The pain was incredible.

Kara, who'd moments before seemed to drift into some kind of haze, now looked at her with clear green eyes. "Are you okay?" Her brow drew together as she looked at Cam limping back and forth across the room.

"It's like someone stuck a hot knife in my leg." She knew it was a muscle cramp, but it sure hurt like something much, much worse. Or maybe she was just being a baby about it because she rarely experienced cramps.

She rubbed her leg again, then noticed the dampness against her fingertips. "What the hell?" Turning her hand over, she stared in disbelief.

Cam held her hand out for the others to see. Her palm and fingertips were covered with something wet and dark. The air suddenly filled with a faintly metallic scent. Blood? How could that be? Why would it be? The four of them had been doing nothing more than sitting around the table discussing the *Book of Shadows*.

Riah's eyes narrowed and she actually took a few steps away. Cam was pretty sure she saw her fangs drop down, but if they did, they disappeared a second later. Right about the time Adriana laid a hand on her arm.

Kara jumped up, her former haze seemingly forgotten. "Sit down. Let me look at that."

Cam's pant leg was sodden, so before she sank to the chair, she unbuckled her belt and let her pants slide to the floor. Her thigh was red and swollen and, strangely enough, seeping blood. This was the weirdest thing ever. She'd never had an issue with wounds. Actually, pretty much the opposite. She never got injured, and in those rare instances when she did get a cut or scratch, it healed so quickly it was as if it never happened. One of the distinct advantages of being a shape-shifter.

Now for some strange reason, she was bleeding all over Kara's dining-room chair. She hadn't hurt herself and she wasn't healing. Something wasn't right. Kara disappeared for a minute, returning with a small pile of towels, one of them wet. Gently, she wiped the blood from Cam's hip. Her touch was feather soft, comforting. More like a nurse than a ranger.

When she'd cleaned the blood away, Kara rolled back on her heels staring. "How can that be?"

Riah once more stepped closer to peer down at Cam's bare leg, any hint of fangs long gone. Adriana was at her side, though neither of them said a word. Cam didn't miss that Adriana kept a hand on Riah's arm the whole time. Not a bad plan. They had enough problems at the moment without tempting the vampire.

This didn't make sense or even seem real. Well, except that it hurt something terrible. After Kara cleaned her up and she could really see it, the angry round wound looked like only one thing: a bullet hole.

Even though she'd never been shot before, it stung as though whatever had penetrated her flesh was coated with a caustic substance. Except nothing had happened to cause the wound, so how could something—anything—have penetrated her flesh? One minute she was sitting quietly around a table, and the next she was trying to stop blood from pouring out a bullet wound.

"Did you hear anything?" Kara was asking Riah and Adriana.

Both of them shook their heads. It was a pointless question. Cam had phenomenal hearing and no one had taken a shot in their immediate vicinity. Whatever this was, it wasn't a normal gunshot injury, if there even was such a thing. No, it was something else entirely, and it scared her to even consider what it might be.

Though Kara's hands felt heavenly as they stroked her bare thigh, Cam pushed her away and started to rise. "I have to shift."

"Are you kidding me?" Kara looked like Cam had hit her.

Once she was up, she put a hand on Kara's arm and gave her a small smile. "I'll heal ten times faster if I shift. Let me run for an hour and then I'll be back. When I do come back, I've got to talk to Dad and Bruce. If anyone knows what the hell just happened, they will."

Kara didn't look convinced. Neither did Riah or Adriana. Didn't matter. She knew what was required, and the sooner, the better. She kicked off her shoes and freed herself from the jeans pooled around her ankles. As she headed to the front door, she flung her shirt and bra onto the floor. Nobody tried to stop her.

Pain, molten-iron hot, jolted Faolán into consciousness. Only once before had he experienced this kind of agony. He didn't need to look now to know what caused it this time around. Someone had shot him, and not with any plain old ammunition. No, someone had shot him with a shiny silver bullet.

Blood ran from the wound on his thigh. Spasms shook his body so hard his teeth rattled. This wasn't from a random shot; someone had known exactly what they were doing. Well, at least partially what they were doing. If they'd wanted to kill him, they'd have sent the shot through his heart. Even with silver, the only way to stop him forever was a hole in his heart. Whether the miss was intentional or not, he didn't know. Either way, he was grateful the wound was to his leg.

But the bleeding wasn't slowing down. The effect of the silver was taking away his blood's ability to clot. Bleeding to death out here in the middle of the lonely woods was a definite possibility. He could barely move and, from where he lay, was nearly invisible to anyone who might be on the trail. Unless they went off trail, no one would find him until it was too late.

The very real possibility that it could be too late already didn't pass him by. Not many people came into the parking area after closing time, so the odds of finding help were pretty slim.

Faolán didn't know when he'd shifted back to human form. All he knew for certain was that when he'd come to, he was lying on the hard ground, all too human and all too naked. The one upside to finding himself incapacitated was, in this diminished state, he couldn't hurt a soul, human or otherwise.

His long life flashed before his eyes as he lay on his back and looked up at the stars. If only he could see Daphne one more time, he could leave this world with one less regret. Thinking about her and how close he'd come to having a normal life made his head hurt. One more day was all it would have taken, and then he could finally offer himself to her. He knew she'd accept. Everything she'd said to him since coming here let him know they had a future.

Until now. Some bastard had just stolen his life. All he could do was lie here and wait, hoping that someone would defy park policy and come his way. The moon hung low and large, beautiful, as if to taunt him. With the silver lodged in his flesh, he couldn't shift. If he couldn't shift, he couldn't heal. If he couldn't heal…he would die.

In the distance, he heard the sound of footsteps and muffled laughter. One male, one female. His heart raced, hope threading back into his heart. Faolán yelled. Perhaps they'd hear him. Then again, given what had been happening in the park, they might run. The footsteps stopped and silence fell. Faolán cried out again.

The footfalls began again, this time at a run. Tears welled up in his eyes as he continued to call out. In a moment, a couple came into his field of vision. He'd never been so happy to see anyone.

"Whoa, dude, what the fuck happened to you?" The man looking down at him couldn't be more than twenty-five with jet-black hair and a nose ring. A shower hadn't been on the man's agenda for a while, his ripe scent hitting Faolán right between the eyes.

The girl beside him giggled, the dozen or so piercings in her ears and face tinkling in the moonlight. She smelled only slightly better. "You're naked."

"He's also bleeding," the man snapped at the same time he slipped out of his jacket and laid it over Faolán. "Roni, go back up to the trail and call 911." He knelt beside him and used both hands to put pressure on the wound.

The young woman looked at Faolán and then up at the road, her pale-blue eyes ghostlike in the moonlight. "Alone?" she said on a whine.

Mr. Nose Ring didn't look up. "Yeah, alone. I gotta keep pressure on this so the guy don't bleed to death."

"Why can't I call from here?" She chewed on a nail.

Even in the darkness, Faolán saw the man roll his eyes. "Duh... look at your phone."

The girl glanced down at the phone in her hand. "Oh, no signal."

"Yeah, now go call."

She hesitated before turning around and stomping up the slope to the trail. The young man turned his attention to Faolán's leg. His hands pressed against the T-shirt he'd pulled off to lay against the wound. The pressure sent a new wave of agony through his leg. It took every ounce of self-control not to scream. The darkness threatened again.

"Don't worry, Roni'll get 'em here to help you. Man, how did you end up here butt naked and shot up? Who'd you piss off?"

Talking was good, kept him from drifting into unconsciousness again. "I don't know," he managed to get out. "Can you take me home?"

"Are you kidding? You've been shot. Ya gotta see a doctor, man. I did EMT training and, trust me, you need a hospital."

Through the haze of pain he wondered in what world this stinky man would be an EMT. "No doctor." He hated how wheezy his voice sounded.

"Yeah, right."

"No doctor," he said again, louder this time.

In the darkness he could see the young man's expression. "Man, I don't think you get it. You're fucking bleeding all over."

"Get me home," he rasped. "Home."

"Roni," he yelled. "Fuck the call. Come help me."

"It'd be nice, Ray, if you could make up your mind," she muttered as she came back down to where Faolán struggled to push himself to something resembling a sitting position.

If he could just get to his feet, they could help him back to the house. By the time he was up on two feet, sweat glistened across his forehead. Liquid fire roared through his leg as Ray supported him. Faolán draped an arm around his shoulder and his other arm around Roni's shoulders. His stomach rolled as he tried to find his equilibrium. Hard to do with silver coursing through his body.

He managed to keep it together long enough to collapse into the backseat of Ray's car, which thankfully was parked in the nearby turnout. The car reeked of weed, and the only thing that kept him from puking all over the cluttered floor was sheer willpower.

His muttered directions weren't great but were apparently good enough to point Ray to the right roads. In a just few minutes after leaving the parking lot, they pulled into the driveway of his little rental house. He breathed a sigh of relief. Still alive.

Ray got out and began talking. "Hey, you guys know a Fay or Fag or something like that? Couldn't quite understand through the dude's freaking accent. Anyway, he's been hurt pretty bad and didn't want to go the hospital. Crazy, if you ask me. He's bleeding like a sonofabitch."

Then he heard Daphne's voice and tears welled up in his eyes. Some vicious werewolf he was. He cried when he heard the sound of his lover's voice. The car door was ripped open and then she was there, the sweet scent of her filling his nostrils and pushing aside the stench of his rescuers, the stink of the stale weed pervasive in the car.

Her hands stroked his damp hair. "What happened?"

His voice was thready. He didn't like it. "Shot."

"Sweet Jesus, Faolán, we need to get you help now."

"No hospital." He was surprised at the strength behind his words.

"Yeah," Ray said from behind Daphne. "He's been kinda vocal about that, like all the way here."

Her hands still stroked his head and he could feel the tremor in them. "I don't know what to do." She fretted.

"Conrí…" Sounded like the old dying man again. Felt like one too.

"I haven't seen him since you two took off."

His vision began to blur. Not good. He needed to stay conscious, yet the effects of the silver were rippling though his entire body and dragging him down. He tried to tell Daphne to just get him inside. The words wouldn't come. His thoughts were muddled, his muscles weak and unresponsive. Nothing felt right. Daphne was fading away as his eyelids fluttered and then he saw nothing.

❖

Riah's eyes narrowed and she shivered as if an icy wind blew through the small house. She didn't like it. Something was off here. Something dangerous. Cam's mysterious injury was just one indication, the vibrations in the air another. Every nerve in her body was tingling as if they were trying to signal her.

Whatever was happening, she decided she better listen to her gut. "We need to leave."

Cam, naked with one hand on the front door and ready to head outside to shift, paused. Adriana and Kara, likewise, stared at her. She knew her barked order came out of left field. Couldn't help it. She'd had a lot of years to develop her instincts and she wasn't about to ignore them now.

"Why?" The question came from Adriana.

"It's not safe." She nodded in the direction of Cam's leg. "That's just the beginning."

"Of what?" Cam asked, not opening the door just yet. "What are you seeing?"

"Whatever's after Kara."

Kara spoke up. "I'm confused about all of this but Riah's right. I'm not feeling warm and fuzzy about my happy little home right at the moment. Let's get the hell of here."

"The estate?" Adriana asked.

"It's the safest place."

"I've got to shift," Cam pleaded, her dark eyes filled with pain.

Riah understood using a preternatural talent to heal the body. But it was more than imperative to get out of this place. "As soon as we get to the estate, you can shift and run."

Tremors ran through Cam's body. "I don't know if I can wait that long."

"You'll have to."

Cam stepped back inside, gathered her clothes, and returned to the front door. "I'll grab my bags from next door and meet you at the car."

It took less than ten minutes for Kara to pack a bag and Cam to collect her things. Taking the seldom-used gravel back roads west off Four Mound Road, Adriana had them pulling through the gates of the estate twenty minutes later. Even as long as Riah had lived in this area, she didn't know these roads existed.

When they pulled into the circular drive and stopped, she noticed lights ablaze in the second-floor windows. Colin and Ivy were up and about. Good, they would be helpful. The more the merrier when it came to werewolves.

Ivy met them on the first floor and flung open the double doors, light spilling out onto the portico. "This is her?" Her dark gaze was on Kara.

"Yes."

Kara had her arm around Cam's waist as she brushed past Ivy to help Cam hobble in. "First things first," she said as Cam dropped to a chair just inside the massive doors, her chest heaving with effort. "She needs to shift."

Ivy tilted her head and studied Cam. "Shift?"

"She's a shifter—"

"Jesus Christ, she's bleeding," Ivy said. "What the hell happened to her and why didn't you treat her wound?"

"Just let me shift," Cam told her. "I'll heal if everyone just gets out of my way."

Ivy wasn't to be deterred. "How did you get hurt? Where's my bag? Where's Colin? He can get my bag—"

Riah laid a hand on Ivy's arm and turned her toward the library. "Long story, let's talk in here."

Ivy hesitated, looking first at Cam, then Riah, and back at Cam. She looked about to protest but then followed Riah.

She hadn't even made it to the fireplace when she heard the front doors open and close once more. No doubt a pile of clothing lay in the entry with a very nervous Kara pacing beside it. Only a matter of time to see if Cam's shifting helped. Through the years she'd been acquainted with other shape-shifters, and she was pretty sure Cam would be able to heal. But the wound worried her. She didn't recall something like this ever happening.

When Cam returned, hopefully in better shape, perhaps they could all figure out what just happened and, more important, why? Now they had to wait. As they did, she updated Ivy and Colin, who'd come into the library a couple minutes behind them.

She wrapped up by telling them, "We're running out of time."

Kara leaned against the doorframe, an almost imperceptible twitch to her eye. Riah sensed that Kara wanted to tear out the front door and follow Cam. Instead, she waited too.

"Do you have any sense of what's going on?" Riah asked Kara.

Kara's eyes cleared. She appeared grateful for something to concentrate on besides the wounded Cam out in the dark alone. Or worse…if not alone, then in the company of a bloodthirsty werewolf. Not a pleasant thought.

"A little." She came in and dropped to one of the sofas, then tapped her right foot on the Persian rug.

Adriana knelt in front of the fireplace, laying kindling and logs on the grate. Before long, she had a fire going. The crackling wood and the slightly smoky smell comforted Riah. It reminded her of long-ago times when her mother was still alive and they would sit before the fire talking softly of life, love, and things to come. Of course, her mother died when Riah was a teenager, leaving her with little but a few precious memories.

Tonight, she was with the only other woman who had ever loved her unconditionally. Of course, whoever coined that phrase probably didn't think it would cover things like falling in love with a vampire. Didn't matter because it worked even if that unconditional love extended to preternaturals.

Kara sat on the sofa, her elbows resting on her knees, her chin on her clasped hands. Her eyes were troubled, her face pale. At least she'd stopped tapping her foot.

"She was betrayed," Kara said a bit distractedly.

"She?" Adriana looked up from the hearth where she still tended the fire.

Kara studied Adriana for a moment before saying, "Her name was Moira. He loved her, he screwed her, and then he left her."

"Nothing new in that story. It happens in every century, every country," Riah commented dryly. She'd been in enough of those multiple centuries to know.

"True, but she was also pregnant, angry, and hurt. She lashed out the only way she could—with her powers. I saw it all in a vision. Her sorrow and heartbreak were so powerful. Almost like it was happening to me. I think he loved her, but she had nothing and he wouldn't marry a penniless old maid."

"Typical man," Adriana said.

"Hey, I take exception to that," Colin said from the doorway where he was propped against the doorframe, Ivy right beside him.

Ivy's smile was genuine. "You, my love, are a special man, and regular-guy rules don't apply to you." She patted his arm.

He screwed up his face and surveyed the all-female cadre in the room. "Thanks...I think."

Ivy hugged him, then plopped down by Adriana in front of the fire. "Sit down, handsome, and let's see how we can all save the world tonight. It's a dirty job but somebody's gotta do it. Might as well be us."

Colin shook his head. "I don't think we'll save the world tonight."

"No," Riah chimed in, "not the world, but if we're lucky we can save a life."

Chapter Nineteen

C am ran, her legs stretching out, her heart racing. The sights and sounds of the forest comforted her and normally would give her an incredible high. Not tonight. Something wasn't right. The pain in her leg was part of it. If it was just her wound, she'd get it, but something else quivered through the night that smelled of rot and danger.

To her right, a noise made her stop. Her muzzle up in the air, she sniffed, then stiffened. Cougar. Really not good. She could smell her own blood, the wound still oozing and, despite the change, not healing. Now it appeared she wasn't the only one who scented blood. The snap of a twig startled her, then spurred her into action. She whirled and retraced her path.

She ran to the house as fast as she could push her body. Nothing worked as smoothly or quickly as normal. Whatever caused the injury still flowed inside her body, taking a huge toll on her physically and mentally. Behind her the crash of the large cat sounded like an earthquake, the power of his run vibrating through the earth. She pushed even harder, not sure she could make it.

Rocks bit into her paw pads and her tongue lolled as she breathed heavily, saliva running from her lips. The scent of blood grew stronger, thanks to the cuts in her paws. She was a racing dinner bell for the hungry cougar. In the distance, a speck of light finally appeared out of the darkness. Blocking out the sound of the advancing cat, she focused on the light, which grew larger as she flew across the ground, barely feeling the pain in her leg and paws.

Behind her the growl of the cat grew louder, closer. She didn't dare give in to fear.

Heart pounding, Cam flew up the steps and, as she was airborne, called the change, drawing on every ounce of her power. It worked. In human form, she smashed into the huge doors and promptly crumpled into a heap at the threshold. The cat was roaring up the steps as the doors flew open and someone yanked her inside.

The adrenaline that gave her enough strength to fly up the steps crashed almost as soon as she was safe. Even if she'd wanted to, she wouldn't have been able to stand. Every muscle in her body screamed in pain as she lay in a panting heap on the entryway slate, bleeding and weak.

"It hasn't healed at all," Kara whispered, her voice trembling. "Is that normal?"

"No." Her voice was so soft, she wasn't sure any of them even heard her.

Riah and Ivy knelt beside Cam. Though both were doctors, they specialized in the dead, not the living. Dealing with those like Cam was far from their normal practices. Still, having two MDs hovering over her when she felt so shitty was a comfort.

What she really needed to do was call her father. This twist was as foreign to her as it was to her current companions. Shifting had always enhanced the healing of a wound. Granted, she'd never had to deal with a phantom gunshot, but her healing capabilities in wolf form were amazing, even for a shape-shifter.

She supposed she could thank Turning Leaf for her amazing healing properties. Never before Turning Leaf had the Crow produced such a powerful woman. Never before had one commanded such respect for her prowess as a warrior and her desire to marry her own gender. She'd been unique and interesting, not to mention respected.

Many in Cam's tribe had likened her to Turning Leaf, and she'd embraced the comparison as a badge of pride. Right now, she was failing her ancestor. Turning Leaf never would have allowed such a thing to happen to her and, had she found herself wounded, she'd have found a way to heal. The more Cam thought about it, the more agitated she became. She hated what was happening to her.

Kara appeared to sense as much. She gently pulled Riah and Ivy aside, to kneel next to Cam. Gently, she covered her naked body with a blanket. Cam welcomed the warmth. Kissing Cam's cheek, Kara whispered, "We'll figure this out together. Can you stand?"

Cam wasn't sure her legs would work. Staying here on the cold, hard floor wasn't much of an option either. With a deep groan, she pushed herself up on unsteady legs. So far so good. At least she hadn't buckled. Kara held her firm, and together they followed Riah down the hall to a small bedroom in the back of the huge home. One step at a time.

The bedroom they went into had originally been designed for a servant, Riah explained. Now they had it made up for emergencies like this. The suites upstairs were large, warm, and comfortable. Far nicer than this small room. But Cam couldn't make those stairs at the moment so the maid's room was just dandy. The walk down the hallway had promptly used up what little energy she had left after the cougar chase.

Lying on her back on the bed, Cam let out a long sigh. Now that she was safe and as comfortable as possible, she had a chance to reflect on the surreal woodland chase. "That was fucking weird."

Kara's brief laugh had a brittle edge. "You should have seen it from my side. That cougar was all but crawling up your ass when we dragged you inside."

"He smelled the blood and sensed my diminished capacity. Can't blame the guy for wanting a tasty meal." Cam understood the big cat, even if he'd scared her senseless. He was only doing what eons of nature had bred him to do.

Kara shivered and closed her eyes. "Don't even put that picture in my head. Once this whole crazy thing is over, I have plans for you that don't include you becoming dinner for a mountain cat."

She felt amazingly calm now that she and Kara were alone. The woman had a very positive influence on her. Now she could think more clearly and mentally screamed for reinforcements.

Cam brought Kara's hand to her lips and kissed the palm. "Don't worry, sugar, not on my agenda either. Can you bring me my cell phone?"

"You want to make a call now?" Kara's eyebrows rose as her gaze pointedly swept over Cam's prone body.

"Yeah, need to call my father. This shit is way out of my area of expertise."

Cam pushed up to sitting, the headboard at her back, when Kara handed over her cell phone. With Kara next to her, Cam dialed, and when her father answered, she launched into a rapid-fire, detailed description of what had transpired since she and Kara left Montana. Then she listened for a minute before closing the cell.

"What?" Kara asked.

"He's got some ideas."

"And?"

"And he and Bruce are on the way." *Thank God.*

"But they're hundreds of miles away."

Cam pulled Kara close, appreciating the warmth of her body. "Who do you think taught me to fly?"

"Yeah…forgot about that plane thing. But wait, don't we have his plane here?"

"We have *one* of his planes."

Kara was shaking her head, repeating, "One of his planes."

Her wound was now just oozing. Still not ideal, but a little better. It needed to be dressed so she swung her legs to the floor, feeling steadier now. "You have any idea where to find a bathroom in this joint?"

Kara jumped off the bed and headed to the door. "Follow me. Saw it when we were dragging you down here."

"You didn't have to drag me."

Kara winked. "Of course I didn't."

In his experience, people were, by and large, stupid. Take the current situation. Bodies were being dropped off the Centennial Trail in Riverside State Park right and left. Did people stop meandering through the park? No. Like right now, two men, big packs on their backs, cans of cheap beer in their hands, stood there, each with a cigarette dangling from his lips. Granted, they weren't the typical nature-loving types that frequented the park, but a person would think they'd give more thought to walking through an area that an active killer was known to frequent. Dim-witted humans never thought it could happen to them. Dangerous for the oblivious. Damned good hunting for him.

He liked the term *active killer*. Had a nice ring to it. Great part was, he'd been an active killer for hundreds of years, and he was good. His father was famous for saying if something was worth doing, it was worth doing right. Dear old Dad was right.

He wasn't simply a werewolf extraordinaire. Through the years, he'd also learned to be successful in life, which equated to having a huge bankroll. In short, he was stinking rich. That made everything a whole lot easier. It took money to feed his habit. Killing with any regularity required frequent changes of address. After he was done here, he'd be on his way. New place to live. New place to kill. He honestly didn't mind. All the moves kept his life fresh and interesting.

His thoughts turned back to another time and place. The most important kill of his life had been a bit of an accident. Who knew it would also be so violent. Oh, perhaps someone with knowledge of the Old Ways could have predicted it. Certainly not him. Certainly not his father. The blue moon had caught him unprepared for its influence on him and how his need for blood became greater than ever before. His prey never saw him coming. It worked out well for him…not so much for his father. Even after all this time, he could still taste his father's blood on his tongue. Something about the blood of the man who was his sire stuck in his memory. It wasn't a bad memory. It drove him year after year, century after century. He was always seeking the ultimate high and had yet to experience it again.

Not that it was a big problem. Each kill had its own reward. The flesh, the blood, the rush of euphoria. Not even sex could re-create it, and he liked that a whole lot too—with men or women. Didn't really matter to him. Sex was sex. It was all good.

Killing was better.

He paused in the deep shadows of the trees and tilted his head to the sky. The moon was big and bright yet still a sliver away from being full. The thought sent a shiver through him. Though infrequent, the hunt for that special one intoxicated him almost as much as killing his father. He had a feeling this one might be the kill that at last broke through mere satisfaction to ambrosia.

He'd been waiting for the woman they called Kara since his birth. He'd watched her for days, and the aura that surrounded her was like none he'd ever seen. The deep-orange glow that emanated from her body told him she was the special one. With her gold halo, he had no doubt who she really was. Only the seventh daughter of a seventh daughter carried an aura that powerful. She was strong, commanding, and unique. When she reached ultimate power at the apex of the coming full moon, she would be unstoppable.

Too bad she'd never get the chance to even feel those powers. When the next moon rose, he'd be waiting and would take the two things she had to give: her life and her power. He'd studied the Old Ways until he understood what he needed to do to end the threat. Only by stealing her powers could he ensure the end of the Magauran family legacy. Once he took from her, he would never again have to wait and worry about another witch. He would end their reign and become almighty.

He didn't want freedom from the moon. Didn't want to relinquish the power that made him better than mere men. What others considered a curse, he knew was a gift. Only by gaining the power of the witch could he ensure his own immortality.

In the distance, the footsteps of the two hikers stopped. They would undoubtedly be setting themselves up for a night in the woods, complete with cheap booze and smokes. He knew the type well. Easy pickings when he was bored or hungry. Chances were no one would even miss them once they were gone. The drunks and the druggies of the world weren't quite as tasty as those whose lives were more civilized, but sometimes it just didn't matter. Right now, he was bored and he was hungry. He'd enjoy what was put before him and appreciate how he didn't have to work very hard to get it.

Stretching out his front paws, he ran. As he leapt into the clearing, he didn't worry about sneaking up on them. Already drunk, neither man even looked up.

CHAPTER TWENTY

"If you won't go to the hospital, we need to find Kara. She's the only one who'll be able to help you." Daphne didn't try to hide her exasperation with his continued refusal for medical help.

Faolán wasn't sure he wanted to come face to face with Kara either. Quite frankly, he was frightened. His father had told both him and Conrí the story of Moira Magauran's curse at least a thousand times. He knew it as well as if he'd actually been there. Granted, Kara wasn't Moira...not exactly anyway. Still, just the thought of her made him queasy.

Somewhere along the line, he wasn't sure when, he'd come to think that Moira Magauran was coming back someday and finally set him free. Everything he'd observed about Kara had him almost believing she was the one. He'd seen the others before her. He'd even hoped they'd have the power, and might have, except their untimely deaths cheated him out of the knowledge and the hope.

This time it would be different. Now, it was even more important. He needed her not only to set him free, but to save his life before the silver made its way to his heart. He needed her to set him free so he might have a chance with Daphne. He just wasn't a hundred percent sure she was the one. That tiny bit of doubt was pretty powerful.

"Aye," he finally answered. It was the only option that made sense.

Daphne kissed him on the top of the head. "Come on, let's not waste any more time. The sooner we get you fixed up, the sooner you'll be healed."

"We should probably wait for Conrí." Despite their differences, they were in this together. Meeting the witch for the first time didn't seem right without his brother.

The way she rolled her eyes didn't surprise him. Daphne and Conrí weren't exactly what he'd call friends. They didn't get on at all. Maybe it was because, for a change, Conrí wasn't able to seduce a woman that Faolán loved. Conrí didn't handle failure well, particularly when it came to women. And he got the sense Daphne thought Conrí was too full of himself. She was a down-to-earth kind of woman. His brother just wasn't her kind of man…or werewolf.

She snorted. "Conrí is a big boy and, besides, he should have been back by now. He never thinks of anyone but himself."

"He needs to run. It burns off his excess energy." Nobody wanted a wound-up Conrí around for any length of time. The longer he ran, the calmer he became.

"Why do you always defend him? He's an ass and you know it."

Faolán did know that about his brother. Conrí far too often thought only of himself. He had everything going for him—looks, personality, money—yet it was never quite enough. He always looked for more and at the expense of anyone and everyone, Faolán included.

Still, blood was blood. They'd been by each other's side for nearly seven centuries. He could always count on Conrí. Nothing could change that, even if he irritated the hell out of him more often than not. Even if, in the far back of his mind, he wondered if he could really trust his brother.

"He is an ass, but he's still my brother. We've been through too much together. I could never turn my back on him."

She smoothed the hair from his face, her fingers gentle and loving. "I get it. I do. I feel the same way about my sisters, except we simply don't have the luxury of time right now. You have to get help, and soon. How's this? Even though I still think he's an ass, we'll leave him a note. Then we're leaving. No more excuses."

He brought her palm his lips and kissed it. *"Mo chroí."*

She wrote a brief note and left it on top of Conrí's folded clothes. Daphne helped him outside and they both stopped. "Damn." Faolán had forgot all about Conrí's rental car, which was parked in the driveway right behind his, effectively blocking them in. "Maybe he left the keys in his jeans."

He leaned on the car as Daphne jogged back inside. Maybe thirty seconds later, she was back, a set of car keys with a rental-company tag attached hanging from her fingers. "We're in business."

Instead of getting in and moving Conrí's car, Daphne paused and appeared to consider something. He wasn't sure what was going on. At least not until she led him to the passenger's side door of Conrí's vehicle.

"Aren't you just going to move it?"

"Not a chance. You rented a puddle-jumper while your brother opted for comfort. Right now, you need comfort much more than he does. I'll run back in and leave him your keys. If he wants to follow us when he gets back, he can."

"He'll be pissed we took his fancy car," he said at the same time he opened the passenger side door and slid in. Daphne made a very good point after all.

"He'll get over it." She kissed him before she closed the car door and once more jogged into the house to leave the keys to the economical little car he'd been driving since he got here.

Settling back into the comfortable leather seat, he decided that Daphne was a very wise witch.

❖

Cam calmed down the minute her father walked through those magnificent front doors. If he was weirded out by sharing a drink with two vampires, a former vampire hunter, and a newly unveiled witch, he covered it well. Kara was as impressed with him now as when she first met him. He was a classy guy.

With Bruce it was a little different. He came into the library and surveyed the group. Then for probably three full minutes, he stood completely still with his eyes closed. His breathing was even and everyone was silent as they watched him. They weren't offended or afraid but, in an odd, unspoken way, respectful. Everyone simply waited.

When Bruce opened his eyes, he cocked his head and Kara felt the heat of his gaze on her. She hadn't been uncomfortable before, but now his expression made goose bumps rise on her arms. Everyone else followed his gaze. Nothing like being front and center.

"What?" she asked, to break the silence.

"The answer is within you," Bruce said slowly.

"Everybody keeps pointing at me, but I don't have a clue what I'm supposed to do. If I am this powerful witch it would have been nice if somebody had let me know before the world started falling apart."

"You'll find it here." Bruce tapped his chest.

"You know, I like you, Bruce, but you're a little too cryptic for a basically average park ranger. I deal with wildlife, hikers, campers, and nature. Not so much with the voodoo magic crap."

He smiled. "When it's time, you will know."

Nobody else in the room was jumping in to help her. She had the distinct impression everyone here agreed with Bruce. So what exactly did they all know that she didn't? Actually, it was kind of a stupid question, considering the nature of the four in the Spiritus Group. They'd been dealing with this kind of shit for years.

Cam's family and the tribal members weren't far behind. Or the Crows might actually be far ahead of Riah and her group of preternatural fighters. Bruce was almost scary in his psychic abilities. And Cam? Shape-shifting wasn't exactly a run-of-the-mill personality trait either. Yeah, the more she thought about it, the more she figured the Crow might have a leg up on the Spiritus Group, at least in this present predicament.

"Well, I got nothing," she said in a petulant voice that was almost embarrassing. "But if you say I'll get it before the shit hits the fan, I'll trust you. You better be right, Bruce."

He shrugged. "My record's pretty good."

"Pretty good...great!" She was hoping more for perfect.

"Dad." Cam broke up the exchange between Kara and Bruce. "We need to talk."

Lee Black Wolf took Cam's arm and began to lead her from the room. "No, Dad, I'd like everyone to hear. This is affecting us all so the more of us in the loop, the better."

Riah nodded and gestured Lee toward a chair. "Your daughter is right. The more information we all have, the better armed we'll be. Mr. Plainfeather might be correct that Kara holds the key, but stopping this one will take all of us."

Lee accepted the offer and sank into the oxblood leather chair. Like Cam, he was tall and handsome, with black eyes filled with intelligence. Kara had the impression everyone in the room liked him as much as she did, despite having just met him.

He said, "Let me tell you a story about a beautiful maiden and a pale stranger."

❖

Dawn was beginning to break over the mountains in beautiful shades of gold. Riah didn't want to rest. They had so much yet to do, to get ready for. The air literally buzzed, though she had to wonder if she was the only one who felt it. Ivy, ever in tune with Riah's moods, picked up on it and gave her a look she recognized well. Time to rest whether she wanted to or not.

Riah hadn't been able to tell what Colin and Ivy were thinking when she left them downstairs. They were a good match, both bright, attractive, and introspective. Like Riah, Ivy would need to rest in preparation for the coming night. Colin would have his hands full getting Ivy to pull her nose away from the *Book of Shadows*. Though in her previous life she'd been an excellent coroner, she was, at heart, a researcher. She'd been Riah's best student during her years as an instructor, bar none. Now, Ivy was able to put her love of research into practice. She'd been doing a damn fine job of analyzing the unique book.

Between Ivy's research and Bruce Plainfeather's psychic abilities, they might just get to the bottom of the rogue werewolf problem before anyone else ended up dead. Riah didn't like not knowing what went on around her, and right now, she was forced to rely on others, a predicament she didn't appreciate. Sometimes it didn't matter what she wanted. Her days and years of relying solely on herself were long gone.

With the impending full moon only hours away, they had to pull their game plan together. The fact that it was also a blue moon made things even worse. The danger potential of a werewolf during a full moon was crystal clear. If they failed to figure out how to stop it before nightfall, she didn't even want to think about what would happen. Even though they were making ground, at the same time something important was just out of reach.

Riah sank to the bed and began to unbraid her hair. She massaged her scalp, hoping something would come to her. So far, nothing. The door to the suite opened on silent hinges, but she caught the imperceptible sound and looked up. Adriana slipped in, closed the door behind her, and locked it.

"Baby," she purred. "You've got to relax."

"No time." The hours were clicking by too quickly.

Crawling on the bed behind her, Adriana began to knead Riah's shoulders, which felt heavenly. She kissed Riah's neck, murmuring, "You think a whole lot better when you're relaxed."

Adriana made a good point. She already felt better. "Keep that up and I'll be brilliant."

"Genius," Adriana whispered as she reached around to unbutton Riah's shirt, then pulled it from her shoulders.

Riah didn't resist. Adriana's touch soothed her, excited her, and made her want to be human. But if not human then this, for nothing else ever felt this glorious.

For hundreds of years, she'd accepted that love had been lost to her. With impressive patience, Adriana had waited her out. Love had come again slowly, and with the slowness, it seeped into every inch of her. The dark-skinned beauty with mysterious black eyes had won her heart. Adriana loved her as she'd never been loved before, which gave her hope every day.

It also made her want more. She wanted back what had been stolen from her that rainy night on the dark, rutted road. She wanted to live again. For centuries, she'd simply existed, maybe because nothing had ever made her want to do more or be more. Until Adriana. Now she wanted to lie in the daylight and feel the warmth of sun as it tanned her skin. She wanted to see wrinkles appear around her eyes. To watch as strands of silver begin to thread through her long, dark hair. She wanted, in short, to grow old, and she wanted to do it with Adriana at her side.

Tonight her wishes felt empty because no one could give her what she desired. Except that wasn't quite true. She couldn't be human but she could be loved, and for the present, that was more than enough. This was the closest she'd been to happy in over five hundred years.

Her clothes now in a pile on the floor, Riah stretched out on the bed and watched as Adriana slowly, teasingly took off first her blouse and then her jeans. She ran her hands slowly down her sides, her eyes intent on Riah's face while a smile played at her lips.

Adriana arched one eyebrow. "See anything you like?"

Riah could barely breathe. Oh, she could see one or two things she liked. She beckoned with one finger. "Come closer and I'll let you know."

With a laugh, Adriana launched herself on top of Riah, who didn't waste any time cupping Adriana's full breasts. With her fangs down ever so slightly, she raked them over hard nipples. Adriana gasped and her whole body quivered. Riah smiled.

Then she rolled them both over until she was on top. Her eyes on Adriana's, she pushed her legs apart and moved her lips, and her fangs, down smooth, dark flesh. At her inner thigh, she nipped, not breaking the skin, but making Adriana jump and then laugh.

Her laugher turned to moans when Riah flicked her tongue over her clit. Adriana gripped the bed cover, and Riah wondered briefly if the beautiful fabric would hold up. It didn't matter. Only this mattered.

Riah loved Adriana, with her hands, her tongue, her mouth. Her skin was slick against her palms, her sweat salty against her tongue. This is what kept her sane and pushed her to keep searching for the cure that would set her free. This woman and the incredible emotion that touching her, tasting her, brought into her life. This hated immortality delivered to her a gift she'd be forever grateful for. Adriana's pure love had the power to banish even the cruelest memories of Rodolphe. Riah held Adriana, coaxed her until she wrung every ounce of pleasure from her body. Only then did she come up and lay beside her, holding her close. "I love you."

Adriana was a little breathless as she murmured, "You're okay too, for an old bat."

Riah was still smiling when she slipped into darkness.

CHAPTER TWENTY-ONE

Even though he wasn't operating at full speed, Faolán caught the subtle change in Daphne once they stopped in the driveway of the tidy cottage. He had the sense she didn't even notice the dam or the beautiful old houses. He'd been awed the first time he'd caught sight of them, but so many things had changed since that day. Including his chances of survival. With every passing minute, he felt his life slipping away.

Her body stiffened and her head tilted as if she was hearing something on the wind. He heard nothing. Couldn't go by him though. He was so far out of whack he wondered if he'd ever feel right again, even if he did survive. The silver of the bullet in his leg was sending out webs of poison, reaching every part of his body. He ached in ways he never had before. His thoughts were cloudy, his vision blurred. He didn't feel like he'd even make it through until the moon rose tonight.

Daphne stroked his cheek. "Stay here. I'll be right back."

He didn't argue. Normally, he'd be the one bouncing out of the car and racing to the door. He was a werewolf, king of the beasts, master of the forest. He and others like him ruled the shadow lands. The power could be intoxicating, particularly on the nights of the full moon. Running, hunting, coupling—unbelievable thrill when in wolf form.

Well, that might not be true anymore. He'd made love to Daphne as a man and never, in all his years, had he felt such joy. He didn't want it to end. Ever. Yet now he feared it would all fade into a darkness he wouldn't be able to escape. The longer he sat here, the weaker he became.

It felt like Daphne had been gone forever when she finally reappeared, though it probably hadn't been more than five or ten minutes. The time didn't matter. It only mattered that she was back with him. The softness of her palm against his cold cheek was more comfort than he deserved. She really didn't know him, despite her protestations to the contrary. He was a killer, and for that he feared his recompense was to die here among the beauty and splendor of eastern Washington.

"She's gone," Daphne said against his hair. "It's dark and quiet. I don't think she's coming back anytime soon."

In a way that was good. She'd be safe. He said as much to Daphne. If her sister was safe then she'd be alive to remove the curse at long last. It would be great. If he lived that long.

Sensing the direction of his thoughts, she said, "No, Faolán, you don't understand. She can't lift the curse without these." From her pocket, Daphne pulled out two bones, each wrapped with brown hair.

He stared at them, not quite comprehending. What did Kara need with old bones and crunchy old hair? The bloody silver was sending his thinking processes into total chaos. Nothing was making sense.

"Oh, darling, stay with me." She kissed his lips. "These are from your father."

Despite feeling as though the world rested upon his shoulders, Faolán reared back and stared. "What do you mean they're from my father?"

Daphne's eyes grew somber. "When he died centuries ago, my family retrieved these bones and hair from his burial site."

"What! You robbed his grave?" He thought of his father as he had been, tall and powerful with a deep voice and confident stride. These pales bones and brittle hair held nothing of the man he'd worshipped, and the thought of someone violating his body after the terrible way he died tore at his heart.

Her voice was tender. "If you want the curse to lift, it's the only way. We've passed these on to generation after generation, waiting for both the time and the one. This is the time and Kara is the one. But, without these," she held out the bones in her hands, "none of it will make a difference."

❖

The sun was beginning to crest the mountains to the east and Cam was still sitting on the balcony that overlooked the river far below. Everyone else had wandered inside hours ago. Kara fell asleep on the sofa in the library, a lovely throw pulled up to her shoulders. Bruce and her father had been shown to rooms on the second floor. Riah and Adriana disappeared to their suite while Ivy and Colin were another room close by, the murmur of their voices carrying on the still air.

She wondered why Ivy wasn't resting. Surely the sunlight would hurt her. At least that's what she understood from both Riah and the elders of her tribe. The elders, her father included, were long acquainted with the vampires. Her own knowledge was relatively new.

Cam's shape-shifting ability didn't manifest until she was about seventeen. She'd spent the next few years learning what it meant in her life. By the time she mastered shifting, she'd finished her undergraduate studies and was on her way to the veterinarian school at Washington State University. The elders didn't begin her real education until she'd finished and returned home to open her practice.

Now, she understood so much more about the world, both seen and unseen. During her training, she'd received instruction about the blood-drinking creatures and, until Riah, she'd thought of them as creatures and wanted to destroy them.

Meeting Riah had changed her opinion a great deal. She hadn't expected Dr. Preston to be a vampire. She was about as far away from creature status as one could get.

Cam had the same sense about Ivy. Her Latino heritage made her stunning and it wasn't hard to understand why Colin was so smitten. His protectiveness of her amazed Cam, considering he'd been a vampire hunter. The way she understood it, he'd convinced Riah to turn Ivy in order to save her life. That was a pretty big leap for a guy who made his living taking the heads of vampires.

Still, in the short amount of time they'd been together, Cam was impressed by the couple and the closeness that couldn't be faked. She'd always wished for that kind of relationship and knew it would never come her way. Her tribe didn't frown on being a lesbian. No, it wasn't that at all.

Being a lesbian certainly set her apart from most of her friends. Being a shape-shifter set her apart from just about everybody. Tonight the final nail had been driven into her coffin when her father revealed the true extent of her heritage. No wonder she could shift like no other in her tribe. No wonder she always felt apart from her friends and colleagues. She wasn't just the descendant of a great lesbian warrior chief. No, she was also the direct descendant of a werewolf.

It wasn't fair. She tried to do good work. She'd learned to live with the path the universe had laid out for her. This…was too much. As she sat on the balcony even the ache in her leg ratcheted up, as if to remind her that her father's story wasn't fiction but cold, hard reality.

Who, in their right mind, would consider getting involved with her? More than one had turned their back on Cam as soon as they learned what she was. She'd trusted a few with her secret and they'd broken her heart time and again.

In contrast, Kara had been as accepting as others had been horrified. Not since Bonnie had another woman been so in tune with her. Beautiful, sexy Kara, as strong as she was, could hardly be blamed if she ran as far away from Cam as she could get. Christ, considering what Kara had learned about her own life, she'd be a fool to complicate it even further by keeping Cam around. Especially now.

No, she needed to be honest with herself. Less heartache. By this time tomorrow, it would all be over. They only had to keep Kara safe a few more hours. Then Kara could return to her job in the park—after Cam's dad brought Winston back, of course—and Cam would leave for Montana. She would have wonderful memories of their night together and would have to make the memories be enough.

The voices from inside the house grew louder. Cam turned, surprised to see Colin and Ivy hurry back into the library. Ivy was crying. Cam struggled up and limped back inside. Kara rose, sleepy-eyed, from the sofa.

"What's wrong?" Cam asked, looking from the crying Ivy to Colin.

Ivy's hand was shaking as she held a cell phone in her palm. *"Mi abuela."*

"Her grandmother," Colin said.

"I'm sorry," Ivy said as she wiped a tear away with the back of her hand. "My grandmother is near death."

"You should go to her," Kara exclaimed.

Ivy shook her head sadly, her lips trembling. "I cannot. She still lives in a small village in Mexico."

Cam filled in the blanks. "And she doesn't know what you are."

"Si."

Kara got up from the sofa and wrapped her arms around Ivy. "I'm so sorry."

Cam was thinking. "Isn't there any way you could sneak in and see her, even for only for a few hours?"

Colin gave her a relieved look. "That's what I've been telling her. We've got passports, we've got access to a private plane. We could be in and out tonight and no one would be the wiser."

"You should go." Kara gave Ivy a squeeze. "Seriously, we can handle whatever shit's going to come down here tonight. If it was my grandma, I guarantee you, sister, I'd be on a plane."

Ivy's eyes glistened. "You are lovely people."

Cam gave a dry laugh, then groaned when she put weight on her injured leg. "I don't know about lovely, but you know what? Family is family and it trumps everything else. Go and don't worry about us."

"Come on." Colin pulled Ivy by the hand. "You get a little rest and I'll arrange for the flight out as soon as they can get the plane ready."

Ivy still didn't look completely convinced. "You're sure you'll be all right if we're gone?"

Cam looked over at Kara, who gave her a confident nod. She turned back to Ivy and smiled. "Yeah, we're gonna be just fine. By the time you get back, it'll be a done deal."

Despite the smile, Cam wasn't as confident as she put on for Ivy. Danger lurked somewhere outside; she just wasn't sure where, and she didn't know how to stop it. Honestly, it would be helpful to have the full complement at the ready, and that included Ivy and Colin. Except if it was her grandmother ailing, she'd be on the first plane out as well. Ivy didn't owe a damn thing to either Kara or Cam. They'd have to work things out without the assistance of Ivy and Colin. That was just the way it had to be.

He sat near the bodies for a long time, gazing at them from a spot behind several trees. He had a clear view of them while he was essentially hidden. It would only be a matter of time before someone would find them, but for the moment, they were his to enjoy. All things considered, this was a pretty good place to hunt. Even with the warnings of local law enforcement to stay out of the park, people came, as he knew they would.

Danger drew people. He'd seen it again and again, the morbid fascination with death. The adrenaline rush of being on the edge of disaster. Some ran hard and fast in the other direction, and then others, like the two spread over the forest floor, came looking.

Despite the draw of relishing the slaughter, he'd be on his way soon enough. One more kill and it would be time to catch a plane. Alaska, maybe. Or perhaps New Orleans. He really liked New Orleans, and he hadn't been there in a very long time. It might be a good time to make another visit.

The sun was almost completely up, bathing him in warm sunlight. In the distance, he heard the sound of an engine. Normal traffic was blocked from this portion of the park, but the rangers could unlock the barrier and drive the small park-service vehicles deep inside here. So far, he hadn't seen any of the service trucks come in this far, but considering the fun he'd had the last few days, he wouldn't be surprised to see one now.

As he waited, letting the sun warm him, a pickup with the distinctive colors of the state park service drove slowly down the trail. One man was behind the wheel and a second was in the passenger's seat. Each stared out the windows, searching with grave intensity. This morning, their search would be fruitful.

At first he frowned, thinking they'd missed his gifts. A few yards past his spot behind the trees he spied the sudden appearance of brake lights. The truck began to back up slowly. It came to a sudden stop and then both men were out and running. He heard voices on a radio and, a little quieter, the sound of retching. One of the rangers had just lost his breakfast. Yellow tape started to appear as they wrapped it around trees, enclosing the bodies inside the visual barriers. Johnny Law was in the house.

He'd like to stay and watch. It was interesting how law enforcement worked. It was different in each country, different even from county to county. Certainly through the years it had changed a great deal. In the old days everything was so much easier. The biggest threat in the early years was the rumors. A couple of times, the rumors got a little too close to the truth and he'd had to take steps to stop the chatter before the trail led to his doorstep. His pleasure, really. His pleasure, literally. These days, technology was a pain in his ass. Too many techies with too many toys. Still, it did make more of a game out of it, and he sure loved games.

Footsteps heading his direction put him into motion. Silently, like the predator he was, he faded into the shadows of the deep woods and disappeared. It was time for a little sleep anyway. Tonight would be filled with excitement and challenges. He was so looking forward to it. But, right now, it was time to get some z's. He'd have plenty of time later to feast and once more relish his victory.

Chapter Twenty-two

Kara wondered if she looked as crappy as she felt. A couple of hours of sleep on the sofa had helped, which wasn't to say it rejuvenated her. No, she still felt like she was running at forty watts when she really needed a hundred. Perhaps a shower and a couple nice strong cups of coffee. Couldn't hurt. Might even help.

"Hey, Cam," she said when they were alone in the library. "I'm going upstairs and clean up. I feel like shit and I'm hoping a nice hot shower will make me feel human again."

Cam was preoccupied and Kara wasn't sure she'd even heard her, until she turned and smiled. "Good idea."

Kara didn't like the gray cast to her skin or the dark circles beneath her eyes. The wound was certainly hurting her, but there was a lot more to it. Exactly what did one do to make a shape-shifter with a bullet hole in her leg feel better?

When Kara left the library, Cam was staring at the window where the morning sunshine had filled the room with a sunny glow. Kara wished a little of that sunshine would rub off on her. A dose of UV rays would go a long way toward clearing her head.

Her body buzzed as if she was high on something. She wasn't. If she'd had doubts about everything she'd learned in the last few days, they were gone now. A change was coming and it flowed throughout her entire body, affecting her mind, body, and soul.

Worse, she could almost feel the danger closing in on her. Would she be alive to see tomorrow's sunrise? She hoped so. She really did. Despite all the unnerving revelations, one incredible thing came out of the craziness: Cam. She really, really wanted to see where she and Cam's relationship was headed.

Her clothes in a pile on the floor, she stepped beneath the shower in the massive bathroom that adjoined the room Riah had shown her to earlier. It was like something from a five-star hotel. A girl could get used to a shower like this.

With her eyes closed, Kara let the warm water slide over her naked body. Her shoulders relaxed. Yeah, this might be the ticket. It wasn't sunshine but it was pretty darned close.

Her eyes popped open when the shower door slid sideways, letting in a rush of cool air. A scream started in her throat and died just as quickly when Cam stepped in and once more shut the door. Strong arms slid around her waist and Cam's firm breasts pressed against her back.

"I thought a shower sounded like a good idea."

"Great idea."

Cam kissed along her neck and shoulders, making Kara relax against her. The touch of her lips against her skin was pure magic. She reached back and ran her hands down Cam's sides, pressing her even closer. Cam's hands came up and cupped her breasts, her thumbs rubbing her nipples until they grew hard even under the warm water. Would she ever get tired of her touch? She didn't think so and hoped she'd have a long time to test her theory.

Kara couldn't stand it. She turned and grabbed Cam's face, kissing her hard, pressing her tongue inside to taste her sweetness. Cam took Kara's ass in her hands and pulled her close as she returned the kiss.

"Your wound," Kara said against her lips. "I don't want to hurt you more."

"Honey, you can hurt me like this any day of the week. Trust me, I'll be fine."

It took Kara only a second to take Cam at her word. Honestly, she wasn't sure she could stop even if she wanted to. It felt too damned good. The warm water cascading down her body, Cam's gentle fingers against her skin, the taste of her lips. No, there would be no stopping this morning. She couldn't ignore her need for Cam's body against her own.

Cam's hand slipped lower until it was between Kara's legs, her fingers stroking her clit. A sigh drifted up from deep within her chest and she pressed herself against Cam's palm. The stroking picked up and soon the wetness between her legs had nothing to do with the shower water. The intensity grew quickly, and before she could stop herself, she cried out, her orgasm rippling through her body like an ocean tide.

She rested her head against Cam's shoulder. "God, you're incredible. How do you do that to me?"

Cam kissed her wet hair. "Fortunate, I guess."

Kara didn't think so. This wasn't luck or a casual hookup. She'd had other girlfriends, women she'd admired and even loved. Yet nothing with any of them ever came close to this. In the short time they'd been together, Kara had the sense they'd known each other forever. It was nice and exciting yet as comfortable as though they'd been a couple for years. She didn't even want to think how she'd feel when this was all over and Cam returned to Montana. Just the thought made her heart hurt.

"Come on." Kara lifted her head at the same time she reached back and turned off the water. "Let's continue this in the bedroom."

Cam's smile was sexy. "Let's, birthday girl."

In the chaos that defined her life in that last few days, she'd forgotten today was her birthday. Thirty years old didn't seem possible.

"I like your birthday present so far," she said with a smile.

Cam raised an eyebrow. "We're not done yet."

Just as they fell back on the bed together, Kara's cell phone rang. She groaned but picked it up anyway. Jake's number was on the display.

"Please don't tell me there's another one."

"There are two this time."

"Oh, Jesus, Jake." She sat up and ran a hand through her wet hair, a habit that was getting very old.

"It ain't pretty, Kara. Can you bring the Doc with you?"

"Yeah. Where?"

She ended the call and dropped back against the pillow. Cam caught the drift of the conversation and was already getting dressed. The wound in her leg didn't look much better but, noticeable limp aside, it didn't seem to be slowing her down. She'd put a new dressing over it and was now pulling her jeans up. She grimaced a little when the stiff denim slid over the dressing.

"This has got to stop," Kara muttered. "Now."

Cam stretched out a hand to pull her up from the bed. "We'll stop it, Kara. I promise. You'll stop it. Now, come on, birthday girl, time to kick some ass like we promised Ivy and Colin."

She wasn't all that certain she could keep that promise. In fact, she wasn't sure what to think or feel. They all looked to her for answers. Shit, she didn't even know who she was anymore, let alone what she was. Park ranger, yeah, that part was good. Daughter... sister...witch...those were all a bit muddier. Things were revolving around her, and though the changes she felt certainly let her know she was different, she was having trouble reconciling that with stopping a killer werewolf. Hard to stop something she hadn't yet seen with her own two eyes, let alone even knew existed until a couple days ago.

Plain and simple...things were fucked up. She hoped she could find the answers everyone looked to her for before it was too late.

The slam of a car door brought Faolán awake with a start. The early sun was bright, the sky clear blue and cloudless. He glanced out the window looking for the source of the noise. Down at the end of the short street, a green Park Service truck was taking off down Charles Road.

He groaned as he shifted in the seat. Every bone in his body ached and he felt as though his blood was on fire. What else could go wrong? Kara's house was as still and quiet as when he and Daphne first got here. Nothing had changed in the hours since he'd fallen into sleep.

In the backseat, Daphne was also asleep. He watched the gentle rise and fall of her chest, the way her red hair draped across one pale, flawless cheek. Though she lay in an awkward position, she looked like the angel she was. Witch or not, she'd always be an angel in his book regardless of how things turned out. At least if it all ended for him tonight, she'd be at his side. That was something, wasn't it?

As if she sensed him watching her, she opened her eyes and blinked. Her smile was sleepy yet very sexy. A man could spend the rest of his life waking up to that face.

"Good morning," he said as he smoothed the hair from her cheek.

Daphne struggled to a sitting position and he laughed a little as she peeled a piece of paper off her face. Apparently it had been on the car seat and she'd fallen asleep on it. He laughed and she threw it at him. Catching the paper, he crumpled it and absently stuck the wad into his pocket.

"We're still alone," he told her.

"Damn it," Daphne said as she opened the door and came around to the driver's side. She got in behind the wheel. "I really hoped she'd be back."

"Do you have any sense of her at all?" He didn't like the panic that was squeezing his chest. If Kara was gone, there really was no hope left for him. Even if she didn't lift the curse, the silver coursing through his veins would kill him before the next sunrise. After all these years, his time was finally drawing to a close.

"A little," Daphne whispered as she rubbed her face. "It's faint but she's still in the area somewhere."

"We should wait."

"That's all fine except I've got to use the bathroom."

"Check the back door." The words were out without any conscious thought.

Daphne looked at him oddly. "Why?"

Faolán didn't know why. He shrugged. "Call it a hunch. Come on." He opened his door and swung his feet out. As he tried to stand, his knees nearly buckled. It surprised him how quickly Daphne made it to his side, her arms amazingly strong. He was beginning to wonder if he'd survive till sundown.

"Let's try that back door."

By the time they made it there, he was sweating like a pig. That would certainly endear him to Daphne. Some strong, hot guy he was turning out to be. Hundreds of years as a virile werewolf, and in less than twenty-four hours, he'd turned into a wobbly-legged pup. Things couldn't get much worse, could they?

The door was locked, his hunch apparently way off. But as he watched, Daphne muttered a few quiet words and the next thing he knew, the door swung open. Once inside he stretched out on the sofa, and she paused long enough for him to ask, "How did you get that door unlocked?"

She touched his cheek. "We all have our own little magic."

"I suppose we do." Although he sure didn't feel very magical at the moment.

He squeezed her hand and lay back against a throw pillow, closing his eyes. The seat of Conrí's rental car that had felt so soft when he'd first gotten in had become uncomfortable and awkward after hours of sitting in it. In contrast, the sofa felt like heaven. He just wanted to close his eyes and give in to sleep, even if he ran the risk of never waking up again. He was so tired.

The press of her lips against his forehead nearly brought tears to his eyes. It simply wasn't fair that when he finally found *the one* he probably wasn't going to live long enough to savor the treasure. Figured. His luck was always of the crappy variety. The one time Conrí couldn't steal his woman and he ends up on death's door. The universe had a sick sense of humor.

"Sleep," she murmured.

"I can smell a dog," he muttered.

Daphne's laugh was light. "Judging by the fancy dog bed, I'd say my little sister has one, but he or she isn't here now. So, my handsome wolf, you can rest easy."

It wasn't just the strong scent of a dog he picked up. Beneath the dog was the faint scent of another. It wasn't another werewolf, but still a wolf of some kind. If he were stronger, he'd be able to distinguish what it was. Right now, he couldn't think. The last thing he heard before darkness claimed him was the fading sound of Daphne's footsteps as she went in search of the bathroom.

❖

The closer they came to Kara's house, the more Cam's body buzzed. Something wasn't quite right. She almost told Kara not to even turn down her road. She kept silent at the sight of a strange car in the driveway. Probably a friend. She hoped.

"Wonder who that is?" Kara said as she pulled behind the car.

"You don't recognize the car?" Now her senses came to full alert.

Kara shook her head. "Nope. Doesn't belong to anyone I know. Almost looks like a rental, don't you think?"

Cam put a hand on her arm. She did think and didn't like it. "Let me go first. This could be dangerous."

Kara rolled her eyes. "Oh, right, with your injured and bleeding leg, you're going to rush in and protect me. Seriously, Cam, do you get that you're not exactly a hundred percent?"

She was a bit insulted. Just because she had some strange-ass injury didn't make her any less a warrior. "I'm still a shape-shifter. That makes me better able to assess the danger."

Kara got out of the car. "Yeah, you got the sensing-danger thing down pat. It's the any-chance-at-stopping-said-danger that's in question. We'll go in together."

Okay, now she was just trying to piss her off. "I'll go first."

"Together."

Cam had to hurry to keep up with Kara. Talk about a stubborn witch. Grudgingly, she had to admit she found that quality appealing. Irritating, sure, but appealing too. Go figure.

When the front door swung open, she found herself staring into a face that looked so much like Kara's, she did a double take. "What the hell?"

"You must be Kara," the woman said, without so much as a glance in Cam's way.

"Who are you?" The wonder in Kara's voice was thick.

She held out her hand. "I'm your sister, Daphne. Come on in, we need to talk."

Cam hesitated, a hand on Kara's arm. "Who's in there with you?" She could smell him, the scent thick and heavy. Not just wolf, but also blood. *Werewolf.*

Daphne held the door open wider. "Please, you'll understand soon."

"No!" She was absolutely not stepping into a trap or allowing Kara to either. A werewolf was in her house.

"You have nothing to fear from us."

"Us?" She didn't like the sound of that.

"Please, it'll all make sense if you just come inside."

"Come on." Kara pulled at Cam's arm. "My *sister* has some explaining to do, and I want to hear it sooner rather than later."

"Werewolf," Cam whispered, still not moving.

"Yes." Daphne confirmed what she already knew. "But he's not here to harm you."

"How can you be sure?" Cam wasn't. She had yet to meet a werewolf she trusted. They all had their own set of rules, their own code of conduct, and it rarely resembled anything even close to what Cam lived by.

"I just am. Please." Daphne motioned toward the living room.

Kara literally dragged her inside. The smell thickened as they walked in, and finally Cam realized she smelled not only a werewolf, but also an injury. The werewolf was hurt. Maybe that was why Daphne insisted they had nothing to worry about.

On the sofa, a man lay still, his dark hair contrasting with his pale skin. Though he was supine, Cam could tell he was athletic, perhaps average height, and maybe thirty-five or thirty-six. Nothing about him screamed dangerous yet she could still smell the wolf on him.

"What's wrong with him?"

"He was shot." Daphne sat carefully on a cushion beside him, her hand resting on his shoulder. "The silver bullet is still in his thigh. If something doesn't happen soon, he'll die."

Cam and Kara stared at each other. It couldn't be…could it?

CHAPTER TWENTY-THREE

Samhain was always one of his favorite nights. From the time he was just a child, he'd loved the festivals and, most of all, the people. Even hundreds of years ago when he was just a small boy and coming into his powers, father allowed him the freedom to hunt on Samhain as much as he wanted. So many people were out and about, it made for easy and plentiful hunts. Father was always pleased by his efforts and, for a long time, he did all he could to earn that pride.

Somewhere along the line things changed. He supposed he simply outgrew his father's strict code of conduct. All his rules became suffocating to the point of intolerance. Something had to change.

That day came, though he was well over a hundred by the time he helped Father to his grave. Despite Father's well-intentioned lessons and guidance, he wanted more. He tired of hunting far in the forest where game was scarce and often unchallenging. Only on Samhain was he allowed to hunt those who didn't live on the fringes. Waiting for that once-a-year chance to really live was torture.

Father was such a stuffy old thing with no sense of fun. Even worse were his ties to those without the gift. His allegiance to humans got tiresome after a good ten decades, so he'd helped his patriarch to eternal rest.

Even to this day, whenever he was home, he would visit the spot where his father's bones were buried. Despite everything, he'd made sure the old man had a proper burial. Freedom from rules and restrictions didn't mean he took his familial obligations lightly. Family was tended to even when they were dead. His father's headstone was much admired over the years, thanks to his own fine tastes. He'd do the same for any member of his family.

Too bad Father couldn't have been more like him. Things would have turned out much different. If only he could have seen the beauty in their awesome power. He'd like to have the old man by his side tonight. At times they'd had such fun years ago. He knew the old man though, and he'd never have changed. If he were here today, he wouldn't approve of what was to happen. He wouldn't have understood the earlier necessity of eliminating the ancestors of the witch he hunted now. No, Father would have objected to all of it. Pity, for the kills had been so satisfying, just as tonight's would be.

As his moment of reflection passed, he stepped beneath the shower spray. The water soothed his muscles and washed away the dirt and sweat. He stood there until the water ran clear and cool. Only then did he quit and step out. Once dry, he walked naked to the bed. Sunset was hours away. When it came, he'd be fully rested and ready to go.

He should be furious at finding himself alone in the small house, but he wasn't all that surprised. If Faolán wasn't here, the witch wouldn't be either. He'd have been more surprised to find Daphne here without his brother. Surprisingly, the two of them traveled in a pack. Not exactly the natural state for a werewolf. Traveling in a pack, certainly. The wolf in any form preferred a pack. Traveling with a witch in the pack? Not so much. His brother always did run to a different tune.

Stretched out on the bed, he relaxed. He slid his hand down his stomach and soon began to stroke himself, smiling as his cock hardened. It was actually quite nice to be alone.

Kara was still in a bit of shock. Finding herself face-to-face with a sister she didn't even know existed until a couple days ago was tough. To find that her sister looked enough like her to be a twin was downright spooky. She was so glad Cam was with her.

Funny thing about Cam. In the short time they'd been together, Cam's mere presence gave her strength. She'd always considered herself a strong woman. Compared to Cam, she was a marshmallow. Cam was incredible. Beautiful, educated, powerful. Just the kind of woman Kara always thought she should be.

As if those attributes weren't enough to impress the hell out of Kara, her *extra* abilities put her over the top. Until Cam came into her life, she'd never even thought about the existence of shape-shifters, let alone considered the possibility of being attracted to one. And attracted was putting it mildly. She was so hot for the woman, her blood boiled. Maybe the wolf in Cam drew Kara to her. Or maybe she'd finally met the one person who completed her, corny as that sounded.

The one.

God, what a frightening thought. Particularly considering everything happening around her. People were dying. A werewolf was lying on her sofa. Her *sister* was in her home. A few days ago, she was an ordinary park ranger living alone except for one feisty bulldog and looking forward to a quiet winter in the park-service cottage.

Well, all that changed in a heartbeat. Now, she was falling for a shape-shifter, she knew she had six sisters, and she was at the center of something really important and, as of yet, unknown. Yup, her life was definitely screwed up at the moment. Kind of exciting.

It took her a second to realize Cam had gone deathly still. She put a hand on her arm. "Hey, are you okay?"

"Is that who I think it is?" Cam asked, and she wasn't addressing her question to Kara.

Daphne looked up at her with a quizzical expression on her face. "I'm not sure I'm following you."

The man on the sofa didn't open his eyes but spoke quietly. "Yes."

"Motherfucker," Cam said, slow and quiet.

The man laughed softly. "Nice to meet you too, granddaughter."

"This is…" Kara looked from Cam to the man.

"The pale stranger," Cam filled in.

"The what?" Daphne looked confused.

He struggled until he was sitting up, his face pale and haggard. "My name is Faolán Maguire."

He held out a hand to Cam. She took it and a strange look crossed her face. Kara wanted to step in and pull Cam away, but she sensed it would be the wrong thing to do.

"He's my many times great-grandfather," Cam told them.

Faolán nodded, then looked directly at Daphne. Kara could see the unadulterated love in his eyes as he stared at her sister. "Years ago I left Ireland to come to the New World. I met a beautiful woman who lived on the Great Plains of what is now Montana. With Moon Flower, I found a life I'd never had before. She and her people accepted me for what I was. She loved me and I loved the life she offered me. For five years, it was heaven."

"What happened?" Kara asked.

Raw pain crossed his face. "Moon Flower died giving birth to our son. I couldn't stay. I couldn't take my son. For five years, I had the chance to live a life as close to normal as I'd ever get, but without Moon Flower, I was back to being nothing more than a werewolf. I left my son in the care of the tribe knowing that, somehow, he'd be fine."

"You knew about me?"

He looked at Cam and his lips curved into a sad smile. "I've always known."

"So why come back here?"

"I didn't really come here to find you. I came to find Kara. You're just a wonderful bonus. You know you look like her—Moon Flower."

Kara noticed how pale he was and couldn't help asking, "Are you hurting?"

Daphne answered for him, her hand stroking the hair from his face. "It's a silver bullet."

Then it hit Kara and she turned her gaze to Cam. "Your leg." It was incredible yet not impossible in this crazy reality. What else could explain what had happened?

Cam nodded, apparently making the same leap Kara had. "Yeah, my leg."

Daphne and Faolán stared at Cam, confusion written all over their faces. She promptly unzipped her jeans and slid them down, exposing the wound.

"Holy Mother of Jesus," Daphne murmured, and crossed herself. Kara's cell phone rang and she jumped. "Oh shit," she said when she looked at the display. "I forgot about Jake."

She put the phone to her ear and assured Jake they were on their way. "We'll be back as soon as we can. You stay here." Somehow that sounded a little like she was talking to Winston. Come to think of it, even with all the people in the house, it was a little empty without the click of Winston's nails on the hardwood. She'd be glad when he was home again.

Cam was pulling her jeans back up. "Ready."

It only took ten minutes to find Jake inside the park. The yellow tape was becoming a familiar though still very unwelcome sight. This madness had to end.

Jake was pale and dark circles dipped low beneath his eyes. For a guy with a normally very cheerful demeanor, he was far from that now. Not that she blamed him. Having a serial killer in the park was bound to unsettle even the most optimistic. Probably a good thing he didn't know his serial killer was also a werewolf.

Kara and Cam ducked beneath the tape and inched toward the ME's investigator. The closer they got, the more difficult it was for Kara to breathe. It was like something was sucking the breath right out of her. Cam noticed.

"Are you all right?" She was looking at Kara through narrowed eyes.

"I'm okay," she said weakly, right before she crumpled to the ground.

Riah came up with a start. Something the Crow Elder, Bruce, mentioned had stuck with her, and she'd been puzzling over it since coming upstairs. She got sidetracked making love to Adriana and then had drifted into slumber.

Now, her mind buzzing, she was done with even attempting to rest. She swung her feet to the floor, then headed to the refrigerator, expertly disguised within the bookcases, for nourishment. It was difficult to think logically when she was hungry. After the workout with Adriana and a long night of discussions with their unexpected guests, she was famished. She drank two of the plastic packets before she felt clear-headed and strong again.

After peeking through the shutters, she drew back when bright sunlight touched her face. She grimaced and ran a hand over her eyes. Right now, it was too early to get up, yet she was done for the day. Too much on her mind to even consider rest. She began to pace, her thoughts whirling.

So many threads to the happenings in the park and so many of them reaching out to touch the two women: Kara and Cam. It wasn't strictly coincidence, she was certain. The universe had a strange way of connecting the dots. Sort of like the theory about seven degrees of separation. She'd lived long enough to know it was more than a theory…people really were all connected, whether they wanted to accept it or not. And often in the most surprising of ways.

Certainly, the chain of events brought Kara and Cam together because of their respective professions. And, while it was true that free will was still an option, fate also brought them together. Decisions made by others years and years ago had set this whole event into motion. It was, however, free will that turned Cam and Kara into lovers. The thought made Riah smile. The two women hadn't announced that they were together, but they didn't need to.

They probably didn't even know it yet, but they were falling in love. Give them time and they would. She just hoped they'd have the time. Two things were really clear to Riah. Kara was truly at the center of everything, and Cam was somehow intricately tied to the solution.

She just couldn't put all the pieces together. It was like a chess game where only one move could save her queen. Any other move… game over.

Naked, she strode into the huge walk-in closet. She rarely lost a chess game, and she sure as hell didn't intend to lose one now. Between them all, surely they could keep Kara safe and stop the werewolf.

She hoped.

CHAPTER TWENTY-FOUR

The heat touched her skin, the smell of burning wood strong, pungent. Kara looked around and wondered where she was. A cold breeze made her shiver despite the heat of the roaring fires. At first she thought she was alone...then she saw her.

Outside the two bonfires, a circle had been drawn and fortified, ready for the confirmation of the spirit. A full moon hung large and swollen in the black sky, its light showering down upon the circle. A leg bone, wrapped with dark hair, in her hand, a masked woman with red hair the same color as hers, flowing down her back, opened her eyes and walked between the two fires. She cast the bone into the center of the fire on her right. She then reached back into the bag, pulled out a second bone, also wrapped in dark hair, and cast it into the fire on the left.

Her arms raised, her face tilted toward the sky, the woman began to speak. "I invoke and conjure thee, oh spirits of Osthariman, Visantiparos, and Noctatur, and command thee to lay a curse upon one most wicked and deceitful. That the man known as Ian Maguire shall, from this sacred night of Samhain on, take the form of a creature of darkness, transforming each and every night of the full moon into a wolf, hereafter hunted and despised. I, by the power of seven, do command thee to lay this curse upon Ian Maguire until the one whom he has betrayed is made whole once more. Within this circle, I invoke thee, oh spirits of Osthariman, Visantiparos, and Noctatur, to do my will."

The flames from both fires shot high into the night, crackling and spitting, lighting the sky as though day had suddenly appeared. The woman pulled the mask from her face and threw it into the fire, watching until nothing of it remained but flakes of charred ash. In the distance, the faint sound of voices carried on the night air and she moved quickly. It took her but a moment to destroy all trace of the magic circle, all evidence that she had stood on the magic ground this night.

The voices grew louder—closer—and with one last look around, she began to melt into the darkness. Just before she disappeared from view, she paused and locked eyes with Kara. "It is in your hands now." Then she was gone.

Kara came to with a start. For a second she couldn't quite get her bearings. Not until Cam helped her to her feet and brushed pine needles out of her hair.

"I got it," she said in a firm voice.

"Got what?" Jake asked, looking at her like she'd gone a bit nuts. "You probably got a knot on your head from that fall. Both your falls. What the hell is up with you? I don't need anymore bodies and, at the rate you're going, you'll be next."

"Sorry, Jake."

And she was. This thing was tough on her boss, and he didn't really have a clue about any of it. She couldn't—wouldn't—tell him. Kind of a need-to-know basis in her book, and she didn't think Jake needed to know. Was pretty sure he'd write her off as crazy if she did tell him.

Cam, on the other hand, did need to know what she'd just seen. This vision thing that kept happening to her was a royal pain in the ass. Then again, this last one was killer. She finally got it. As in GOT IT! The thing was, she needed to be somewhere else. Nothing they could do here would help.

The two men whose mangled bodies were strewn all over the forest floor were long past help. She was sorry they were dead. They didn't deserve what happened to them. They were simply in the wrong place at the wrong time. But she now knew what to do to make things right. She hoped she could use it in time to make a difference.

She could lift the spell that kept the Maguire family prisoner for all these centuries. She could set them free. The only niggling doubt was that she was pretty sure the spell would only release the Maguires. If the werewolf who made these kills wasn't one of them, well, they'd be shit out of luck.

It was still worth a try and worth a try right now.

Easiest way to get out of here was to feign illness, which she did, very convincingly, if she did say so. Cam didn't catch on until they were back in the car. Kara was excited as she explained it all to Cam and confused when she didn't get the expected excitement in return.

"What?" Kara asked. "You don't think it'll work?"

Cam stroked Kara's hair. "I know it'll work."

"Then what's the problem?"

"You need to have reached your thirtieth birthday."

"It is my birthday."

"Yeah, but what time were you born?"

That stopped Kara and she tried to think. Nothing came to her. She just didn't know the answer. "Where's my cell phone?"

Cam reached around her and pulled it from the holder at Kara's waist. "Here."

It might be illegal in Washington to drive and talk on the cell phone, but sometimes breaking the law was a necessary evil. She punched in her mother's number and waited.

"Mom, quick question. What time was I born?"

A few seconds later, she snapped the phone shut.

"Well?" Cam prompted.

Kara frowned as she drove. "She doesn't know."

❖

The last thing Faolán wanted to do was move. He could lie on this sofa until the end and it would be just dandy with him. Nobody was giving what he wanted even the tiniest consideration. Ten minutes earlier, Kara and Cam had burst through the front door and started talking machine-gun fast, both at the same time.

Daphne managed to slow them down and, one at a time, they explained what they thought. That turned out to be loading both him and Daphne into the car and heading to some castle. Or at least castle is what he thought he heard. In Spokane?

That couldn't be right. Since when was a castle found on America's west coast? And in a place like this? He had to have heard them wrong. He wasn't quite firing on all cylinders. Even so, he got up at Daphne's urging and followed the little band out the front door.

In the car, he rested his head on Daphne's shoulder, breathing in the intoxicating scent uniquely her. So clean and unmarred by the violence that defined his life. He wanted to take her in his arms and pretend he was worthy of the kind of love she had to give. Even if that was true, it wouldn't matter. Dying had a way of making everything else irrelevant.

One upside to his being on his way out…no more innocent people would die. "Everyone will be safe now," he murmured against Daphne's shoulder.

She stroked the hair from his forehead before she kissed him. "No one was in danger from you."

"All those innocent people."

His voice was barely above a whisper, yet it reached Cam, who shifted in the front seat so she could see him.

"What's he talking about?"

"I killed them."

Daphne put a finger to his lips. "He thinks he's the werewolf killing all those people in the park."

"No!"

He and Daphne both stared at Cam. Daphne found her voice first. "How can you be so certain?"

"I'm a shape-shifter and my senses are as sharp as the wolf whose form I take. I know what I smell, and it wasn't Faolán's scent I caught at the crime scenes."

"Do you have another reason?" he asked.

"You. Or, rather your connection to me. If our connection is strong enough that I'm mimicking your wounds, I guarantee I'd know if you were running around killing people. I'd have felt it."

He hadn't thought about it like that. Now that he did, Cam had a point. Except if he wasn't the werewolf killing these people, then who was? He could think of only one other option, and that simply wasn't possible.

Thinking out loud, he said, "Conrí's the only other werewolf around, and since it's not him, could it actually be wolf attacks? Wolves are repopulating all over the place these days. Maybe they're moving into the park."

Cam's eyes darkened. "No, these aren't wolf attacks. Who's Conrí?"

"My brother."

"Why didn't you tell us there was another werewolf with you?"

"He didn't exactly come with me. I did the scouting and he came in after the first two murders, so it couldn't be him. Besides he wouldn't do something like that."

"How can you be so certain?"

Cam wasn't about to give it up. It was impossible to explain to people who lived normal lives how close people, no, brothers, became after spending centuries together. If he could explain, he wouldn't need to say anything else. He had the feeling the only thing they'd accept was something in black and white.

Then he remembered the paper Daphne had peeled off her face…Conrí's rental-car receipt. He was just about to dig it out of his pocket when Kara brought the car to a stop. He hadn't been paying attention. Damned if what they told him wasn't true. She'd just pulled up and parked in front of a place built to resemble a small castle. Somebody with more brains than money had constructed a castle on the bluff overlooking the Spokane River.

A petite black woman came flying out the huge front doors and met them at the car. Kara paused only long enough to introduce Adriana James to him and Daphne. Pretty was all he could think of, as his energy poured out of him like water through a sieve. It took both Daphne and Kara to get him up the steps of the long entrance and inside. Gratefully, he collapsed on a cushioned sofa.

Another woman stepped into the room, and he wondered if all the women in the castle came in miniature. This woman, with long black hair and pale skin, couldn't be much more than five feet tall. Despite her tiny size, it didn't take a brain surgeon to figure out she was the one in charge. She oozed authority.

Even though his faculties were greatly diminished, he also caught the scent of death and realized in a flash the woman in charge was a vampire. Not typically an ally. Would she finish him off?

Holding his gaze, the woman said, "No, Mr. Maguire, I have no intention of killing you."

"Riah." Adriana scolded her. "That's no way to make the man feel at home. Excuse my partner, Faolán. Sometimes she gets a little too blunt."

"No offense taken." In her shoes, he'd have reacted exactly the same way.

"See." Riah raised a delicate eyebrow. "The werewolf gets it."

"He's not our problem." Cam was talking from the doorway where she'd propped herself with both hands stuck in the pockets of her jeans. "His brother's the problem."

Faolán pushed himself up until he was sitting. Sweat broke out across his forehead. The effort just about did him in. "I was trying to tell you in the car, it can't be Conrí. He hasn't even been in town long enough to be the one killing people. See!" He'd managed to dig the paper out of his pocket and held it out to Cam.

She took the paper, smoothed it out, and read. Then she handed it back to Faolán without a word. The expression on her face was dark and he didn't understand why. Not, that is, until he looked down.

❖

He slept deeply. Outside the window, the day was winding down. Occasionally, he'd awaken and peer out between the blinds. The light ranged from the warm morning glow to bright afternoon to fading sunlight.

The glorious undisturbed sleep had rejuvenated him. He'd need all his strength for the evening's activities and appreciated the fact that he was alone to recharge.

Now, time to think about the evening's plans. Without little brother around to help—like usual—he'd have to take things into his own hands. He was used to it. Had been doing it for years.

He was a natural-born leader. He'd been acutely aware of his exceptional leadership abilities for as long as he could remember. Others noticed too and responded accordingly. Through the years, he was the one people came to for insight and advice. He always had the answers. The right answers—just as he did now.

Enjoying his solitude, he strolled naked into the kitchen and opened the refrigerator door. Cold air poured over his hot skin as he studied the contents. Not a steak anywhere. He finally settled on a bottle of tomato juice.

Sinking to the sofa, the half-empty bottle in one hand, he propped his feet on the coffee table and gazed out the window. As he sat there watching and waiting, the sky changed from blue to gray to scarlet. Finally, the brilliant color disappeared and all that remained was a black sky and a full, round moon. Tremors tripped along his muscles and he smiled.

Dropping the empty bottle on the floor, he stood. He'd be leaving here soon...very, very soon. His arms extended over his head, he stretched, feeling the pull of the moon that was sending warm light into the inky darkness. The heat of the rays called to his wolf. His fangs began to lengthen, his bones shifting and changing. The shift came so easily and quickly.

On the porch, he raised his head and inhaled deeply. He wished he could experience more nights like this one. They came too rarely and the high didn't last nearly long enough. Tonight, though, he would taste the magic one more time. The blood, her blood, would run hot and thick down his throat. He would take her power and then he would take her life. The prize would be worth the eternal wait.

Dropping to all fours, his body began to change. Bones shifted, muscles moved, teeth lengthened. With a forceful leap, he cleared the steps and was running toward the river, the trees, and the place where she waited.

Chapter Twenty-five

K ara was so dumbfounded at finding herself facing a sister, the rest of the conversation going on around her barely registered. Overwhelmed was an understatement. She barely heard anything. At least until the werewolf roared.

Tears streamed down Faolán's face and Daphne was distressingly pale. A piece of paper that he held, white-knuckled, was the obvious source of their distress.

"What?" Kara finally asked. Time to tune back in.

"Conrí," Faolán muttered. His whole body shook so hard the paper rattled in his hand.

"As I said before, his brother Conrí is our problem." Cam took the paper and studied it.

"He's been here all along." Faolán put his head in his hands. "All along...the bastard."

Kara was just about to ask what that even meant, when it hit her. "He's the one killing people in the park?"

"He's the one who marked your house," Cam added.

Daphne was stroking Faolán's hair as she looked up at Kara. "He tried to make Faolán believe he was guilty. I knew it couldn't be true but I never suspected Conrí."

"Why would you?" Faolán asked.

Daphne sighed and said softly, "Because he's done this before, Faolán."

"What! He couldn't have. I'd have known. Besides, why would he?"

Kara got it even if he didn't. "He doesn't want to change," she said quietly. "He doesn't want me to stop it."

Faolán stood unsteadily. His skin was such an unhealthy color Kara wondered if lifting the curse would make a difference for him. Just since he'd arrived, his unhealthy pallor had deepened.

"No…he wants to be free of the curse. Too many have died and it all has to stop. Conrí is on board with that too. I know he is."

"Please," Daphne said softly as she stroked his cheek. "Sit down. Search your heart. You know what she says is true."

He sank to the sofa. "It can't be," he said weakly.

Riah interrupted the conversation. "The silver has to come out. He won't make it otherwise. Where's Ivy? She can help."

"They're gone," Adriana told her.

"Gone? What do you mean?"

"Her grandmother is dying. Colin has taken her to Mexico."

Riah closed her eyes and breathed deeply. When she opened her eyes again, she turned her gaze on Cam. "Come on, I'm pretty confident what they teach you in vet school will help."

After they had Faolán on a stainless gurney in a rather well-appointed lab in the basement, Riah shooed both Kara and Daphne out. Upstairs, they found Lee and Bruce on a balcony overlooking the river.

"My," Bruce said as he studied them. "Would never know you two are related."

Daphne nodded. "Aye, we all have the look."

"All?"

Again Daphne nodded. "In good time, you'll get to know us all. Everyone is excited to meet you, but first, you've got to make it through this night."

"About that," Kara said. "I know what I need to do. I just need to get a few things ready and find out exactly when I turn thirty."

"You know?"

Kara inclined her head toward Bruce. "I have him to thank for that. He took me through some sort of past-life exercise, and after it was over, I've had more little episodes, if you will. Pretty weird and pretty detailed. I think Moira is showing me the way."

Daphne looked at her as if seeing her for the first time. "You are the one." Her whispered words were barely audible before howling drowned them out.

❖

Riah talked as she worked. "What do you know about Faolán and Daphne?"

"I've told you what I know."

"Bullshit."

Ting. A silver slug landed in the small stainless pan, blood splattering up the sides. The wound was angry, ragged. Two bullets had done a powerful job of damaging Faolán, and they'd been in his body far too long. She wasn't sure she'd be able to save him. He might not be responsible for the deaths in the park, but he could have many other deaths on his soul.

One didn't live as long as Riah and not see every preternatural creature that walked the earth. Her experiences with werewolves weren't full of pleasant memories. Like the wolves they came from, they saw themselves as the top of the food chain. They were powerful, beautiful, and elusive. Unlike vampires, they'd been better able to assimilate into the human population for centuries. That alone imbued them with powers it took vampires years to obtain.

But Riah didn't think they were superior. Every one she'd met was a narcissist. For pack animals, they were far too often concerned with only themselves. Point in fact, the brother of the werewolf currently on her table.

She'd heard of the curse on the Maguires many, many years ago. Nothing too unusual. Get a strong witch pissed off bad enough, and things like this happened. What made this one unusual was the longevity of Ian Maguire's offspring. How these two brothers managed to stay under the radar for centuries, she didn't know. It was unusual and also said much about their cunning and resourcefulness. It proved how dangerous they could be. Or how dangerous Conrí Maguire could be.

Finishing up the sutures, she stood back. Cam proved an extremely capable assistant. Not that she was shocked. The woman's air of competence was born of experience and professionalism. Riah appreciated that combination in people. She had little doubt Cam was an excellent veterinarian.

Of course, that she was a Crow healer and a shape-shifter made her all the more interesting. Little surprise Kara was so attracted to her. She almost smiled, thinking back on how she'd been drawn to Adriana. When things were right…they were right, and she had the distinct impression things between Kara and Cam were more than right.

At the moment though, it might be a good idea to try to keep this werewolf in one piece so they could all help Kara stay alive long enough to do her thing. Cam studied the werewolf, her hand on his bare shoulder. Small spasms had rippled through his body the entire time he lay on the table, until Cam touched him. The second her flesh touched his, he stilled. Briefly Riah marveled at the power of family. For just a flash, sadness touched her heart for the family she'd never been allowed to have. But only for a moment, then her thoughts returned to the here and now, to the witch upstairs who was the magnet for all the recent turmoil.

Riah was familiar with humans, vampires, werewolves, even the occasional time walker, but witches? Frankly, they made her nervous. She was never quite sure what one was capable of, which didn't typically leave her with a warm and cozy feeling.

Kara was different, maybe because she'd spent her life not knowing she was a witch. She was stunned by the news, though Riah gave her credit. She'd stepped up to the plate without complaint. Riah, and the rest of the Spiritus Group, were talented in their own ways, just not the way that was needed tonight.

"What are you thinking about?" Adriana asked from the doorway.

Would the sight of her lover ever get old? Riah doubted it. "I'm thinking about Kara."

Cam, who'd stepped to the stainless sink, finished washing her hands and turned around. "I have to get to her. She needs me."

Adriana shrugged. "She's undergoing witchcraft one-oh-one right at the moment."

"What?"

"Daphne's filling her in on all the dirty deeds she'll need to perform tonight. Oh, by the way, she was born at eleven straight up."

"So we've still got hours to go. Damn."

Cam had been heading to the door and now stopped. She turned and looked at Riah, her eyes bright. "No, I don't think so. Wasn't she actually born in Ireland?"

Riah glanced up at the clock. Eight. "Which makes it the wee hours in Ireland."

"She came into her full powers four hours ago."

Riah looked back at Faolán, who, despite her careful ministrations and Cam's touch, was fading. "Let's get this party started."

CHAPTER TWENTY-SIX

Kara knew what she had to do and didn't have a minute to spare. As the seventh daughter of a seventh daughter she was powerful in her own right, but to make this work, she needed the power of seven. It would be better with her sisters, but five of them were thousands of miles away. As an alternative, seven whose hearts were true could make the difference.

In addition to Riah and Adriana, Cam, her father Lee and Bruce, Daphne and Kara rounded out the group of seven. Together, they could create magic powerful enough to lift a seven-hundred-year-old curse. No one had to tell her time was running out. Seeing how pale and weak Faolán had become, even after Riah and Cam removed the silver bullets, filled her with a sense of urgency.

"The bonfires," she yelled. "We need to build two bonfires."

Silence fell and everyone stared at her. No one moved. "Now," she said, feeling a bit like a teacher trying to get through to a classroom of kindergartners.

Motion appeared to happen all at once. Riah headed to the French doors leading out to the back. "This way," she directed them. "We'll build the fires on the bluff."

Kara wondered how she knew. Moira had shown her how it happened so long ago. Though miles away, this place had the same elements she needed to make her magic. Her first magic. Her stomach rolled. What if she got it wrong? What if she wasn't the special one and she was reading everything wrong? What if? What if? She didn't dare stop long enough to let her doubts settle in or she'd never be able to go through with this.

As the group gathered fallen branches from the woods that bordered the property, Cam came up, wrapped her arms around her, and held her close. Warm and comfortable, she smelled faintly of disinfectant, yet somehow the acrid scent soothed Kara and she held on.

"You can do this," Cam whispered against her hair.

"I don't know." For all her brave talk, doubts were beginning to thread through her confidence. What if she really was wrong?

Cam took Kara's face in her hands. "You can do this. You have to." She kissed her slow and long.

The reassurance, the kiss, and Cam's loving touch gave her confidence. She didn't want to let her down. She didn't want to let any of them down, including Moira Magauran. She had an odd feeling that her ancestor had been waiting all these years for both Kara and this night. She felt the truth of it in her heart.

"I will," she whispered against Cam's lips. "I will." Saying the words out loud made them more real.

Cam gazed at her for another long moment, then stepped away. "Come on, we're wasting moonlight."

Lee and Bruce had managed to get both fires roaring. She worked to picture the vision and Moira as she'd been on that Samhain night. She recalled the fires, the mask, and the bones. Everything looked right. Sort of. She walked around the fires a couple of minutes before it hit her.

"I need salt," she said to no one in particular.

Adriana didn't hesitate. She sprinted back into the manor house and returned shortly with a large container of table salt. "Is this all right?"

Kara nodded. "Perfect."

With everyone watching, she opened the pour spout and began to walk until she had both bonfires contained within a closed circle. A magic circle that pulsed as if it was alive. The buzzing in her body grew louder.

"I need the bones and the mask."

Daphne took off the bag she'd had draped over her body as she'd worked to gather wood. From inside she withdrew two bones, both wound with dark hair, and a painted mask—exactly as she'd glimpsed in the vision.

Kara put the mask to her face and turned so Cam could secure the ties at the back of her head. Then she took the bones from Daphne, holding one in each hand. The buzzing kicked up a notch.

Careful not to disturb the salt, Kara stepped inside the circle. Power washed over her, pulsing, throbbing. All her previous doubts fled. Inside the magic circle, everything was different. She was different...no longer Kara. No, she *was* Moira Magauran and had stepped back in time. She felt her anger, her betrayal, but most of all, she felt her forgiveness. The time had come.

"Let's do this," Kara said, and the heat in the palms of her hands grew more intense.

Outside the circle, the six joined hands, forming an unbroken line of defense, and their combined power of seven sent the flames of the fires soaring skyward.

❖

Sounds were everywhere. All Hallows' Eve and the Americans loved the holiday as much as his Irish ancestors. Children were running from door to door, laughter everywhere. It assailed his sensitive ears and filled his nostrils with tantalizing scents. Children, so many children. And, right behind them—their parents. A party he so hated to miss.

As much as he hated to forgo the delectable hunting tonight, it was time for his date with the lovely little witch. He could certainly understand how Father was taken with the first one. They were all pretty little things with pale, flawless skin and hair the color of an autumn sunset. But, this witch, like the ones who'd come before her, had to die. The game was to let them think they'd live long enough to grab their powers. Perhaps the wolf in him enjoyed the hunt, letting the prey think it had gotten away before making the final leap and sinking his fangs into all that lovely, tender flesh.

He'd enjoyed this last week. Each kill had nourished him, helping keep him strong and virile. The entertainment factor was off the scales. Nothing made him laugh more than watching law enforcement run in circles as they tried to figure who was murdering the fine members of their community. The game never got old no matter how many times he played.

Of course, not just the police entertained him. His brother was such an obedient and stupid little pup. He'd never been quite sure why Father didn't put him down when he was born early and underweight. Any good bitch would abandon a pup like that, but not dear old dad. He nursed the little bastard and damned if he didn't make it.

He still remembered the first time little Faolán shifted. Father had been so proud and they'd had a great celebration. His first time, Father patted him on the head and told him he'd done a good job. After Faolán came along everything was about him. He became part of the background.

He didn't go to the background without a fight. After all, he was a great silver wolf, larger than any other he'd ever seen. Drab little black-and-tan Faolán resembled a common shepherd rather than a wolf. He could run with a pack of dogs and no one would notice the difference. Not Conrí. He was the master—an alpha—yet no one ever cared.

Only when their lives were about to end did they notice him or care. But then it was too late.

Holding his head in the air, he searched for her scent. On the porch of her small bungalow where inside all was dark and silent, he sniffed. Her scent was heavy here and, surprisingly, so was Faolán's. He'd been here and recently. Probably dragged his scrawny ass here to die after Conrí loaded him full of silver. He'd been waiting years for the right time to put little brother down. It ended up being much more satisfying than he'd ever imagined. Almost as good as the day he'd killed their father.

Now, to find the witch. His head down, he began to run, following the scent of his prey. He raced through the park and along the hillside. The scents grew stronger and he followed them up and up. In the distance he saw the flames, and the smell of burning wood mingled with those of his brother and the witch.

Checkmate.

❖

As a healer and a shape-shifter, Cam possessed her own fair share of power. This, well, this was something altogether different. The ground beneath her feet shook, and with each tremor, the flames of the bonfires shot to the sky. Each time Kara got close to the fire, the flames danced.

Outside the circle, they stood together and waited. Not quite sure for what, but she figured Kara had a plan. Since they'd gotten here tonight, Kara'd had a crystal-clear vision of what to do.

Cam understood. The first time she'd shifted, it all came to her as if she'd always known. Despite being kept in the dark her whole life, the last few days had changed everything, and Kara had taken it all in with astounding ease. Incredible to watch, a privilege to be a part of.

She held her father's hand on one side and Bruce's on the other. Standing between the two elders, she felt energy surge. They might not be witches but damned if they couldn't summon their own magic. Right now, they needed every little bit they could get. Danger still lurked out there beyond the trees. She wouldn't feel safe until Kara cast her spell and Conrí was stopped.

In a painted mask Daphne had brought for her, Kara looked exotic and beautiful, just plain erotic as she moved and swayed between the fires. Cam's heart raced from either fear or arousal…or perhaps a little of both. Awesome, whatever it was.

Her father squeezed her hand and she looked up at him. His dark eyes caught the light of the fire.

"Shouldn't she be doing something?" Cam whispered.

"She's gathering our power to her," Bruce said quietly.

He was right. The air grew thicker as the ground trembled more violently. The vibrations soared up through her body. Between the two fires Kara stiffened. She was feeling it too. Cam wanted to let go and run to her. Suddenly, despite the obvious strength they possessed as a group, she had to keep herself from grabbing Kara and pulling her to safety.

Safety was an illusion, though, and Kara wouldn't come even if Cam begged. The woman in the center of the magic circle, the one she'd kissed and made love to, existed in the here and now, and at the same time in a century long past. This night had to happen as it was unfolding, and Kara had to orchestrate it. Cam couldn't rush in and save the day. This was Kara's show, start to finish.

Fate had brought her here and to this woman. Fate had brought her father and Bruce, combined their powers, enhanced and contributed to the magic Kara needed to bring the universe once more into balance. As hard as it was for Cam to let go, that's precisely what she had to do right now.

Bruce squeezed her hand and leaned close. "Be patient, little wolf. She will bring us all through this."

"I'm scared," Cam whispered. "What if something goes wrong? What if Kara gets hurt? I hate this, hate being this scared."

"Fear is pain arising from the anticipation of evil."

He so got her. "You always know the right thing to say."

"Naw, stole it from Aristotle."

This time she squeezed his hand, incredibly glad these two men were here tonight.

Kara paused in the middle of the two fires and locked eyes with Cam. "I'm ready."

CHAPTER TWENTY-SEVEN

Tears slid down Kara's cheeks. Emotion had no place in this night, yet she couldn't help it. She needed to harness the greatest of her powers, not cry for a woman who'd died of a broken heart many centuries ago. Heat from the bonfires made the mask feel claustrophobic, and bits of ash from the charred wood of the fire, carried skyward by the wind, clung to her hair. Unlike Moira, she wasn't alone on the high cliff, so she choked back her tears and let the power of the dark half wash over and through her.

Time was growing short. Somewhere out in the darkness he was coming, just as he had come for the others—her ancestors. She knew that now. Knew how he had killed them before they could undo what Moira set in motion so many years ago. It was all up to her. She must hurry. Taking a deep breath, she cradled the bones, one in each hand.

Outside the bonfires, the circle had been drawn and, with the help of Cam and the others, fortified, ready for the confirmation of the spirit. High above her, the full moon hung large and swollen in the black sky, its light showering down upon the circle. Kara pulled her gaze away from Cam's face and started to walk between the two fires. She cast the first bone into the center of the fire on her right. With her other hand she cast the second bone into the fire on the left.

Her arms raised, her face tilted toward the sky, Kara began to speak. The words came from a voice giving gentle guidance inside her head. "I invoke and conjure thee, oh spirits of Osthariman,

Visantiparos, and Noctatur, and command thee to remove the curse upon Ian Maguire and that from this moment, on this most sacred night of Samhain, no longer take the form of a creature of darkness…"

The words stalled as a sound from the darkness made her spin. A moment later a man's cry shattered the night. The circle was broken as something yanked Bruce backward and dragged him into the darkness. Immediately, the power weakened. A cold breeze blew over her skin despite the heat from the two roaring fires she stood between.

"Keep going," Cam yelled.

Cam was right. She began again, picking up where she left off. "That no longer on the night of the full moon, or any other night, shall he or his offspring transform into a wolf. No longer will he be hunted and despised. I, by the power of seven…"

Her words trailed off again when she realized they were no longer seven. How could she make this work? Another scream made her whip her head around. This time something yanked Lee off his feet and dragged him, like Bruce, into the trees, where he disappeared into darkness. Another colder wind whipped over her flesh.

Power faded as if a glass was being slowly emptied. She didn't know how to do this without the others. She didn't know how to do this alone. Her hands started to tremble and she really, really wanted to rip the mask from her face. She would too, except that voice in her head urged her on. She refused to let *him* win. Not when they were so close. She'd just found out she had sisters, and she was damn well going to live long enough to meet them.

She also had every intention of seeing more of Cam too. That woman had future written all over her, and Kara intended to see if it was true. Cam was special in a whole lot of ways, and if Kara didn't end this all tonight, she would never get to find them all out. Somehow, she had to keep going.

❖

Faolán rolled from the table and hit the floor with a thud that sent spasms of pain up his legs, fanning out to the rest of his body.

He steadied himself, gripping the edge of the table. When he felt more sure-footed, he headed to the door. By the time he got there his heart was racing and his limbs trembled. He vaguely wondered if this is what a heart attack felt like, then pushed the thought from his mind.

He'd sensed Conrí getting close and knew he was here by the very subtle change in the air. It was always the same when his brother arrived—everything was just a little left of center. He should have gone out sooner, the second he realized Conrí was near enough to be dangerous. If anything happened to Daphne, he'd never forgive himself. He should be there to protect her, not laying around like a baby. He was a werewolf, for Christ's sake, except he was a werewolf with the effects of the just-removed silver bullets still threatening his life.

Halfway across the library, he noticed the French doors hanging open. It made sense. Whatever would unfold would have to happen outside under the moon. When he stepped out on the flagstone patio, he turned his face up and closed his eyes. The full moon bathed his body in golden light. It helped even if he was too weak to call the change.

Opening his eyes, he followed the sound of voices, the smell of burning wood, and the glow of the blazing fires. Each step shot spikes of pain up his leg to radiate throughout his entire body. He wanted to stop and had to keep going. Conrí was near, and even though the thought of his brother's betrayal made him sick, he knew the truth in his heart: Conrí was a killer. Only one thing would stop him, and that was Faolán.

He'd come here hoping to keep Kara from the fate that had befallen the seventh daughters who'd come before her. He wanted her to live, and most of all, he wanted her to make him human. He'd been convinced that Conrí wanted the same. How he could be so terribly wrong was enough to make him physically sick.

As he staggered across the grass, he could hear Kara's voice growing louder as he neared the fires. Around the outside, the others stood, hand in hand. Maybe it would be all right. This time, the witch would live and he'd be free at last.

He stumbled over a fallen branch and fell to his knees. Pain once more shot up his legs and nausea rose. Hands on the ground, he gasped and waited to move until his breathing evened out and he was fairly certain he wouldn't vomit. As he rose, he was close enough to see Daphne's face in the glow of the firelight. She was so incredibly beautiful. His heart ached at the knowledge she'd be lost to him before the night was over. He'd be lucky to survive the next hour.

He just had to stick around long enough to protect Daphne and her little sister. Only that mattered now. He owed them that much.

Movement caught his eye and he whipped his head around in time to see one fall. A moment later, a second one was taken down. Faolán roared and, despite his weakened state, did the only thing he could: he called the change.

He screamed as his body began to change, the silver that was coursing through his veins making the shift pure agony. He didn't have a choice. The only way he could protect his love was to become the wolf one last time, even if it killed him…and it undoubtedly would.

Cam shook from head to toe. The intruder had yanked her father and Bruce from her grip so quickly, so powerfully, she never had a chance to even try to protect them. She'd caught his scent before his first attack, yet she hadn't been able to stop him.

She touched the medicine bag at her waist, hoping to draw power from it, and tried not to let her imagination run wild. The werewolf didn't have time to hurt them. He had to come back here to stop Kara. That's what they all had to focus on, the only advantage they could capitalize on.

Kara was looking at her now, the mask obscuring her beautiful face, but her eyes windows to her soul. "Keep going," Cam urged. "We have to stop him."

"We've lost the power of seven." Kara's voice shook.

Cam shook her head. "You don't need us. You can do it on your own."

The emotion in Kara's voice tore at Cam's heart. "I'm not strong enough to stop him."

"Yes, Kara, you are."

Cam looked around frantically, trying to find something, anything, she could do. Riah, Adriana, and Daphne still stood with their hands clasped. Cam took Riah's free hand. Despite stretching as far as she could, she couldn't reach Daphne.

"Try," she urged Kara. "Hurry, before he comes back."

Cam couldn't wait much longer before she'd have to go find her father and Bruce. It was killing her as it was. They were out there, in the dark, at the mercy of a werewolf. Then again, they were Crow elders, both powerful and wise. They could hold their own. She hoped.

All of a sudden, movement came from behind her. Cam whipped her arm up as if it could protect her from the beast. But the werewolf wasn't going for her. It was trying to breach the magic circle Kara had cast around the fires. Cam hoped the circle magic was strong.

She didn't have to worry if it would hold because as the silver wolf flew through the air straight toward Kara, another flash, dark and large, came out of the darkness to tackle it. Faolán, it had to be.

The dark wolf had the silver one by the throat and they rolled in a tangle of fur and vicious growls. Cam leapt out of the way as they fought. For a minute, Faolán appeared to take control, then suddenly the tide turned. Conrí grabbed Faolán by the neck with his massive jaw, shaking him, then tossed him into the scrub. Daphne cried out and ran toward where Faolán lay in a crumpled heap, beginning to change back to human form.

His silver fur glowing in the moonlight, Conrí swung his head back toward Kara. Cam noticed that the fury of the battle had disturbed the magic circle and made an opening. An opening big enough for a wolf to slip through.

Cam screamed at the same moment the wolf leapt through the circle.

CHAPTER TWENTY-EIGHT

Until the one he has betrayed has been made whole once more.

The words came into her head like a whisper on the wind. Everything appeared to happen in slow motion. A few minutes ago she'd known what to do and say, but then everything went terribly wrong.

Bruce was gone. Lee was gone. Faolán tried to help them and now he was probably dead. A few more minutes, and the werewolf could kill them all. Even Riah didn't seem a match for this creature.

Then, as her sister cried out in distress and ran to Faolán's side, Kara got it. Love. It was about love in 1370 when Moira cursed Ian and his family, and it was about love now. Though she didn't know how Cam felt about her, she knew she was falling in love with her. The love between Riah and Adriana was clear even to the blind.

But more important than anything else was the love between Daphne and Faolán. Love between the descendants of Moira and Ian. Betrayed and betraying in long-ago Ireland, they had found redemption in the twenty-first century. Kara didn't need anyone else; the power of the seventh daughter of a seventh daughter was hers.

She stared into his black eyes as he flew across the circle between the fires and directly toward her body. She recognized those eyes as she'd known she would. No mistakes and no regrets.

"I command thee to remove this curse from Ian Maguire for the one he has betrayed is made whole once more. Within this circle, I invoke thee, oh spirits of Osthariman, Visantiparos, and Noctatur, to do my will."

The flames from both fires soared high into the night, crackling and spitting, lighting the sky as though day had suddenly appeared. Kara pulled the mask from her face and threw it into the fire a second before Conrí's massive body struck her, sending her backward into darkness.

She opened her eyes to the sight of the star-filled sky and the bright full moon. It was hard to tell if she was alive or dead because she couldn't breathe or move. As everything came into focus she realized she couldn't breathe or move because a naked man lay sprawled across her body.

Conrí's scream set her into motion. Strength she didn't even know she possessed sent him flying off her to tumble on the grass until he stopped just short of a fire. She jumped to her feet. As he turned his face toward hers, the fury in his eyes was something she'd never seen before. She was looking into the windows of hell. His roar was just as chilling, and when he lunged at her, hands reaching for her throat, she stumbled back.

Another flurry of motion, then a snap sounded. Conrí's lifeless body dropped from between Riah's hands to land on the ground with a thud.

"He won't harm anyone else." Riah wasn't even breathing heavy.

Something was wrong though. Conrí lay dead on the ground, naked and human. Daphne was helping a tired but, thankfully, very much alive Faolán. Together, Adriana and Riah picked up Conrí's body and began to move toward the house. She didn't even want to know what they planned to do with him.

Then it struck her. Cam. She whirled and searched the night, staring at the place where the silver wolf that had been Conrí had dragged Lee and Bruce. She took off running.

Before she made it to the edge of the woods, Lee limped into the clearing. *Thank God.* Cam followed him, tears flowing down her cheeks, the lifeless body of Bruce Plainfeather in her arms.

Epilogue

Riverside State Park
Two months later

Kara stood on the porch of the little cottage and smiled. Hard to believe everything that had happened over the last couple of months. Jake was happy because once again his park was safe, although Kara's decision to leave hadn't pleased him.

Riah and Adriana had set Conrí up as the Riverside State Park serial killer. The DNA matched, the physical evidence matched, and the story they'd spun to cover his particular signature made all the local law enforcement happy.

Kara thought it was too convenient and that everyone bought into it too easily, except obviously Dr. Riah Preston was far more than just a vampire. The good doctor had learned a trick or two in her centuries of life and, thank goodness for everyone, chose to use those skills for the greater good.

Despite Riah's offer that Kara become a member of the Spiritus Group, she'd had to decline. Not that she had an issue with the group's work. On the contrary, she was impressed. No, she wanted to spend some time in Ireland and get to know her sisters. Mom and Dad had been pretty forthcoming once the truth was out there, and so many things now made sense. Her hand strayed to her silver necklace. These days, the touch of it against her throat brought only a smile. It no longer made her feel unwanted. She felt love when she ran her fingers across the beautiful design. Love and sacrifice, and, most of all, hope.

For some, the truth of a birthright could be downright scary. Not for Kara. She was enthralled to discover who and what she was. She thirsted for knowledge.

And for Cam. During that few minutes it took to locate her on the bluff that night, her heart had nearly stopped. She was so afraid she'd lost her. She'd never forget the sight of Cam walking out of the woods alive. She'd vowed to herself right then never to let her go.

Everyone felt the loss of Bruce Plainfeather deeply, but none more than Cam. Bruce had been her mentor, a friend, a guiding light, and when he was gone, it was as though a piece of her died with him. Kara had gone back to Montana with Cam and participated in the ritual burial. She swore she heard his voice, and when she said as much to Cam, a light of pleasure sparked in her eyes. Together they mourned him and together they said good-bye to him.

Though not sure how Cam felt about her, Kara sucked it up and professed her feelings, only to be delighted to find out Cam shared them. Tragedy had touched them both, but joy waited just on the other side.

Now, Cam emerged from the house lugging the last of the boxes. Kara was officially out of the little cottage and out of the park service. She and Cam would be leaving tomorrow for Ireland, while Winston, the little traitor, would stay with Lee. When they'd returned Lee's plane to Montana, she'd been certain Winston would be coming home with her. Didn't happen. Her once-faithful companion had taken such a liking to Cam's father that Kara didn't have the heart to separate them. As much as she loved him, she was convinced that Lee loved him even more. So Winston took up residence in the charming house in Montana.

Cam loaded the boxes into the SUV, then returned to the porch. Putting an arm around Kara she asked, "You ready to say good-bye to all of this?"

Kara took one last look around. The house, the trees, the dam were all so beautiful. But when she looked at them she saw her past. She turned to Cam and saw her future.

"Yeah." She smiled. "I'm ready."

About the Author

Sheri Lewis Wohl grew up in northeast Washington State and though she always thought she'd move away, never has. Despite traveling throughout the United States, Sheri always finds her way back home. And so she lives, plays, and writes amidst mountains, evergreens, and abundant wildlife. When not working the day job in federal finance, she writes stories that typically include a bit of the strange and unusual and always a touch of romance. She works to carve out time to run, swim, and bike so she can participate in local triathlons, her latest addiction.

Books Available from Bold Strokes Books

Burgundy Betrayal by Sheri Lewis Wohl. Park Ranger Kara Lynch has no idea she's a witch until dead bodies begin to pile up in her park, forcing her to turn to beautiful and sexy shape-shifter Camille Black Wolf for help in stopping a rogue werewolf. (978-1-60282-654-0)

Love Life by Rachel Spangler. When Joey Lang unintentionally becomes a client of life coach Elaine Raitt, the relationship becomes complicated as they develop feelings that make them question their purpose in love and life. (978-1-60282-655-7)

The Fling by Rebekah Weatherspoon. When the ultimate fantasy of a one-night stand with her trainer, Oksana Gorinkov, suddenly turns into more, reality show producer Annie Collins opens her life to a new type of love she's never imagined. (978-1-60282-656-4)

Ill Will by J.M. Redmann. New Orleans PI Micky Knight must untangle a twisted web of health care fraud that leads to murder—and puts those closest to her most at risk. (978-1-60282-657-1)

Buccaneer Island by J.P. Beausejour. In the rough world of Caribbean piracy, a man is what he makes of himself—or what a stronger man makes of him. (978-1-60282-658-8)

Twelve O'Clock Tales by Felice Picano. The fourth collection of short fiction by legendary novelist and memoirist, Felice Picano. Eleven dark tales that will thrill and disturb, discomfort and titillate, enthrall and leave you wondering.(978-1-60282-659-5)

Night Hunt by L.L. Raand. When dormant powers ignite, the wolf Were pack is thrown into violent upheaval, and Sylvan's pregnant mate is at the center of the turmoil. A Midnight Hunters novel. (978-1-60282-647-2)

Demons are Forever by Kim Baldwin and Xenia Alexiou. Elite Operative Landis "Chase" Coolidge enlists the help of high-class call girl Heather Snyder to track down a kidnapped colleague embroiled in a global black market organ-harvesting ring. (978-1-60282-648-9)

Runaway by Anne Laughlin. When Jan Roberts is hired to find a teenager who has run away to live with a group of anti-government survivalists, she's forced to return to the life she escaped when she was a teenager herself. (978-1-60282-649-6)

Street Dreams by Tama Wise. Tyson Rua has more than his fair share of problems growing up in New Zealand—he's gay, he's falling in love, and he's run afoul of the local hip-hop crew leader just as he's trying to make it as a graffiti artist. (978-1-60282-650-2)

Women of the Dark Streets: Lesbian Paranormal edited by Radclyffe and Stacia Seaman. Erotic tales of the supernatural—a world of vampires, werewolves, witches, ghosts, and demons—by the authors of Bold Strokes Books. (978-1-60282-651-9)

Tyger, Tyger, Burning Bright by Justine Saracen. Love does not conquer all, but when all of Europe is on fire, it's better than going to hell alone. (978-1-60282-652-6)

Words to Die By by William Holden. Sixteen answers to the question: What causes a mind to curdle? (978-1-60282-653-3)

Haunting Whispers by VK Powell. Detective Rae Butler faces two challenges: a serial attacker who targets attractive women, and Audrey Everhart, a compelling woman who knows too much about the case and offers too little—professionally and personally. (978-1-60282-593-2)

Wholehearted by Ronica Black. When therapist Madison Clark and attorney Grace Hollings are forced together to help Grace's troubled nephew at Madison's healing ranch, worlds and hearts collide. (978-1-60282-594-9)

Fugitives of Love by Lisa Girolami. Artist Sinclair Grady has an unspeakable secret, but the only chance she has for love with gallery owner Brenna Wright is to reveal the secret and face the potentially devastating consequences. (978-1-60282-595-6)

Derrick Steele: Private Dick The Case of the Hollywood Hustler by Zavo. Derrick Steele, a hard-drinking, lusty private detective, is being framed for the murder of a hustler in downtown Los Angeles. When his best friend Daniel McAllister joins the investigation, their growing attraction might prove to be more explosive than the case. (978-1-60282-596-3)

Nice Butt: Gay Anal Eroticism by Shane Allison. From toys to teasing, spanking to sporting, some of the best gay erotic scribes celebrate the hottest and most creative in new erotica. (978-1-60282-635-9)

Worth the Risk by Karis Walsh. Investment analyst Jamie Callahan and Grand Prix show jumper Kaitlyn Brown are willing to risk it all in their careers—can they face a greater challenge and take a chance on love? (978-1-60282-587-1)

Bloody Claws by Winter Pennington. In the midst of aiding the police, Preternatural Private Investigator Kassandra Lyall finally finds herself at serious odds with Sheila Morris, the local werewolf pack's Alpha female, when Sheila abuses someone Kassandra has sworn to protect. (978-1-60282-588-8)

Awake Unto Me by Kathleen Knowles. In turn of the century San Francisco, two young women fight for love in a world where women are often invisible and passion is the privilege of the powerful. (978-1-60282-589-5)

Initiation by Desire by MJ Williamz. Jaded Sue and innocent Tulley find forbidden love and passion within the inhibiting confines of a sorority house filled with nosy sisters. (978-1-60282-590-1)

Toughskins by William Masswa. John and Bret are two twenty-something athletes who find that love can begin in the most unlikely of places, including a "mom and pop shop" wrestling league. (978-1-60282-591-8)

me@you.com by K.E. Payne. Is it possible to fall in love with someone you've never met? Imogen Summers thinks so because it's happened to her. (978-1-60282-592-5)

High Impact by Kim Baldwin. Thrill seeker Emery Lawson and Adventure Outfitter Pasha Dunn learn you can never truly appreciate what's important and what you're capable of until faced with a sudden and stark reminder of your own mortality. (978-1-60282-580-2)

Snowbound by Cari Hunter. "The policewoman got shot and she's bleeding everywhere. Get someone here in one hour or I'm going to put her out of her misery." It's an ultimatum that will forever change the lives of police officer Sam Lucas and Dr. Kate Myles. (978-1-60282-581-9)

Rescue Me by Julie Cannon. Tyler Logan reluctantly agrees to pose as the girlfriend of her in-the-closet gay BFF at his company's annual retreat, but she didn't count on falling for Kristin, the boss's wife. (978-1-60282-582-6)